The rawness swamped everything. But through it ran the thread of another emotion: relief. It was wrong, a sin. But—Hun was dead. He would never touch her again.

"How…" Alina tried to soften the question, but could not find the words. There were none. No acceptable way to ask the man you loved how he had killed the foul creature you had been given to, sold to. But she had to know. *"How…"*

"You want to know how I killed him?" Brand questioned.

"Yes. I want to know how it was." *How you set me free.*

Brand moved, her dream creature, and there was nothing left either in his eyes or his body but the warrior. "I will tell you, but not now. Not here. Come. We are wasting time. It is a long ride to Bamburgh."

Alina gasped. "You cannot mean to take me back. Hun is dead. It…it is all over—"

"All over between us?" Brand leaned over, holding her captive just with his size. "No. It is not. Not yet."

HELEN KIRKMAN

EMBERS

HQN™

ISBN 0-373-77017-0

EMBERS

Copyright © 2004 by Helen Kirkman

To "The Hussies," wonderful historical authors, for allowing me to share in the laughter, tears and joys of being a writer.

CHAPTER ONE

Wessex, southern England, 716 A.D.

HE WAS A FIRE SPIRIT and he had come for her.

Everyone else in the small chamber of the Wessex nunnery stepped back. Not Alina. She knew him.

"The woman is mine. I will take her and none shall stop me."

Alina's breath choked. He would do what he said, this creature made out of light and fire and unstoppable force. He had proved his words before.

Her gaze caught his face, fixed on its fierce, brilliant planes. She had loved this man with all she had, through the wild extremes of joy and sorrow.

She had destroyed him.

Love was no debt payment for that.

He had come for her, her wild-souled Northumbrian, and he would take: not love, but vengeance.

Her betrayal of him had been absolute. He had no reason for forgiveness. She would give him none. Not if it meant her life.

She stepped forward, out of the press of shivering strangers clustered round her.

"Brand," she said. It was the Saxon word for fire. Living fire.

He moved. Just the tread of one heavy warrior's foot, and the cold empty space round her gaped wide in the sudden rustling retreat of a dozen people. She stood her ground in front of them, just as she had come in from the orchard, her rough, plain tunic and kirtle stained with purple sloe juice, streaks of wild dark hair escaping from the uncomfortable restriction of her coarse veil.

A nun's wimple in front of the finest, the best, the highest-hearted man in all the lands of England, of Britain.

"You remembered."

It was a killer, that understated Northern English irony. She had forgotten. It would bite through steel, just like the snake blade sheathed at his hip. His hand rested on the hilt like something that belonged there. It did.

He strode forward. Sunlight from the open window glinted on his flame-bright hair, dazzled on the gold twisted round his wrists, on the sword hilt, on the buckle of his leather belt. Her aching eyes stared in disbelief.

But it was there: all she had robbed him of by reason of who she was. Wealth, position, riches, all the very foundation of his life had been restored.

"You seem surprised."

"Stunned."

She raised a dark-winged brow in exactly the expression she had used on importunate vassals in her uncle's palace at Craig Phádraig. Never let any inappropriate emotion show. That was life's teaching.

She smiled. That was because she could not get another word out. If she did, he would read the fear in her voice.

The gold light of his gaze flicked at her.

"Nay, stunned is what I should be, looking on the living dead."

Her insides jumped. For one instant she thought she saw in the luminous golden depths of his eyes some reflection of what her forced deception might have done to him. It seemed greater, different, deeper a thousandfold than she had expected—

"The lost Princess of the Picts. Or am I addressing a phoenix risen from the ashes?"

There was nothing in his eyes but fire. He thought she had been killed and her body burned. She had made sure of that. He was not supposed to pursue her. He was a creature of impulse, not cold calculation. Everyone said so.

"Aye," she said in the voice that matched the haughty turn of her brows. "Restored, it seems. Just like you."

She forced her gaze to take in the deep blue dye of his tunic, the pure gold thread decorating its edges, the fine dark cloth of his trousers, the leather shoes. She kept coming back to the gold and the garnets. Just what he wore at waist and wrist would have bought more land than this small abbey owned.

She would not let herself look on his face, because if she did, he might read all that she would conceal. Bright metal clinked as he moved his hand.

He would see terror.

"So? Is the past wiped out?"

She raised her head.

"Yes."

His eyes glittered. All the gold about his person, the twisted thickness of the arm rings, the belt fittings, the plated scabbard chape, dulled into leaden grey beside that living brightness. His eyes were the colour of light-shot amber. Liquid fire.

"Indeed? Shall we see if that is so?"

She tried not to look at him.

"Of course it is so. The past is gone. What would you expect me to remember? Flight? Loss? Disaster?"

He walked toward her.

"Such things stick in my mind."

He kept moving. Power leached from him, from the broad shoulders and the thick warrior's hands, from a body that belonged to a hero from some blood-thirsty English saga. Its strength spoke the language of fear; the splendour that adorned it brought awe.

None of it mattered beside the fire in his eyes.

No one could hold the gaze of such eyes. There was a faint rustling noise around her like the sound of a dozen indrawn breaths. A dozen people shrinking back.

They must have been plastered against the wooden walls by now, the abbess, the priest, the nuns, the servants, all the inhabitants of the southern Wessex abbey that had given her sanctuary. By the time the fire spirit reached her, he and she could have been the only two people on Middle Earth.

She took a breath that scorched her throat. She had no words left. Nothing to frame the truth that she still loved him, that that was why she had left him.

"Brand." It was all she could get out of her mouth, just his name, like someone repeating an enchantment that might be deadly. "Brand."

He stopped, almost touching her but not quite. She would never have that again, the wild frightening magic of his touch. Her body ached for it, even now, pierced through with longing. Everything, words, even the sound of his name, was burned away.

He was so tall that she had to look up at him. She remembered having to do that. Always. Her heart remembered everything, all that there was to know about him. She had stored it deep inside because the thought of him, the idea of his presence, had been the only thing that had stopped her from going mad in her self-imposed exile. That was how it was for her. His face, the first time she had seen it across the opulent palace hall at Bamburgh, her prison, had been like light.

It was so now. Light and fire. Except then the fire had warmed her, right through to the most secret hidden part of her being, to a place she had never believed existed in a creature like her.

Yet now that same heat burned her. It was so strong

it ate up the very air around her so that there was none left to breathe.

That was why her mind dizzied, as though she would faint.

"We have naught left to say—"

Somewhere beyond her in the abbess's chamber she could hear feet shuffling in the thin covering of rushes on the earth floor. It made her turn. Faces, pale, fascinated, terrified, stared back at her. She wondered whether she looked like that in her borrowed clothes, chalk-faced, wild-eyed and desperate.

"Get out," yelled Athelbrand, Prince of Bernicia, at the crowded room. "Now. Leave me with the woman."

There was a moment when she thought either the priest or the man who had come to mend the sheep pen would not, that they would try and help her. That they did not realize it would be impossible.

She saw the jewelled hand tighten on the gilded, snake-patterned hilt. There was a sound like no other in the world: the sliding rasp of steel freed from wood lined with leather.

"Leave."

They went. No other choice existed. She watched the guilt in their faces. Their stiff backs. The latched door. Nothing.

Brand placed the gleaming feral length of the sword down on the rough-wood table. He did not need it with her. There was nothing she could do. He leaned one shoulder against the wall. He was still too close to her. She could see the rapid shallow movement of his breath, the deeper breath that meant he would speak.

"Welcome back, Alina."

The English, rough-smooth voice dropped into her language, Celtic. He spoke it beautifully, but not like a Pict or a Scot. Like a Briton. It was the kind of accent she had heard in the best part of her childhood. It was like a song. Enough to shatter all her resolve.

"I have come to take you back."

"Back…"

They were the words he said to her every night, in her dreams. But dreams had nothing to do with what was real.

"Alina. I have come for you. I will take you back."

She closed her mind against the shape and the sound of his voice, against a happiness that no longer existed. This was now. Her future was different.

She forced herself to concentrate on the words and their meaning.

"Back where?"

"Bernicia. Bamburgh."

You could not say those words in her language. They were English, just as he was. Like him they belonged to Northumbria.

The kingdom that warred so often with hers.

"I cannot go back." She spoke it in English. Because it was a Northumbrian catastrophe that divided them.

"There can be no going back. Not for—" Her voice

stumbled over a word so filled with danger it had no right to be spoken, a word that had been drowned in bitterness. *Us.* "Not for me."

"You still believe you belong to that *nithing* your fool of a father betrothed you to. To Hun."

Alina stepped back. She could not help it. Her fingers, hidden in the patched folds of her borrowed skirts, twisted painfully into fists.

"My father made a lawful betrothal—"

"To a killer?"

Her nails dug into her palms.

"My betrothal to King Osred of Northumbria's kinsman was arranged to benefit my father—"

"So you did manage to work that much out—"

She flinched. "Maol is a prince of Pictland. He had a duty to protect his country. My—" her voice tripped on emptiness "—from yours. *My* land has always been beset with troubles, either from the Scots over the western border or from the English in the south. The duty was mine as well, to do what I could."

"Duty? So it was an attack of conscience that made you go back to Hun?"

She stared at eyes that had known loss more brutal than it seemed possible to survive. Such a thing should not happen again. Not through her.

One person was already dead.

There was no other decision.

"Yes," she said. "It was conscience."

The bright flame in the gold eyes turned savage.

Her heart beat and the floor beneath her feet shifted like something living.

The saints give her the strength she needed for this.

"But even if I had not seen my duty at last, I would still have gone back to Hun." She did not blink. "Not because that is my rightful place, but because I choose to."

She tilted her head. The walls seemed to close in.

"I was wrong to let you take me away from him, wrong to run away with you. That is why I left you. I let you think I was dead so that you would not follow me. What we did was a mistake, just a mad, foolish, impulsive mistake."

Brand was ruled by impulse. He would see—

"I came to my senses. I knew Hun would be ready enough to welcome me back. Just as you must have known that."

Her head was tilted at the same arrogant angle. So many years of practice. But her feet were walking backwards. To escape him. Or to escape the deadly bale of falseness that now poured out of her mouth. She did not know.

How could she explain why she was in Wessex?

His stride followed her stumbling footsteps, pace for pace, crowding her in the small space of the crude bower. The burning eyes were relentless.

"I know well enough what was."

"Then—" Her mind was reeling, both from the shock of his presence and the hunted desperation of her thoughts. "Why—" Her voice choked.

Why are you here? How much do you know? Have you...have you caught out any of my lies?

What *was*. The sense of that word penetrated the hell inside her head. Her gaze fell to the sword resting on the table: the tempered blade, the gold-chased hilt carved with twisted snakes to give protection. Deadly.

The laws of revenge.

"You found Hun...." Her voice cut off and her gaze sought his, wild, cornered, desperate to discern how much he knew.

"Aye. I found him. What was he thinking, Alina? That a diplomatic mission to the south would keep him from me? Did he truly believe I would not follow him here?"

"Here?"

"What a mask of surprise. Was that what you believed, too, when you came to Wessex to be with him? That I would never find you here?"

Her mouth opened and shut, soundless, without a breath.

"It amazes me, what you and your lover must have believed. Hun did not even know King Osred of Northumbria was dead. He did not know his diplomatic mission in Wessex for his master was over. He was just as surprised as you look now."

But it was not surprise that made her look so, like a terrified madwoman. It was the rawness of shock. She had fled the length of Britain to be safe from Hun, and he had come south in her footsteps, without her knowing. Or him.

"Then—"

"You know the answer. There can be no other since I am here and Hun is not. The man you were betrothed to is dead. I killed him." The gold eyes flickered. "You must have been wondering why he was neglecting you."

The rawness swamped everything. But through it ran the twisting thread of another emotion: relief. It was wrong, a sin doubtless, especially in this place. But— Hun was dead. He would never be able to touch her again.

Her hands gripped the wall behind her to stop herself from falling.

Brand became quite still.

"You are truly shocked."

He did not understand why. She could see it in his face. Somehow he had failed to realize that Hun had had no idea where she was.

The luck was with her. All she had to do was keep her head. She would somehow come through. It looked so well. She had chosen to flee to Wessex and Hun had come south on some mission for his master, King Osred.

"I should have expected how you would feel."

The rough bitterness of Brand's voice seared her. Yet for all that, she could have fallen into his arms right then, just to hear his voice and feel his touch. Even if he killed her.

The nightmare of fear and loathing that had taken shape the day she had looked into the ice-coloured eyes of her lawful betrothed was over. Finished. Her breath shuddered.

Only Brand had been stronger than that fear.

"Alina…"

He would touch her. Her eyes caught the brief blur of gold as his hand moved. His protection. Like heaven's blessing. No longer hers. She jerked away before he could reach her. Instinct, pure, fast and unstoppable in its strength. She could not let him touch tainted flesh. Not with so much guilt on her. Not him.

"No, I will be well, perfectly well. It was a shock. I did not know—" She swallowed bile.

"How…how…" She tried to soften the question but she could not find the words. Probably because there were none. No acceptable way to ask the man you loved how he had come to kill the foul creature you had been given to, sold to.

But she had to know. If there was more harm, if there had been—

"How…"

"You want to know how I killed him?"

"Yes. I want to know how it was."

How you set me free.

She straightened. But that meant she found the deep honeyed-amber of his gaze, so strong, purer than melted gold. Hot. For a fractured moment, the heat of that gaze scorched through everything, every bitter, ugly catastrophe, so that only the pureness was left.

But then the moment broke because it could not live between them. The shadows claimed all.

She had not meant it to be so. None of it. But life took no account of intentions. Only of what was.

"Then I will tell you what happened to Hun. But not now. Not here. Come. We are wasting time."

"Wasting—"

"Time." He moved, her dream creature, sliding his weight smoothly from the rough-hewn support of the wall and there was nothing left either in his eyes or his body but the warrior.

"It is a long ride to Bamburgh."

"Bamburgh? You cannot mean to take me back to Northumbria, to Bernicia, after all? Hun is dead. It...it is all over—"

"All over between us?" He leaned over her, holding her captive just with his size, big hands on either side of her head flat against the wall. "No. It is not. Not yet." Her heart clenched.

Vengeance.

She could see the width of his shoulders and the sleek, muscled fullness of his body.

But she could also see his eyes. She would look at nothing but his eyes. He had never harmed her.

But never before had she caused an unjust death.

"You will not take me. There is no reason to."

"What a defective memory you have."

She flinched. He did not move. There seemed nothing of joyous, impulsive, high-hearted man who had taken her before. The man whose heart was capable of pity.

His eyes scored straight through the defence of

her plain nun's clothing, straight through to her skin, making her burn, even though there was nothing of the lover in that look, only the predator.

The strength in that warrior's body was absolute. She knew it. There could be no mercy in it. There was no reason for any.

She held his gaze. Tried to think, to work out what she could say.

"If Hun is dead, then it is finished. Done. There can be no reason to want me—"

"What a fool you must think me."

Lethal muscle gathered itself. His hand moved. She had one glimpse of his remorseless face.

His grip was like a band of tempered steel. Inescapable.

"I will not go with you."

Her arm, her whole slight body was wrenched against him. She thought she had known his closeness. She thought she was quite familiar with the measure of his strength. She had not even begun to realize.

He was huge. She could feel him breathe, feel the faint edge of his breath touch the delicate skin of her face, like a mockery of the lover's caress that had once been theirs. But now it was the breath that fed his rage, the overwhelming power of his strength. The fire.

His grip on her arm hurt. She did not think he even realized. The fire burnt too strongly.

She gritted her teeth. She would not make a sound.

But he knew, quite suddenly. The realization came and the terrible grip on her arm abruptly relaxed. So abruptly that her shaking legs would have let her drop. Except that he still held her. Very close. And although his grip no longer hurt her, she knew that she would never break it.

She forced words.

"Do not make me do this." Their breath, wildly uneven, was shared, so that her senses span out of control. Because of his nearness.

"Do you truly wish to stay here?"

She raised her head. The ugly wimple, jammed against his arm, tore, unleashing a swath of heavy, tangled hair. Dark, not Saxon blond, jet-black against coarse white linen.

There was nothing she could do. She could not move.

She watched his gaze fasten on the embarrassing display of what should be kept hidden, and the fire in his eyes took on a different edge. She should be afraid. She was.

Yet the fierce heat in him found its echo in her, the way it always had, unbidden, quite beyond her control.

He knew that. The flare of recognition, of hunger, in his eyes was quite familiar to her. Neither of them had ever been able to disguise it, whatever they wanted.

His hand slid down her arm.

His touch was as unsteady as his breath, heated and

not quite controlled. But that did not diminish his strength. He would take her hand, touch her as though—

She jerked away from him. But it was not allowed. His grip fastened on the thin bones of her wrist.

"We made our choices, Alina. Now we must abide them."

Her hand was engulfed by his, buried in his heat. His fingers closed over her flesh and his touch was...gentle.

It was that which took her resolve, and her strength, all of it, so that her body swayed toward him as though she would fall. But he did not let her fall. His hands slid round underneath her arms, supporting her, smoothly, with the expert touch that belonged only to him. Only his touch could make her begin to melt from the inside so that her body seemed to dissolve, helpless against his.

His hands held her, slid across her waist, the small of her back, took her weight so that the sensation of floating intensified. His hands were warm and his strength was complete. He would never let her fall. He never had. His touch had been the only thing she had had in the world to put her trust to. His strength, his warmth could hold her. Against everything.

If she would let it.

"Were you afraid? Is that why you could not go through with it, living an exile's life with me? Is that why you came south instead?"

Oh, the seduction of that voice, no longer burning

with such anger. Brand's voice. Laced through with the priceless possibility of understanding.

How easy it would be to say *yes*. She had been afraid of everything, even her love.

She could just admit her fear, here in the shelter of his arms, and perhaps he would forgive her. Perhaps it would open the door on the bright light of the present, the greater lightness of him. That light surrounded her. Her sight dazzled against the wild brightness of his hair that seemed to attract every shard of golden sunlight in the room, against the far greater wildness and brightness of his eyes.

Eyes like that lived. It was the only way to describe it. They saw through things. They knew and accepted all the passions and the hopes, all the inadequacies and the contradictions that had been poured into the creation of human beings. Perhaps they would even understand that other fear, the one she could hardly find words for: the fear she had of love, just as great as her longing.

To win that complete acceptance, to have it offered like the most generous of gifts, would be like wound balm over deadly hurts.

Touching him and looking at him, she could believe he would give it, even though he could no longer love her. If she had ever truly won his love. Such a thing did not seem possible to her.

But what then, if he did understand, if he did forgive her? Because he had such a finely balanced sense of honour the burden would begin all over again.

She could not allow that.

The shadows that lay behind the brightness and the strength in his eyes had been put there by her.

She watched him, and his warmth seeped through her bones.

"Aye. I was afraid," she drawled, "but not of Hun. I understood him and I should have stayed with him. The thing that made me afraid was the criminal folly of what I had done with you."

He did not say a word. Did not move. The eyes just stared at her, with a keenness that would draw blood.

"I..." But her voice stopped. Suppose he did not believe her? Even now? Suppose those eyes that saw so much could see through her deception?

She cast about frantically in her mind for something to say, something that would convince him. Something to show why he had found her cowering in an inadequately endowed Wessex abbey. Wessex. Hun.

"I came south to meet Hun." The slow, mocking sound of her voice formed the lie that would seal her fate. "And to get away from you."

The eyes shut off, closing her out. The gift, the possibility of understanding, was gone. All that was left was the frightening strength, the power that scorned all earthly restriction and would take everything.

He said nothing more. Just turned her around bodily and pulled her towards the door. His heavy booted feet scuffed the packed earth floor so that the meagre rushes flew. Her clumsy skirts, her feet, her whole weight dragged after him.

She fought him.

It was the only thing left, a matter of life-preserving instinct. She fought with a single-minded force that did not belong to her but to some maddened wildcat. She burst his grip. She actually burst his grip because she had surprised him and because there was a small and breathless instant when he held back.

She struck out with all the force that she had and his left arm slammed against the wall. It brought a sound of surprise, or pain. Pain. She had hurt him, more than she had thought. It was now. Now or she, *he,* would be lost.

The wildcat hit him again, beat against the arm she had damaged, lunged for the door. She would make it. Her hands scrabbled for the heavy iron latch, the last of her once carefully tended nails breaking.

He caught her. He was so fast. Lightning fast. She twisted desperately, lurched against the table. The table... Her scrabbling fingers found the sword. The snake hilt slid into her right hand. She could not, would not, use it because it was lethal. But neither would she give in.

Because it was not her safety at stake. It was his.

She hefted the blade, but it was overlong, unwieldy and she was jammed into the confined space between the table and the wall bench. She could not make the blade obey her.

"Do not touch me," she yelled with all the strength that she had. But she was a fool and more than a fool to think she could stop a fire spirit like Brand with a mere sword.

"Leave it, woman. Put it down. You will injure yourself—"

But she would rather do that than injure him. She turned for the door, unbalanced, swaying, her feet clumsy in the ill-fitting borrowed shoes. Her arm and her shoulder hit the wall and the blade sliced through the air, falling, falling toward her. The steel-bright edge was in front of her face, filling her vision. She could not stop it because she was falling, too.

This is how warriors die, she thought, just like this. Bright steel and no escape. Just as she hit the ground, something knocked her sideways.

There was silence. Deep. No movement except hers. She tested out each muscle like a terrified animal. She was not hurt, not really—no movement except hers. She gained her feet fast, in one lithe surge, because she was not hurt, only bruised.

There was blood. It oozed out in a small, thin trail from beneath the heap of expensive clothing jammed against the wall.

CHAPTER TWO

HE WAS DEAD.

He had to be dead because she had seen the keenness of the sword blade, right before her eyes.

Just before he had knocked her aside.

She had killed him and the cycle of destruction was complete.

She dropped to her knees beside the motionless form. She was too terrified to touch him. Then she saw it, like a streak of flame in the rushes. The sword he had knocked out of her idiotically dangerous grip was lying on the floor, close to his hand, as though it wished to return to its owner.

It was not tangled up with the crushed remains of his body.

But there was blood.

She touched his face. It was warm. One fingertip moved with delicate, fear-streaked, sense-tingling slowness toward the faintly parted lips; felt the soft, moist-dark warmth of him. Breath.

Her own breath, bundled up in one horrible constricted tightness that scored her throat, came out in a rush that stirred the bright tangled gold of his hair.

A single, light gossamer strand slid across his closed eyes. He did not feel it.

He did not feel her touch.

But he was alive. Her hand rested on warmth. She could feel the smooth texture of skin under her fingertips, the rough line of his jaw under her palm.

Her hand shook. Not just from the aftermath of panic but because she had never touched him so, had never touched any man so.

It had all been of his doing before. And she had let him because she had been spellbound. Because she had been ignorant and desperate and unskilled, and he had been the opposite. He was the only one who had not realized the truth others had known since her birth. That she was not good enough.

She had wanted him to the point of madness.

She still did.

Her fingers traced their way back very, very slowly over the unmoving flesh, caressed the pure, fierce outline of the Northumbrian Brand's face. She brushed the soft threads of his hair aside. The seductive warmth was there, under her fingertips. It penetrated through the frail barrier of her skin, up her arm, and then inside her in a small swift rush, tingling, melting. Real.

His warmth had a generosity that overwhelmed. Even now, she could sense it. It was something that called to her, even though she had never been able to give it fair return and had now given away even the chance to. Nothing could stop her yearning for his warmth. It had a power that both exhilarated and frightened. Something clenched deep inside her with a force like pain. She snatched her hand away.

It was Saxon *wiccecræft*, the man heat that lived in her Northumbrian lover. It possessed absolutely. Witchcraft.

He did not move, was lost in that otherworld of darkness. But he lived. He was strong. He would be well. The blood had stopped. She should leave him, now, before she did a harm that was worse than this.

But she could not.

Not after what he had done. He must hate her and he could have left her to the consequences of her own dangerous folly with the sword. He could have let her fall and that would have been the end. It would have solved everything.

But he had not.

Because of that, she could not leave him.

She could not leave him because he was Brand and though her love was like a thing maimed, she was bound to him by a cord she could not break, whatever she did.

At least she had to help him out of this.

She touched his shoulder. It was massive. Her hand settled round the familiar-unfamiliar shape. She knew him so well and yet she did not know him at all. They had touched as yet so very little and yet when they had, it had threatened to plunder sense and every feeling and every emotion. She had felt alive in his arms, all at once, in one intense, dizzying, life-consuming rush. Just for a moment. A moment that could not last.

He had kissed her. Once. That was all she had had
of him in return for breathless, willing abduction and
terrified flight and all the bitter consequences of pursuit. It was probably all she could give him.

He had wanted to wed her.

"Brand."

Her hand on the massive shoulder tightened, the
damaged and useless second finger tangling in his
tunic. He lay in a twisting uncomfortable heap on his
left side. She could not see where the wound was,
where the blood came from. She could not move him.
He was too big, too heavy, and she was terrified of
making the damage worse.

"Brand."

Helplessness, fear for him, twisted through her
belly. She bowed her head over his. "Brand…" Her
breath shivered across the heat of his skin, across the
clear rise of his cheekbone.

His face was the comeliest she had ever beheld.

Her hand moved round from his shoulder, sliding
upward, burying itself in the wild tangled mass of his
hair, seeking the strong curving line of his skull,
cradling his head.

"I will not leave you to be alone." The words came
out of nowhere, raking through the thick heavy silence of the room. The last words she had any right
to say. She bit her lip and tears sprang stinging against
the backs of her eyes.

She should not still be with him, but some things,
some feelings, admitted no reason.

Her lips trembled, a breath above his flesh, because being with him, holding him was wrong. He was not hers, just as she could never be his and yet—Her mouth touched him, her touch so light that it would scarce have been felt had he been conscious. It was next to nothing. Could be counted so.

But she could not be content with that. She kissed him.

Because this was the only way she could, when he did not know, when he could not feel the uselessness of what she did. Could not respond.

He would not want to respond.

But she could not stop herself. Her mouth fastened on his skin with a desperate greed that held nothing of grace, only the measure of her despair.

Then she felt it, what she should have felt before through her touch if she had not been so frantic to sense his living warmth. His skin scorched her mouth.

It was so hot it burned. He burned.

She drew back in terror.

"Brand…" Her voice was no longer a pleading whisper. It shouted. Her hand slid down, seizing the great bulk of his shoulder.

"Brand, you must wake up. Otherwise I shall not be able to help you. You must hear me. You must wake."

She swapped her damaged left hand for her right and shook him.

He did not respond. Her unsteady fingers moved to touch his brow. It burned under her hand, as though all the fire that lived inside him would scorch through the finely-wrought covering of his skin.

She had to get help. The abbess, the priest. Whoever she could find who knew more than her about healing. Even his own men standing guard outside. Even if they killed her. Someone had to help him.

He moved. Her hand. She had left her hand resting against his heated skin. Touching him. Her fingers moved with the turn of his head, sliding across his face, touching the moistness of his lips like some indecent caress she had no right to. She was staring into gold-flecked eyes, dark with confusion.

"You…" She felt the whisper of his breath.

The eyes were deep, so achingly deep. Their deepness held her, just as it had the first time she had seen him, when nothing in the world, her world, had existed except him.

Just for one instant it was like that again and her heart leaped with a hope and a strength that had no relation to any decision of her mind. But then it was gone, that moment. It had not belonged to anything real, not even to what was real in the mind of the man she loved.

She saw the instant when full consciousness returned and when it did, it wiped out that frail, fathoms-deep connection as though it had no existence.

"Making sure I was really dead?"

She gasped, dragging her hand back. Guilt, the renewed savageness of loss, nearly paralyzed her. Blank impenetrable eyes watched every awkward, clumsy, shaking movement she made.

He tried to straighten up. A small wrenching sound of pain and surprise escaped the lips she had just touched.

She grabbed his shoulder. Regardless of what he wanted.

"Wait! You fell. You took some hurt." She swallowed. "The sword…" It came out on a thin, keening sound of terror.

He looked at her fingers twisted in his tunic.

"Hang the sword, woman. If it had been the sword I would be dead." He raised his head and her gaze was caught in a mesh of burning gold. "Disappointed?"

She blinked, trying to tear herself out of the golden net.

"Yes." She raised her head, but despite the show, her voice choked. She was not naturally good at lies.

She was learning. She untangled her hands out of his sleeve.

He sat up.

She choked back what would have been a shriek. She saw the blood welling down his arm, so much it had soaked out from underneath his body in that thin, life-sapping stream and she had seen it. She remembered how he burned.

"Saint Dwyn preserve—"

"Saint Dwyn? Does that not seem an unlikely choice? A virgin saint?"

Hun's whore.

She flinched. He watched it.

"But then your Saint Dwyn is also the patron saint

of ill-fated lovers. Or do you perhaps prefer the fact she had her own importunate suitor frozen into ice?"

Of all Englishmen, only Brand would be able throw a Celtic saint's name back in her face.

And ice could, of course, burn through flesh like fire.

"She unfroze him afterwards."

"Aye. But she did not marry him."

"No." But then Dwyn had been a saint. It would not have burned her heart out that she could not marry in mortal love. Her gaze slid away from molten gold that burned like ice and fire all at once.

She saw the trail of blood. She swallowed.

"What happened?"

"It is an old injury. Naught to do with this and naught that matters."

"But…at least let me see. I can help you."

He became very still.

Healing had not been an accomplishment of the Princess of the Picts.

"I learned healing from the abbess."

The worst thing she had helped with had been the broken arm of a travelling goldsmith. She had been squeamish all the way through. The man's gratitude had been an embarrassment. She smiled with a confidence she did not feel.

"And you use your…skills on those who pass through this place?"

Her smile became bland.

"Why not?"

The subtle eyes flickered.

Do not do this, Alina. Do not tread on dangerous ground.

Her perfect smile remained intact. She had never taken advice in her life, least of all her own.

"Well, then? Do I practice my skills on you?"

"It is not necessary." The eyes blanked off. He got to his feet. She stepped back, watching his pain, both physical and of the mind, obliterated, consumed by the flames inside him as though someone had poured oil on hot coals. "If you really want to be useful, just find me a cloth to bind it."

She crossed to the carved chest in the corner, found clean linen. She thought his gaze followed every move. Doubtless ready to fall on her if she attempted escape.

She could not. Not yet. Not while he was so hurt.

She ripped cloth into strips. "Let me see."

He was sitting, propped up on the wall bench. The sword, laid out next to him, was unsheathed. She averted her eyes from the gleaming, lethal length of metal that had so nearly killed her. Killed him.

She took his arm. She half expected some further outburst of the scarce-contained wrath scorching inside him. But her touch was permitted. The gold eyes held her, like a giant beast of prey toying with its victim before it drove for the kill.

"You really are going to minister to my hurts?"

His voice was cool and quite calm, but inexpressibly dangerous. Her insides clenched.

"I know how to do what is necessary."

"So you say."

"Then—"

"Just bind it. There is no time for anything else."

"But you need—"

"Do it."

He was already reaching for the fallen sword. The danger in his voice was in that movement, locked down in every muscle, ready to take the fire that burned inside him.

She looked at how much blood there was.

"Give the cloth to me. I can do it."

He must have seen how much she was shaking.

Her fingers tightened on the linen strip.

"You have the onset of fever from this wound. If you cannot tell that you are a fool. If you do not do anything about it you are an even greater fool."

"You mean I am running true to form?"

"Stop it." Northumbrians. They could kill you with their impenetrable irony.

"The wound will need cleaning, for all I know it needs stitching. If you want to live, it needs care and herbs against elf shot. If none of that bothers you, do as you suggest. Bind it and leave it."

"None of that bothers me." And she saw what she had only glimpsed before, the consuming darkness that lay behind the feverish brightness of his eyes.

A chill ran through her because she recognized what it was: the kind of bleakness that saw only a blank future. She recognized that because it lived inside her.

It was so bitter. It did not belong in a strong and beautiful creature like him.

"You must—"

His fingers hauled the cloth out of her hand.

"I shall not die yet. I have got a job to do first and the jaws of hell would not stop me. Tie this."

She caught the trailing end of the cloth flung at her. She tried not to think about the probable mess underneath his blood-soaked sleeve. She straightened the cloth, reaching round, leaning toward him so she could see. Gold arm rings, strong fingers, the intensity of his eyes. Their fingers tangled. She stifled a gasp.

"Hold it steady. That is not tight enough."

She pulled, biting her lip just as he did. As though she felt the pain. His fingers hauled on the cloth, compensating without thought for the weakness of her left hand.

"There."

It was done. Finished. She surged to her feet while he was still sick and helpless with the pain. It was less than three steps to the door. Simple— An undamaged arm snaked across the opening, blocking it. Her heart seized up. He could not have done it, could not have moved like that.

"Bit precipitate are you not? I might have thought you were trying to go without me."

"I will not go with you."

"Really? Have you worked out who is in charge of the sword at this moment?"

She stared at it, sheathed at his side, ready again to his hand. Her face set. If that was the only way to cut the lethal tie that bound them, then so be it.

"That does not bother me."

As an attempt at Northumbrian irony, it was masterly. The repetition of his own careless words struck a chord. Either that or he read in her face the underlying truth. She saw the moment that the bitter irony in his eyes gave way to shock, then something else she could not define. Except that it was weary, so gut-wrenchingly exhausted, like someone pushed past the end of their endurance who yet went on.

"Nay, life does not stop, Alina, regardless of what we want. It is we who must shape it. There is only one thing left that matters to me. The lands that are mine, the lands that make up Northumbria, will not slide back into the bloodbath that was King Osred's reign, not for your father's foolishness or for yours."

"*Mine?* I was the—" She bit off the word *sacrifice*. "I was betrothed to Hun to foster an alliance, because he was King Osred's kinsman. King Osred is dead. *Hun* is dead—"

"And his brother is not. Do you think I am not aware he is following me south, coming here—"

"Goadel? Coming here?" That foul, spitting, red-haired creature? "But he cannot..." Her voice rose out of control at the very thought of Hun's brother. Coming after her.

"He cannot claim you? If Goadel has you, he believes he is halfway to persuading King Nechtán, your uncle, to help Osred's kindred reclaim the Northumbrian throne. It is the best way to get rid of a new king, is it not? With outside help? Pictish help?"

"No…"

"No? Why not?" The eyes watched her: a falcon measuring its prey. "There is always a chance. And think of the benefit to you. You would be related to two royal houses. That is exactly where you wanted to be, is it not?"

Her blood froze. She could not say anything, could not get a word out of the tightness of her throat. The thought of being used, all over again, in some greedy, murderous power struggle was a horror she could not permit. Never.

Her gaze, fixed on the deadly snake hilt that swung at Brand's hip, became focused with a sharpness she had never known. The sharpness of her vision was frightening, but at the same time oddly strengthening in its finality, as though the sword were bound up with her future. The rune carved into the cross guard became visible, glowing in the sunlight close to his hand.

Runes were English devices. They were not of her people. But she recognized this one: elk sedge. It symbolized protection. But it was also dangerous, an Atheling's rune. It was a link to a higher world and full of force. That force could overcome people if they could not control it. Only Athelings knew how to merge with it and turn it into protectiveness.

Brand was an Atheling, a prince.

She was a princess. Equal.

She could feel his gaze on her bent head, the back of her neck. He moved, so that the sunlight diced with the shadows, like the mirror of her future.

"You really wish you had killed me, do you not? Then you would be free. Free to follow what you have found you desire. But there is just one thing you may not know, Alina, one thing you should take into account before making your sweeping decisions. Do you realize who your uncle's ambassador is at the court of Bamburgh? Your brother Modan."

Her sight blurred.

"Modan? In Bernicia? But he was my uncle's ambassador in—"

"The Kingdom of the Britons in Strathclyde. Your uncle had him recalled. Then sent to Northumbria."

Her uncle? Or her father? Maol of the Picts did not forgive. She knew the reach of his bitterness where Strath-Clòta was concerned. Where she was concerned and… "Modan…"

It was as though she was calling his name, as though he could hear her. The dark-eyed face of her older brother obliterated the sword. Modan had been the only member of her family who had ever cared about her. He had had no part in her marriage arrangements. He had been in Strath-Clòta, with their mother's kindred. Safe.

"My brother—"

"Your flesh and blood. Just think on it, Alina. What do you believe Modan's life would be worth if you do not come back to Bamburgh with me? If Goadel launches a rebellion with you as part of it? How long do you think it would be before the new King Cenred or his retainers at Bamburgh had your brother killed? They would not keep him alive for one day. He is already a virtual prisoner."

"A prisoner?"

"I should have said an honoured guest. Naturally he would not be harmed. Not unless what everyone suspects Goadel is planning actually happens. Not unless you make it happen."

The irony in his eyes and his voice, even the anger, were subsumed by a deadly earnestness that she had not seen before.

"Think. Is it worth pursuing what you want over your brother's blood? Will it be worth waking up each day even in the midst of all your power and all your riches knowing what you have done?"

The shadow of that other unjust death took shape between them. The power of a brother's sacrifice. The sound she made was not human. It came out of the mouth of some crazed animal writhing in its trap. She could see why wolves caught by iron would bite their own limbs off just to escape the pain and the darkness closing in.

If she went back to Bamburgh they would keep her there forever, a prisoner in all but name. Or else they would send her back to her father in the palace at Craig Phádraig. To let him plot another marriage for her. If even the most greedy and ambitious of prospective husbands would have her now.

If she took one step out of this door in Brand's keeping she would place him in appalling, merciless danger just as she had done before. Until he got her across the length of Britain and possibly even after that.

If she did not go they would kill Modan. Sooner or later. Because Goadel would not give up his ambitions.

Is it worth pursuing what you want over your brother's blood?

That was what Brand had done, unwittingly. Caused his brother's harm. For her sake. It was what she had already done. Killed an innocent man.

And now what would she do? What choice did she have?

"Come. You will be quite safe from a repeat of my importunate advances if that is what you are worried about. Someone else claims he was...seeking to find you. He is here."

She looked at the burning eyes.

"No doubt he will see to your welfare."

"Who?"

"You will see."

He did not touch her again. He did not need to. She took the first step by herself, the step that set her on the road back to the past, to the beautiful, deadly palace set on the impregnable sea-girt rocks at Bamburgh. The place where it had all begun.

There were half a dozen Northumbrians waiting outside. And one Pict. It was her half brother Cunan.

The hellhound of Craig Phádraig.

CHAPTER THREE

THEY WOULD HAVE TO STOP.

Brand could see it in her face. He cursed. He had wanted to be much farther away before they halted. Farther north. He knew he could push himself until the daylight faded, beyond, despite the wound to his arm. The men would follow. They would have to. But Alina...

He called a halt. The first to protest, naturally, was the yapping creature Cunan. The word meant "hound-like." If ever a man had been more aptly named...

A torrent of badly-accented English poured from lean and snapping jaws. He turned his back. Even a bitter, illegitimate half brother ought to have some feelings for his sister. The man should have been demanding that they stopped hours ago, not that they went on.

He strode off without looking, trying to mask disgust. Behind him the complaints continued.

His shoulders flexed with the urge to knock a set of predatory teeth down a snarling throat.

Alina said nothing. She had said next to nothing to her brother since she had seen him. Whether that meant she resented him, or whether she would not converse with her kinsman in front of a band of Northumbrians he did not know.

He stopped beside her mount and held up his hands. "Come here."

He thought at first she would refuse his aid. She probably loathed him enough to do so. But then she changed her mind. He realized the full measure of her tiredness. She simply fell from the saddle into his arms without the slightest resistance, or, he suspected, the slightest control over what she did.

He braced himself instinctively to swing her weight against his right side. He need not have bothered. He could have held her against his injured left arm without effort. Her weight was wrong, not nearly enough for her height.

His hands tightened on her body under the threadbare sack she seemed to consider passed for a gown.

"Cuthbert's bones."

It was an appropriate expression because that was all that seemed to be under his hands, a collection of very small bones. Had they starved her at that miserable-looking nunnery where she had chosen to wait for Hun, or what?

He could not believe this was what the smooth, curvingly voluptuous body had been reduced to. But then neither could he believe the coarse sack a creature of silk and fine cloth and bright gems was wearing. That creature had dazzled an entire court. And himself. She had struck straight through his heart.

But she had done that to a person who no longer existed.

The small frame pulled away from a grip that was too close. Strands of her night-black hair slid across the backs of his hands like remembered silk. Remembrance. A hunger beyond limits. The tightening in his loins was instant, tearing.

"Let me go…." The words were breathless, whispered low against his ear. Her rapid breath fanned across his heated skin, enough to send the desire twisting deep inside.

Desire born of memory. There was nothing else left in him.

Or in her. She spoke so low only because she would not struggle with him in front of his men. A princess to the last. He let her move away but kept hold of her wrist until the camp was made and she was settled.

She sat, stiff-backed, between Cunan the Pict in his long cloak and brightly coloured clothes and Duda the Northumbrian dressed in what could only be described as rags. If you were feeling charitable.

Duda's various mismatched coverings twitched, which meant Alina's bastard brother had irritated him. Cunan's hound nose flared in response. Brand did not bother to intervene. Cunan would find out. Everyone did eventually. Duda was both the most cunning-minded and the most ruthlessly disgusting fighter he knew.

He was also the most trustworthy of his men.

He left them. Because he could not bear yet to be too close to the risen phoenix, to the woman he had believed dead. Because he must. To see whether he could really hear it, or whether it was imagination: the stealthy sounds of pursuit. Nay, not pursuit, it was too circumspect as yet. The sound of a shadow. Someone who watched where they went.

It made no sense. It could not be Goadel yet. Goadel would still be racing down the ancient Roman road that led due south, believing that his prey, his brother's leman, was still hidden away in Wessex. Waiting for him. He thought of his phoenix's stunned ignorance of Goadel's intentions. It had been very well done.

But he knew what it was worth.

The stream among the tall beech was clear, ice against the heat of his face. A coldness you could lose yourself in, as darkly seductive to him as the sense of aloneness. The water drew him, as it always did, at every sudden twist of his life. It was the clearness of it, a clearness that the human world did not allow to those who had to deal with the complex ties of living.

The silence was complete beyond the plashing of the stream and yet… He raised his head because he thought he heard it: the stealthy sound, quick and untraceable.

Just as suddenly it was gone, leaving no clue. It was like trying to find an unseen enemy who would strike out of the dark. It made his skin crawl with loathing. He would deal with anyone in a fair fight in the daylight. But he had never been suited to treachery.

He was starting to learn.

Like Alina.

Treachery. He closed gritty eyelids but the vision he saw was not Goadel racing down the well-worn straightness of Ryknild Street. It was Alina's face. Not as it looked now, in its nun's veil, full of such suppressed anger and bitterness, but as it had been the first time he had seen it at Bamburgh.

She had been the most beautiful woman ever to step into that gilded hall, the Princess of the Picts. So fair of face but with the dark hair and the dark eyes that belonged to night, to the hours full of *wiccecræft* and the private secret shadow world that only lovers shared.

It had been there for all to see, how beautiful she was, that she was formed for love. That had dazzled him. But what had fastened claws in his heart was that which had been hidden. What he only believed he had seen. Her fear of her fate, her desperate, hopeless wish to be free of it. Her apparent loathing for her betrothed.

The other thing that had undone him was the fact that he had known just what a tainted and vicious force Hun was. And he could not bear the thought of a woman like her being at the mercy of that. So he had— He closed his mind against what he had done.

The only reflections in the water were of his brother's mangled flesh. His brother, Wulf, who had sur-

vived because of the strength of his will. It had been
the mysterious power of the water that had led him
back to Wulf. He had believed that Wulf was dead.

He had believed the same of Alina.

He plunged his face into the sharpness of liquid ice,
breaking the images that held him like a spell. The
merciless cold struck his skin, ran down his neck,
streamed off his hair, soaking through the shoulders
of his tunic. He opened his eyes.

He had made his decisions and nothing called back
the past. The only thing that could be changed was
what would come.

It would not be the bloody destruction of another
royal feud. It would not be the wanton cruelty that had
ravaged his home and his country under Osred's
reign. People would not be killed and dispossessed
and driven into helpless exile again.

He watched the moving water.

There were some things that could not be redeemed, and there were some things that could. There
would be no more undeserving deaths.

Not even for the powerless Pictish hostage in Bamburgh, Alina's brother. Alina who— He moved, bal-
ancing himself on his aching left arm, unprepared for
the force of the pain that shot through it. But it meant
that his right hand was free for the *seax*. It would be
much quicker than the sword.

The now familiar stealthy sound came again, but
from the opposite direction this time. Behind and to
the left.

He turned.

The knife, single-bladed, twelve inches long, deadly, embedded itself harmlessly in a tree.

"What," he bellowed, in a voice that would have split the heavens open, "are you doing here?"

There was a small space of silence.

"Dodging knives?" offered the phoenix of the ashes. "What about you?" Her shoulders were hunched into a thin, stiff line but her gaze met his, straight, like someone who had the right. "Why did you miss your aim?"

"What makes you think I did?" he yelled. "I could have split your heart in two at that distance."

"So you could."

Alina's eyes with their well-remembered match-less pride gave nothing, but he could sense the small waves of shock and fright inside her. His empty hand clenched. If he had not seen until a second later that it was her... She knew what the consequences would have been. It was there in every tightly held line of her body. But she said no more, did not so much as move.

He had seen the proof of her courage long ago, strong and high-hearted. Reckless, just like his. They should have been two of a kind.

But what she had used it for in the end... How had she managed to come here after him? Why had she appeared behind him, so silently out of the tree shadows?

She watched him, her head tilted back, her eyes unwavering.

"My guards let me come," she said, as though she could read exactly what was inside his head. "It was Cunan who argued. He… How shall I put this? He does not quite trust you. But there was not much he could say, in the end. I am both his sister and his princess. If he wanted to maintain the value of my rank before all you Northumbrians, he could not stop me. The other one merely grunted. That seems to be the full extent of his word hoard."

He felt an unruly gleam of amusement tug at his mouth. He could see the small scene playing out round the campfire. Just as Alina wished to direct it.

He cut off the dangerous rush of warmth her elegantly practiced high-handedness always invoked.

The other one, Duda, would simply have followed her. Which meant that Duda considered Cunan the Pict's reactions to his sister and his princess should be allowed to play out. Just for interest's sake.

Duda, he would not have heard moving through the trees. Neither would she.

"I have brought this." She was holding a leather saddlebag by its strap. "The medicine bag."

It was perfect. There was no better pretext she could have chosen. The first white-hot reaction was to send her packing back to her guards. He suppressed it. The princess should be afforded the opportunity to play out her game as much as her brother.

Now.

He sat down because it was easier. He would not allow Alina the phoenix to guess how weary he was,

how dangerously light-headed. He did not admit to
the fever that scored its burning path through his body.
He could not allow its weakness. There was no time.
Too many people depended on what he did.

And perhaps, if she could not kill him off, she might
decide to impress him with her good faith and do something that could see him through all that had yet to be
done.

He watched her begin the next stage of the game.

She began to unpack what was in the bag.

ALINA'S HANDS SHOOK.

It was not a good beginning for a scarce competent
healer endeavouring to inspire confidence in her patient.

She bit her lip. He had decided not to kill her.
Twice. But then he had always been cursed with too
much honour. That was what it was. Nothing was
going to inspire trust of her in those ice-bright, fever-
bright eyes.

But she was beyond caring about what was in his
head. Not just because of the exhaustion she felt. But
because there was only one clear thought she could
fix on out of the dealing and double-dealing nature of
her second mad flight with Brand. She had to cure the
wound before it killed him.

She scrabbled through the small hoard of medicines
until she found what she sought. More precious than
gold.

"There is poppy—"

"No."

Her hand wavered, its unsteadiness suddenly embarrassingly obvious. It had not occurred to her he would refuse. Stupid fool that she was. He did not trust her one inch. She had set that up herself.

Saint Dwyn. Did he not realize what was to come? How did he think he could face it if he did not... The gold-flecked eyes that held all the unabated fire that burned within, fierce beyond compare, gave her the truth.

It was she who could not face it. She swallowed gathering sickness. Perhaps if she admitted it, perhaps if part of his decision was for pride, he might agree.

"Then for my sake."

"You consider I should lose my senses for your sake?"

Northumbrians were bastards, with their double-edged words. She had forgotten quite what bastards they were. The way they struck straight through people without the need for anything so unreliable as a flying *seax*.

She forced her mind back out of the terrifying enchanted death trap of Bamburgh and into the present.

"Yes," she ground out, and then her voice hesitated. She could feel its constriction in her throat. "I do not... I find it difficult if... The less of the pain the sick person feels when I tend them, the easier it is for me."

"Nay, it is too late to feel less." The eyes were gold-bright, burning. "If I will abide it, you must."

And that was what they had agreed, from the moment the madness had begun: that they would abide the consequences of what they had done. Together. Always.

It was she who had broken the vow.

He began undoing the makeshift bandage bound over his sleeve, single-handedly.

Because there was nothing else she could do, she took the ends of the cloth from his hand. She tried to concentrate only on now.

"The sleeve will get in the way. You...you will have to take your tunic and your shirt off."

She cursed herself for stumbling over the words, such ordinary, practical words, but—

He stood up, reaching for the gilded belt buckle, garnet-crusted, wrought into the sinuous shape of a backward-looking beast. Shining colours caught the sun.

She folded her hands in the coarse wool of her skirts, and then she could no longer watch.

Of course it was not possible to have given your heart to a man, to have shared pain and grief and loss, to have felt the measure of his courage, all the mad tumult of his passion and your own confused and frightening response to it...and to know less than one of the virgin sisters at the nunnery.

He must not realize that. He must not know that her heart beat and her blood surged like white fire just at the thought of him. And that she was afraid.

He must have had enough time. She turned round.

She had her face schooled into its impassive, slightly disdainful mask. The mask that had hidden every personal thought she had ever had in the dangerous halls of Craig Phádraig.

She did not know where to look.

The first glimpse of his naked skin made her insides clench so that she could scarce draw breath. She had held his body in her arms, taken his kiss, felt all the wild pent-up passion of their dangerous flight.

She did not know him at all.

She should have done.

The tightly muscled planes of his body seemed carved and fitted together to define his maleness, to force her to know what all that strength and fierceness was about. She had never seen, never had to face that, not in this way.

Her mind numbed. That was what he was like. That was what he was. This was what she had loved with all that was in her, and yet never known. Never had the chance to know.

What would it have been like to have all that power and all that raw vital grace and all that fiercely drawn strength surround you, possess you? In the embrace that belonged to lovers. To know it with your body, feel the burning life of it and the maleness, and know no barrier. Just the total elemental completeness that existed between man and woman.

Her skin shivered with such thoughts. But she could not stop looking at him.

He took a step towards her, utterly unconcerned,

completely self-possessed. Sunlight glinted on him. Sunlight and shadows.

She stepped backwards before she knew she had done it and nearly dropped all she was carrying. She saw the brief flash of surprise in his eyes. She looked away. But it was too late. He must have seen how she stared. Like a green-sick maid on her marriage night.

"Ready to begin?"

"Of course." Her voice, at least, was quite as cool and expressionless as became a princess of the Picts. Her face was back in its mask.

Too late. Her weakness had been placed in the open.

He sat down in the sunlight, so that she could see the wound. His movements were smooth and controlled and quite unhurried.

She looked at the blacked mess of his arm. It was appalling, blood-matted. Older.

"It was truly not the sword that hurt you."

She got a Northumbrian sound of disgust.

"The sword. You could not have hit a hay bale with that, let alone killed me. I have never seen anyone with an unhandier grip. You did not even have your thumb wrapped round the hilt."

"I… Then what was it?"

"Call it a parting gift. From some of the late King Osred's hired mercenaries."

"*Osred*'s men?"

"Aye. You are going to spill that."

Her fingers tightened on the bowl of clear water

and she could feel the heat rise in her face. How could he know what she thought? Damn him for that, for being able to see— She set the bowl down before she spilled the contents.

"King's men, or what was left of them after Osred had been killed."

"After—"

The knowing eyes raked her.

"Aye. After. Though they thought I had had a hand in his death. Obvious conclusion, is it not?" She looked down. "By that death, all that I had lost was restored, and now it is my kinsman who sits on the throne."

Her gaze tangled with the jewelled belt, lying discarded in the grass, glittering in the sun like a gold-crusted serpent.

"Changes of fortune come with no warning at all. Like regrets."

"Regrets achieve nothing." She picked up the bowl. She did not spill a drop.

Dealing with the wound took a long time. She hated every moment. She had to stitch it. She was aware all the while of how he watched her, despite the pain and the mess and the sheer unremitting awfulness of what she did to him. It was as though she were on trial.

She thought at first that the test was the obvious one. Whether she planned harm or healing. So she was quite careful to show openly what she did, how she touched him, what herbs she used.

But there was something else. Something she had not fathomed and which she had neither the strength nor the will to think about.

It was all she could do to endure.

How he endured it, how he could even begin to think while all that was being done, how he could possibly have the ability and the sheer will to assess her, she did not know.

All she saw was what she must have known instinctively from the first, that his formidable strength lay not in the hard-chiselled muscles, but deep inside. The thought frightened her.

By the time it was over, she was sick to the stomach and every separate one of her muscles, already stiff from the long hours of riding, was shaking from the tension.

But it was finished, and in the end he had let her do what she would.

She had used all the skill that lay within her power and it would do no good.

She crawled away and left him. In case she was sick before she could get to the mead flask she had found in the saddlebag. She could not possibly stand up.

He needed the mead.

She crawled back towards him, holding out the hardened leather bottle. But all of a sudden it seemed very slippery. There was a scattering of dark spots in front of her eyes that she would swear by all the saints had not been there before.

"Here, give me that." A large hand took the flask out of her grasp and removed the stopper. "Drink."

"It is for you." She could not spare any more words than that. The spots in front of her eyes were getting too large. She hoped he could grasp the logic.

"I am next. Do it."

"But—" She choked.

"Wrong moment to try speaking. Happens to a lot of us. Swallow."

She spluttered, which was the nearest she could manage but some of the mead went down. It tasted like heaven. It had a glow fit to banish black ice. The dancing spots receded.

He was holding her head. His hand was a far, far greater bliss than the mead. It had more warmth. He had more warmth.

She was half lying on him.

That was him underneath her body and her aching shoulders and her neck. Her face seemed to be buried in him.

"You drink it," she said to a patch of very rich golden skin dusted with darker gold hairs.

She could feel him swallow. It made tiny, delightful rippling movements.

She should not be able to feel that.

She tried to scramble up. Her limbs would not work.

"For pity's sake, keep still, woman. You cannot stand up straight. In all probability neither can I."

"But I cannot—"

"Exactly," he said, with his brutal English logic. She digested this.

"But…" Her arm flailed. But her limbs were so

leaden with fatigue she could not lift them properly. Her hand slid with a kind of appalling slow deliberateness across the naked skin of his belly. Like a caress. Fear at the way such an action would look and feel to him gathered at the back of her mind. Fear and the familiar helpless, terrible longing.

He did not want her touch. And then she felt it, the hidden, wildly enticing shiver in the heated flesh beneath her hand. Buried need tore her.

She stopped moving. Her breath came in shallow unsteady pants like a wounded beast's. She felt his muscles tighten beneath her. She knew it was just an involuntary physical reaction, nothing to do with her, Alina. Perhaps nothing at all. Perhaps it was just his pain.

"I—"

"What?"

He was all around her, everywhere she looked, everything she touched. His skin, his hair, his scent, the animal warmth of him.

"I no longer know," she said through dry lips.

He laughed. She felt it as much as heard it. A sort of deep rumbling sound beneath her ear, and the smoothness of his flesh beneath her face rippled.

"I shall remember this. The Princess of the Picts at a loss for words."

But she was quite beyond words. They had no interest for her. All she could think of was him.

He breathed. Much more steadily than her. She felt the firm rise and fall of his chest. Controlled.

He was a wonderful seducer. At the Northumbrian palace he had been the flame that had drawn each woman's eyes, even though people said he was wild, that he was outside King Osred's favour.

Every man had been afraid of him. Because it was said that there was nothing he would not dare.

She had not cared. The danger had spoken to something inside her that she had never admitted. And at a level beyond understanding, it had also touched on the hurts that she had no way to heal.

She had wanted the fierce and changeable charm of someone who lived hard and fast.

She had wanted everything a lame creature like her could not match.

Now it was here, with her. The need to touch him, to fall under that earthy, knowing, masculine spell, to feel its danger, was stronger than ever. She needed to taste what it was like.

Even though she was afraid.

He moved under her body, the heavy contours of him sliding against her. The lure of him was so strong. You could lose everything, every sense of who you were just by touching him.

She could not allow that. Because they were no longer together. Because—

She lay with her eyes shut and tried to believe that her hands did not cling to him, that this was not just some further and more dangerous phase of his testing of her.

She had to speak. She could not give in to the power

of him. She had something to say that was vitally important, and after that she could escape. If her bespelled, exhausted, wildly unsteady brain could just work out the words.

She opened her eyes. She was so close her eyelashes rustled against his skin. Her head swam in the delight of his faint musky scent. She tried to focus.

The first thing she saw was a hand clutching at the waistband of his trousers. It must be hers. She stared at it. It would not move, despite the exercise of her will. It seemed not to belong to her. He seemed not to have noticed it.

"You make a very strange nun."

He had noticed it. He thought she was a licentious and unprincipled trollop. He doubtless thought that she was trying to practice her wiles on him so that she could regain the trust she had shattered, get him to do what she wished.

The idea of practicing her wiles on him sent a wave of heat through her so fierce it burned hotter than the harshest fever could, so strong it would burn through her heart. She buried her face deeper in his flesh and shut her eyelids against tears.

She felt his hand close over hers, thick and solid and strong. Twice as big and wide as hers. But he still had to work at it to prize her fingers away from the waistband of his trousers.

"Or else you make a strange princess."

The thick pad of his thumb slid across the tingling arch of her palm, across the base of her fingers…across the marring ridge of unhealed blisters, scratches from picking ripe sloes, a bruise.

Her breath caught. What a naive, sense-besotted fool she was. There could be naught in him of the seduction she felt. Just the clever, determined paths of his mind. Coldness followed heat, like a fast shivering chill, as though the fever that touched him touched her, too.

She stared at the scratches and the bruised nail, the more recent damage overlying the old.

It was not the hand of a princess waiting in the discreet, hidden comfort of a convenient nunnery for her lover. It was a hand that belonged to a desperate and penniless fugitive. The hand of someone who worked for their keep in a true house devoted to simplicity and usefulness.

She fought for her voice. "Oh, that. That was just an accident. I fell over and scratched my hand."

There was only the quietness of the glade, the faint sound of clear falling water. Running water was so strong. But its pure sound had only one shape in her mind.

Liar.

"It seems fated to be your weakness, this hand."

The coldness stabbed ice through her. He had never mocked at the accident that had disfigured her hand. He was the kind of person whose instinct was to deal with what was, not what should be. She envied that. It was the quality above all others that had scored through the barriers she had set against trust.

He turned her hand to the sunlight. Her muscles tightened in a denial that went all the way back to childhood. Yet his action did not hold the mockery every instinct expected. It was different: an assessment that was filled with deliberation, quite relentless. That was not something she had associated with him.

She had no right to expect anything else.

She could tell from his breath, sense through the fiercely intimate touch of his body against hers, the implacable distrust of all that she said.

She waited. He still had hold of her hand. The warmth of his flesh invaded hers.

"Alina?"

She could not speak. She had broken his trust long ago and the connection between them was severed beyond any possibility of redemption. But he held her hand. Her body. She could not stop him. Neither could she stop her powerful awareness of him. It trapped her as surely as the physical force he was so capable of. *Her father had trapped her mother, in just such a way.*

But it could not have felt like this. Not such warmth, warmth that blossomed on the inside just from the touch of one body against another. A warmth that was frightening, yes, but at the same time intoxicating. A warmth that filled her with a longing so deep it would kill her.

"Naught but a chain of accidents. Is that the way of it?" His voice was as deceptively gentle as his hold on her. Just as seductive. "So many things are not what they seem."

"Aye."

Like you, like the way your body feels to me, the way your arms feel around me, as though carnal desire and trust could exist together.

It was not possible.

"Sometimes I would rather there was only what seems, and not what is—" She shut her mouth. That was the mead talking. Or her longing.

Or her fear.

She was trembling inside. All from the alien touch of male flesh. His flesh. So full of mysterious strength. A vitality that was so uniquely his. A strength that could rend and destroy.

Or be destroyed.

She would not be able to bear that. She had to say what she must, and then she could be free of him. Now. Somehow. She had to think, even though all her mind could focus on was the strangeness of lying on the earth with a man. And all she could see was their joined hands coiled on his lower belly.

She had never lain like this with any man and his body was so beautiful, the chest solid, the abdomen a tight, flat line of muscle over the hipbone. Everything she felt was so different in shape and texture and composition, the thick smoothness of the skin, the soft-rough feel of body hair. She craved him so much that it was like a pain. A pain that burned her on the inside, the way the touch of his skin scorched hers with its heat.

The heat.

The heat was unnatural.

The danger was not just from the wound to his flesh. The flames were inside. She knew them. Knew them for her own. She would rather they consumed her inch by inch than him.

"The wound is fell."

She felt him start, felt the small change in the rhythm of his breath.

"What do you mean?"

The words were bland, expressionless. But she knew that the whole of that sharp intelligence was focused on her.

"I mean that it is powerful." She paused. They were strange words to use for a wound: fell, powerful. But they were how she felt. She sought to express it in a more usual way. "Dangerous."

The broad shoulders shrugged, muscle expanding and contracting against her skin.

"It is hardly likely to kill me. Besides, there is no time. I have got too much to do."

Her heart twisted. He did not know, or he did not admit, even to himself, how he ate his heart out. That the burden he carried was lethal. He just went on. *Because there was so much to do.* She sought for the words.

"The payment for what happened to your brother lies with me, not you."

The sheet of muscle under her body seemed to change out of recognition, reconstituting itself into one terrifying mass of power. He moved, surging up so that she briefly lost his warmth and then she did not. Because he dragged her with him, his hands digging into her arms. She was sitting up, imprisoned against the solid, remorseless wall of his body. Trapped. But that was not the worst.

She could see his eyes.

"What have you to say of Athelwulf, my brother?"

I caused his death.

She would never be able to get another word out of the dryness of her mouth. She had called up the demons of the past and they were there, in the all-consuming fury of his eyes, bright gold fire, burning, like the heat of his hands on her arms.

Fever heat. And because she knew what had happened she could see past the fury to the pain.

"I am saying that what happened to your brother was my fault, not yours. You rescued me because I thought I did not want to marry Hun. You arranged it all. Paid Hun my wergild, my life-price… Yes, you did. I know it though you did not tell me."

She took a breath. She did not know from the burning, feverish eyes whether he heard her. Whether what she said reached through to the fortress of his mind.

"But Hun broke his word and chose to pursue you anyway, despite the honour payment. You sacrificed everything to take me from Hun, and Hun made King Osred destroy you for it, so that there was only exile." *And death.* "And Athelwulf—"

"My brother chose to save both our hides."

"You did not know what he would do. That he

would go back to throw Hun off the scent. It was not your fault Hun caught him." *Killed him, burned the corpse so that there was nothing to be found except bones.* "It was Hun's fault. Mine."

But Brand did not hear her, she knew he did not. What she said meant nothing to the fire in his eyes. She tried again.

"None of this would have happened if I had not thrown myself on your mercy so you had no other choice but to take me from Hun—"

"No other choice? Is that what you think?"

"Yes." It was the truth. Yet she could feel his rapid breath, as he would feel hers. Memory consumed her, and with it all the longing, all the fierce desperation, all the pain. It beat inside her, as though it would not be contained. As though it still existed in the silent Wessex air between them.

She struggled to speak, to go on saying what she must.

"The payment for what happened to your brother is mine, not yours. It is not a payment you can make by throwing your own life away. The guilt is mine."

The power of him, all that savagely leashed intensity would tear the soul out of her.

"Why would you say such a thing?"

Because that much, at least, is truth between us. Because I cannot bear that the weight of guilt that belongs to me should kill you. That is why I ran away from you. That is why I went back to Hun.

I want you to live.

She wanted to shout it out so that it would split the foreign southern air in two. She wanted to say it into the light so that there would be no darkness between them, but she could not. Because if he knew she had cast herself adrift for his sake, he would never leave her. Because he always took her burdens.

She forced breath.

"I can recognize when I have made mistakes. I—" It was impossible to hold his gaze. She had to force the words out of her mouth.

"It was wrong, what I did, escaping with you. Being with you."

His eyes still burned. But differently. He watched her…differently. She thought he would speak. The hardness of his grip on her arms changed. But she could not have moved away from him. She did not have the strength. Her breath was coming in gut-wrenching gasps so that he must think she was ill. Mad. Both.

She got the last words out.

"I realized. So I went back where I belonged. To Hun."

She saw his eyes go totally blank. Lifeless. Black. It was terrifying. His eyes were not like that. They were gold. Gold never changed. It was imperishable.

"I made my decision," she said, through the raw-ness inside her chest. She could not breathe. "That was my choice."

His hands let her go and the shadows were not just around him. They were everywhere. She was falling.

CHAPTER FOUR

ALINA WOKE WITH her head wedged against his chest. She could not move because his arm, heavy, immobile, lay across her waist.

She should leave him be, after what she had said. She wanted to leave him. She wanted to crawl away into some black pit and never come out.·

She raised her head.

There was something wrong with the light. Pearl-grey. Cold. Not the golden, heavy warmth of late afternoon.

"Brand…"

He did not move. Nothing. She stared round wildly at the wrong shapes of the trees. They were not as she remembered. She could not hear the stream. She had no idea where she was. It was like trying to wake out of a nightmare and being unable to.

Her head twisted. Her arm sought instinctively for the now familiar shape of his body. Cool. Almost…cold. A scream, raw and with the power to tear, lodged itself in her throat. And then she felt it: the faint, soft edge of his breath against her cheek.

"Brand…"

But he still did not move. He was deeply, numbingly asleep.

He should not be so cold. She pulled the thickness of the cloaks that covered them tighter round him. There was a fire nearby. Still burning. Full consciousness hit her. The campfire. His men. They were there. Shadowy shapes moving in the half-light. Morning.

He must have brought her here from the glade. And she had not known, could not remember. She still had her nun's clothing and over that, the heavy cloaks. His.

He had taken her shoes off. Her feet were buried in his legs. The solidness of his body curved round hers. They lay, tangled like awakening lovers in the midst of his men.

"He is ill. Is he not?"

The familiar voice, low, sibilant with the sounds of Craig Phádraig, was right beside her.

"Cunan!" Hound. Her brother's breath touched her skin. She could not suppress her startled gasp and she saw the small reward that gave in the triumph of his smile.

She drew away, struggling to raise herself between the lissom heaviness of Brand's body and the tight aggressive barrier of her brother's.

Hellhound. The keen-boned face and the intensity of his eyes suited the name. Her father's unquestioning slave. In his person he managed to combine unbending loyalty with the ability to tear people's guts out when necessary. She swallowed. Her mouth felt as dry as wood shavings.

She sat back, putting a hand to her face, trying to disguise the shudder. She felt appalling. Her eyes burned and her bones ached from the hard ground, from yesterday's exhausting ride.

"Cunan, why are you—"

"How ill?"

The eager, knife-sharp eyes watched not her, but the sleeping form beside her, with an attention that was spine-chilling. The words *more ill than he knows, perhaps dangerously so,* died on her lips.

Cunan was her brother, as much so in her mind as Modan, even if he was not legitimate.

But he was her father's man. His loyalty to that did not include allowance for his sister's shameful and inappropriate attachment to a Northumbrian.

Past attachment.

She moved her hand, as though she would shield the sleeping face of the Northumbrian, as much as her own face, from Cunan's gaze.

"I have tended the wound. It will heal. There is a touch of fever, but that is as you would expect."

She shrugged, to emphasize the carelessness of her words. The movement made the cloak slip from her shoulder. The sharp gaze shifted.

"I am not sure that anything is quite as I expected."

She was suddenly aware that her wimple had been lost somewhere. That her hair streamed over the shoulders exposed by the rumpled cloak. That before her brother's face she had spent the night in the arms of the man she had abandoned her lawful betrothed for. The man she had wanted above all others as her lover.

She fought down the consciousness of where she was, the heat that rose in her mind. She lifted her head. Perhaps it had not been such an ill placement after all, to be here in the middle of the ring of Brand's men. Nothing could have happened without them knowing, without Cunan the Hound knowing.

Even if they did not realize how much cause her supposed lover had to hate her.

She simply stared at him, with the practice of nineteen and a half years spent living in a court that had been more dangerous to her than to an illegitimate offspring.

"There are many things that are not as we might expect," she said. "Sometimes we have to adapt to them."

"But not at the expense of the duty we owe to the land that gave us birth. If that means aught to you?"

Duty.

It had been beaten into her head from birth that she must put duty first. She had tried with all that was in her to do what was right. She had agreed to the marriage arranged by her uncle and her father. Because it would forge an alliance that might pacify Northumbria.

For the first time in her life her father had been pleased with her.

Then she had found out what Hun was. A savage, a ruthless man who would encourage his king to dispossess or murder anyone who got in his way. Hun was the useful retainer who carried out such tasks for ambition and policy, for reward. For the enjoyment of cruelty.

Her uncle and her father must have been aware of that unstoppable savagery. They had known exactly what they were asking. They had not known that in the end, she would not do it.

That had been both her choice and her doom. And then Brand had come, like light out of the dark. But the light had not survived. It was impossible in this world.

"My duty means exactly as much as it should mean." Such fine words. They hissed through the still air. But they were hollow. She had failed in every kind of duty. To her land, her king and her family.

To the foreign Northumbrian warrior who had given up everything for her.

She turned away, so that she would not see the dissatisfied eyes, the face so like her father's. So that she would no longer hear the tongue of Pictland. Bright gold eyes were narrowed on her face.

He had heard.

When had he woken? When she had spoken of her duty, whispering in Celtic with Cunan the Hound?

She told herself it could not matter. Brand already knew she was a traitor.

"What a delight you are in the mornings, lady.

Never at a loss. But I am afraid we cannot linger here. However you charm your companions."

He had heard everything. She knew it. She only wondered that Cunan did not know. She saw her brother's eyes sharpen in anger. But it was only at the obvious dismissal. There seemed no consciousness of the deeper meaning in the English words. The hidden warning to him and to her. But then Brand was wearing his wantonly reckless face, the one that hid all the ruthless intelligence inside.

He was smiling at Cunan.

"I know how eager my lady is to journey on to Bamburgh and her brother. The same eagerness must be yours, of course."

"What else?"

The smile was returned, with a hint of secrets withheld, a knowledge superior to the other man's. And then she realized. It had not occurred to Cunan that Brand spoke Pictish.

She was the only one who knew. The knowledge was there like a weapon in her hand. But like every weapon she had ever held either with or against Brand, it was two-edged. If she gave that knowledge to her brother, Brand would know who had betrayed him.

She got up, fighting life into stiffened limbs. She wished to appear to busy herself getting ready, so that she could do what she really wanted: watch Brand and how he moved, every word he spoke and every gesture he made.

The camp was struck. Fast. Brand's men moved with a disciplined efficiency that should have pierced warnings through Cunan's devious head. The only thing Brand stopped to do without the slightest care for time was to make her eat, more than she wanted to. But it was either swallow the food herself or be force-fed.

Nothing faltered. Nothing went wrong. They rode as fast as they had yesterday, nay, faster, with scouts and in complete silence. They had passed the border into Mercia, the wide kingdom that lay between Wessex and Northumbria. Enemy to both.

She used the only time of respite to seethe herbs for her patient, feverfew, woundwort and blackberry leaves. Pointless gesture. It would not be enough. They both knew it.

She rode and watched and waited for him to succumb. So did Cunan.

She had had time to make her plans.

She made use of the instant when Duda closed up beside her mount and Cunan drifted ahead, drawn away from his eager watch on her by the greater eagerness with which he watched his true quarry.

She turned to the revolting collection of patched wool that housed Brand's companion and began on the stratagem that might have consequences beyond her control.

There were not many choices.

"You realize you will have to do something, do you not?"

Shaggy hair and a beard that seemed to be a refuge for the remains of last night's meal turned toward her. There had to be eyes in there somewhere. A mind?

"About what?"

She glanced ahead. Cunan's brightly coloured cloak caught the wind.

"Dwyn's bones," she hissed. "I have no time for games. You will need to have your plan worked out before Compline…" What did they call it in English? "Nightsong. Otherwise you, all of us, will be taking our orders in Pictish."

Something blinked. Perhaps there were eyes in there. She reserved her opinion on the brain.

"Well, that would not do any good. I do not speak Pictish." *There certainly was no brain.* "Of course, it would be all right for you. Looking forward to it?"

Choices.

This time, she could not tear her gaze away from her brother's unprotected back.

"It does not matter the smallest curse what I think. I am telling you what is going to happen—"

"Ah. You know, do you? Got it timed?"

She gritted her teeth. He probably thought, in his grubby Northumbrian head, that she had added the juice of deadly nightshade berries to the infusion of herbs she had given to Brand.

This was pointless. There was no more she could do. She spurred forward, after Cunan. But as her horse crested the rise, she saw it. What must be their destination: a little group of buildings inside high wooden walls. The unmistakable shape of a house of religion. The single bell suspended above the shingle roof rang out across the evening air.

It was a small monastery. They were allowed inside. It would have been a brave monk who had refused admittance to so many armed men. But when the doors of the refuge shut behind them was when the danger began.

Brand collapsed.

She had been waiting for it. She knew it would happen the moment sanctuary was reached because it was only force of will that had kept him going. Will and the responsibility for his men riding through the open lands of Mercia.

She also knew that there would be a small moment that was hers because the watchdogs would begin rending each other apart instantly. There was room for only one to command. She could not control that. There was only one course for her.

She slid through them, fell on her knees beside the body and flung herself on it, so that it would take the most unseemly show of force to drag her off.

This was her battle, fought on her terms. She would win it. The fire in her blood surged in the strength-giving recklessness that came only with total commitment to one course of action.

She raised her head.

"Father..." She fixed her gaze, a lethal mixture of helplessness and command, on the monk who appeared to have the most importance. "You must help me, please." She let all the emphasis fall on that small word, *me*.

"Lady!" He knelt beside her in the rushes. A gilded cross set with river pearls swung from a cord round his neck. She had not been mistaken. The abbot.

"Quickly. Help me with him. It is fever from a wound. Outlaws. We were attacked…." It would serve. Not one person in their party was going to admit who they really were or what they were doing.

She permitted a sob. It was not difficult. The abbot made distracted noises of comfort but she was pleased to see his hands on the patient, his gaze, were direct and competent. He might have the strength to take her side.

"Thank you." She breathed it.

Only then did she give in to the need to look at Brand. Like Duda and Cunan, she fought tactically.

His face terrified her. The paleness and the shadows round the eyes. She had thought she was prepared for this. She was not.

"Dear heart." It came out without any of the duplicity she had planned. She touched his face. It burned her hand. She thought he was gone, lost in the grip of the fever world, but then the thick-lashed eyes fluttered.

"Brand? It will be all right. There is help for you here that—"

The look in his eyes, one slight movement of his hand, cut that all off as irrelevant.

"Alina…"

She could scarce hear. All she could see was the terrible effort this took.

"Do not speak."

But the eyes held her: gold light, unquenchable. It was as though hurt and betrayal and bitterness no longer existed. It was the look that had passed between them and changed the world's shape for them. For her it had been stronger than the power of isolation, despair and the malice of two kingdoms. Still was.

"Alina...trust Duda. He knows..."

She leant lower, trying to shield him from view with her body. All her senses trained on the strained mouth.

"Do not go with Cunan...betray..."

Her brother, her flesh and blood. Her only link with her home.

"Why..." But it was too late. Someone grabbed her arm and even as she braced herself, clinging to the fever-wracked body she could feel the life of consciousness drain out of it.

"Lady, come away."

Duda. Even his hands were hairy. He had won then. It was hardly surprising. He had half a dozen Northumbrians at his back.

Above her she heard Cunan's voice arguing. He was the one who was supposed to protect her.

But all she could see, all she could think of was the lifeless form in her arms and the fact that his last conscious thought, right or wrong, whatever he believed her future should be, had been of her. All that filled her mind was the bond that had been forged between them those long months ago in Bamburgh. Tested by loss that could not be borne without breaking.

Their bond was shattered, yet even so, her last thought, her last action, would be for him.

Behind her Cunan's voice rose. The werewolf's paw on her arm tightened. There was only one weapon that would keep her with Brand.

She fixed her gaze on the abbot.

"Father, if you could send for the infirmarian to help my husband…" There was an appalled silence behind her. She filled it by saying, "I know something of healing myself and I can help."

She took a strength-giving breath. "My husband is all in the world to me." She let her voice rise in pitch, become shrill, but piercingly clear. "I will not be parted from him." The words rent the air in a male-chilling shriek of womanly desperation.

Her hand, despite the weakness of badly healed bones, despite the grip of the wolf's claws at her wrist, embedded itself in Brand's tunic. The other hand lighted on his unconscious face with a possessiveness none could miss. It was not feigned.

No one moved. She took another breath. She sobbed. The abbot must have thought it pathetic. The others knew precisely what it was: a declaration of war.

The next sob took on an edge that made teeth grate.

"Of course you must stay with your husband and

help care for him. There is terrible danger on the road for travellers. We will do all we can to aid you." The abbot's hand patted her shoulder in a commendable attempt to stem the threatening flood of hysterics. She used the opportunity to shake off the werewolf's paw. Her foot slid back, stabbing into Cunan's ankle.

The abbot got to his feet, filling the small space she had created behind her. "You and your husband are safe now."

She looked up, her eyes swimming with tears and, she hoped, quite luminous with gratitude. Graciousness in victory. Always.

"Saint Dwyn reward you for your kindness, Father."

Even Brand would have appreciated the appositeness of that.

HE WAS GOING TO DIE.

It was so obvious that when the abbot came to administer extreme unction, no one protested.

Alina watched. It did not matter what she had done, neither her strategy, nor her vain attempts at healing. Some things could not be turned aside.

The infirmarian had tried everything, every wort and herb and simple. No one could have faulted his skill. Just as no one could doubt the faithful wife's devotion, or the watchful loyalty of companions, all of them, bristling with weapons. Cunan had had the sense to keep his mouth shut. Duda, his command firmly established, was not in a mood to refer to reason.

She glanced at Cunan's furious face. She did not believe he would be harmed while Brand was alive. But afterwards, if he did something that… She could not think of afterwards.

When the sacrament was over, Duda threw everyone out of the chamber. Healing, he said, had proved useless. Prayers could be said in the chapel with the same effect. Wives could weep elsewhere.

"I do not weep," said Alina, "but I scream very well. The brothers will hear me."

She thought for one moment that the *seax* he was toying with would be stuck through her throat. But in the end Duda did not move.

She brushed past the naked edge of the blade and sat down at her accustomed place on the wall bench with the pitcher of water.

There was no point in going on, but she could not stop. Her arm reached out in the rhythm that had become eaten into her brain. She watched the muscles shake with fatigue. It was quite visible even under the coarse wool of her sleeve.

Soak the cloth with cool water, squeeze it out. Touch him. Smooth the wad of wet linen across the alien-familiar form of his body, the long, sleek, full-muscled shape of arm and leg, the wide chest: smoothly dense skin, dark gold hairs flattened by the water, by her touch. Burning. All burning.

The cloth under her hand heated before her touch could bring relief. Nothing she could do to stop all that brilliant, precisely constructed beauty, all that frightening, virile, masculine strength from being consumed before her eyes.

When she touched him with her hand, his fire burned through the aching wet coldness of her fingers.

Her hand dropped. Mostly because her arm was too heavy for her to move. Mostly because her heart was dead.

She slumped, buried her face in the damp-glittering mass of his hair. So close that her face fitted beside his like the other side of a coin. His heat enfolded her like a shield against the chills that chased over her exhausted body. If she just cast herself on those warm, strong planes, if she placed her arms around his body and held him, she would be safe. Nothing, besides him, had ever made her safe. The urge to do that, just to hold on to him for eternity, was overwhelming.

But she could not. The warmth of him was destructive. The breath that slid so softly across her skin was fought for. The wide, strong chest strained for every inward life-giving gasp of air, so that she was afraid to touch it.

She kept her hand at his head, where the life-force found its home, the force that burned too strongly. Her voice spoke, even before she knew what it would say.

"You must not die." The words whispered into the tangled, sweat-streaked hair were low, but clear as crystal water. "You cannot. There are too many people who need you. Look at Duda."

She raised her head to glance across the room.

"See?"

She had no fear of any reaction from the heap of despair across the room because she spoke in Celtic. Her language, and yet not so. Theirs. Because they had shared it. It was what they had spoken in the night, when they had fled through the dark, when they had shared what small secret moments they had had, in love.

She buried her face again in his hair, as though he had looked with her, as though he could hear her. As though it were not utterly and wildly mad to carry on a conversation with an unconscious man.

"He is loyal to you and he depends on you. He would collapse into a heap of grubby rags and disintegrate without you. He does not want you to go. If he knew how, he would beg you."

As I would.

"Brand?" The heated body moved. As though he heard, as though he knew and would not forsake them.

"Brand…" But it was nothing, just fever dreams. Each time his tormented body moved, each time the dry lips seemed to form words, her heart leaped. But he did not see her, could not return her words.

The only breath of sound she had recognized had not been her name. That name had belonged to the man who had been sacrificed.

Athelwulf.

The division between them was not in the power of either of them to heal.

She touched his brow. But even her touch made him twist away from her, like someone in torture.

Like someone who was cut off, even from what would help them.

Like someone who was alone.

Even when he said his brother's name it was as though he warded someone away.

She picked up the cloth, plunged it into the water, squeezed it out. Her hand shook, from exhaustion, from fear, from pity and helplessness and…soul-destroying rage. The cloth hit the wall with a smack that shocked the rag bundle on the other side of the bed out of its motionless despair.

She did not care. Her hands sank into the heap of discarded herbs on the scrubbed wooden table, horehound and feverfew, henbane, viper's bugloss and the seeds of cleavers. And vervain. Vervain the enchantment herb that staunched bleeding, dispelled fevers and the effects of snakebite, and when it was rubbed on the body granted wishes.

It conciliated hearts.

There was naught it could do here. It was useless. Everything was useless: the cloth, the herbs, the whole skill of the infirmarian. Even Duda's despair was useless. Her hands tightened on crushed leaves.

They were all powerless to fight his illness because none of them understood. It had nothing to do with the wound.

She was the only one who knew the cause. And she was the one who could not heal it.

Because there was nothing else that could be done, she stepped into the flames with him.

She gathered the burning body into her arms, beyond thought of whether she would damage the wound or strain the laboured breath in his lungs. She held him with a strength beyond the tiredness in her arms. The coolness of her body melded with the heat of his until it was consumed and there was only one body tormented by the same pain and the words that came spilling out of her head were the words she had most wanted to say.

"It is me who cannot live without you. You cannot leave me. You have to remember what we said. That we would abide this together, whatever happened for right or wrong."

She took a shaking breath. "I would share all the wrong that has happened, as much as the right. I know what my blame is and I would not leave you to bear what you should not." Her voice was like a thread in the darkness, something he might not have heard had he been conscious. "I am with you…"

Her words sped up, tumbling over one another while she held him. They whispered against his hot flesh. "I have not broken the vow we made, not truly. I might have seemed to because I could not bear the thought of what you would lose for my sake."

Her hands fastened with desperation on burning flesh, fragments of leaf clinging to her damp skin: white horehound, feverfew. And vervain that held magic. The coolness of her breath mingled with his.

"I never left you in my mind, in my heart. You were always there and you always will be. If you leave now, if you pass into the shadows, I will go with you. That is how it will be with us, always."

She was aware, in some other part of her brain, that Duda was on his feet, might be moving toward her. The thought did not stop her, nothing that belonged to the world could. Her hands held him, fragrant leaves crushed against his skin.

"You will not go. You will live. I know you will, because you will not leave with so much still to be done. With so many who need you. Because that is what you do. Abide with people and help them and understand their pain. You will not go. I know it even if you do not. It does not matter if you do not know. I know it for you."

His skin burned.

CHAPTER FIVE

ALINA WOKE in the same position as before, with her head jammed into his chest and her body curled up tightly into a ball, like a frightened child's.

He did not stir.

It was like waking into the same nightmare. Except it was not the pure cold light of dawn against her eyelids, it was a flickering golden glow, and she knew exactly where she was.

She could not have slept. Not at this time. It was not possible. How long? How long had she slept and why had no one woken her? Duda? Cunan? The monks?

The red-yellow glow beat against her eyelids: torchlight mixed with the light from the hearth in the monastery chamber. Fire's heat.

She could not open her eyes.

"Duda…"

He would be there, the Anglian werewolf, lurking on his side of the bed like some angry, despairing spirit. He would be able to tell her.

"Duda?"

There was nothing. Not a sound.

There was no one there. The chamber was empty. They had left her alone.

They had left Brand alone.

How could they have done that?

She twisted round, opening her eyes, forcing her useless limbs into movement. She turned her head.

The aching sobs, suppressed all night, rose chokingly in her throat, found their way out at last, so that her stiffened body was racked with them.

The sobs would not stop. Even though she should not cry. Not now.

But then that was what had the power to rend the heart most truly, not death, but life.

She buried her head in flesh that was scarcely warm, that was cool, blessedly, miraculously cool. She wrapped her arms round it, buried her hands in it, her whole body. Held it close, in her embrace, because just for that moment, it was hers.

He slept. Not like before when she had woken beside him in the morning under the trees, but with a quality that was quite different. Peace. It took her a while to recognize what it was. Because it was something that she had dreamed of all her life and seldom experienced.

It was something they had never had.

She did not want to rob him of such an unlooked-for gift. She should move away, leave him, but she could not go. She was bound as though under a double spell. Caught by him, and caught by that elusive quality you could never hold but which had lighted on him at this moment like a gift from heaven. It was just there in the simplicity and the softness of his breath, in his touch.

She lowered her head with infinite caution, dreading waking him, breaking the spell. She laid her head against his chest, but even with that slight movement, she felt his breathing change. He would wake—

"Alina…" His voice was roughened, fathoms deep, but not harsh. It could have been part of the dream-spell.

She raised her head. His eyes watched her, wide, scarcely focused, their brightness hazed, still half in the dream world.

"You are real."

She smiled. She could not help it. But she was frightened by it because the smile might show what was inside: the all-consuming joy that was the other side of the terrible fear she had felt. She tried to think, to be practical. To pull herself out of the dream that seemed to hold them both.

"It is all right. You will be well now, and—"

But once again, what she would have said was brushed aside, and she could see the same struggle in his eyes to fix on what had to be said and done, what was real.

"You are quite safe?"

"Of course—"

"Duda…"

Her smile became wry. "Won control by strength of numbers and the measure of his rage. If you had died, there would have been blood."

The wryness in her smile found its exact match in the subtle change of expression in his eyes. Her heart jumped because it read that instinctive understanding between them that had never needed words.

A wholly inappropriate heat jarred through her body. She veiled her eyes with her lashes, lest he could see, lest he could guess that she was still slave to the delight of sharing his thoughts and to the rich touch of his body, however fleeting.

"You must drink," she said. "There is a herbal draught I—we—the infirmarian prepared. You will need that."

She slid away, so that he would not be able to feel how she shook, sense the hot trembling rush inside her. In her haste, her hand brushed against the thick, curving muscle of his thigh, sliding across the full length of that solid nakedness. She gasped. It was so different, touching him now, now that he knew, now that she could see his eyes.

She had nursed him for the endless age of the dark night, had touched almost every inch of that naked flesh. She had ached for him, poured all that was of her heart and soul into that touch, and now when he looked at her, her breath choked and lightning flared through her veins. And fear.

"I—"

His hand caught hers as it skittered away from the hard tightness of his knee.

"You were there, were you not, through all that hell dark? It was you...."

The intensity in his eyes, the rough-fierce caress of his voice, the raw unabated strength in the hand that held her, would take everything. They would take her and all that she was. They, he, had that much power.

And then what would she do? If she gave in to all that she wanted more than her life? She could bring nothing but disappointment and then destruction. She could not bring the kind of peace that had touched him before.

"No. At least, not all the time. Of course I helped. It was the infirmarian who had the skill. He prepared this."

She turned away, towards the heavy wooden table that held the spilled herbs, the water pitcher and the leather flask with the healing draught. He let her go. Her hand slid through his so that she could feel the faint warmth of his palm, the hard calluses caused by sword fighting, the firm deft pads on each separate finger.

"I will get the draught." She nearly spilt it. It took all the will that she had to get her shaking hands under control. But she did it, and when she turned, her face was the beautiful and unmoving mask that had always kept her inviolate.

Or kept her trapped.

She watched him drink and then fall again into the blessing of sleep. But the peace was gone.

THERE WAS SOMETHING CLAWING at him, fastening fiend's talons into his shoulder and his arm, sending the pains of hell through him. He could not get it loose. The black, faceless shape of it blotted out the torchlight. It was mouthing something.

"Oy," ventured the shape.

Not a *hell-thane* then, a hell fiend. Duda. Although sometimes there was not much difference. Brand glanced round the small chamber.

Alina was gone.

"What?" he enquired.

"Thought you would never wake up."

"There was a choice?"

"Oh. Sorry. Was that the bad arm?"

Some questions were not worth answering. He stuck to asking them.

"Well?"

"Few things been happening while you were not exactly with us." There was a reproachful glint somewhere in the midst of hair and whatever had not completed the perilous journey to Duda's mouth during breakfast.

"What?" He bit back amusement, adopting the tone of one suitably chastened for willful inattentiveness over the last day and a half.

"Cunan."

He forced his mind to work past the pain and the light-headedness and waited.

"Went off."

"Off? Where?" He hauled himself into something approaching a sitting position. The heap of rags beside him twitched, as though the occupant somewhere deep inside was feeling suddenly uncomfortable.

"You did not follow him." It was a statement of an unpalatable fact. They both knew it. But somehow it still came out sounding like a question because he could not believe what Duda had, had *not,* done. Not with the lives of seven men and a woman at stake.

He closed his mind on the vision of Alina leaning over him, her lithe supple body curving its too-frail warmth against his. Her face and the soft lilt of her voice, both real and imagined in fever dreams.

"I was…occupied."

"You found something more important than discovering what Cunan is planning?" His voice would have bitten through steel. He—

"You."

"Me?"

"Thought you were *fæg,* death doomed."

He did not know what to say to that. He waited until the air currents in the closed chamber stopped moving against his naked skin.

"Not me."

The words would rip something in the sudden stillness. In him.

"I am the one who always survives scatheless, if you remember."

Duda was staring at him. He suddenly recognized the expression in the clever ruthless eyes.

It was the most finely-prized gift in the realm of Middle Earth, the one true and increasingly rare quality that kept the world from collapsing in on itself in chaos. It was the one thing he could no longer stand.

Loyalty.

"I do not—"

"You do not understand yourself, or what you mean to people," said Duda. "It is like a *hell-thane*'s blindness in you when otherwise you see so much." And then before his fever-racked brain could grapple with that, "Cunan was pleased with himself. Doubtless he is a bit more disappointed today with you being on the mend."

Brand uncoiled his fists.

"He is back, then?"

"Aye."

"And the watcher?" The noiseless sound and the formless shape that followed them.

"No sign."

Gone then. Gone to report to Goadel on the whereabouts of his brother's killer and his brother's mistress.

The last question had to be forced out.

"And the Lady Alina?"

"You mean your lady wife?"

THERE WAS NEVER ENOUGH hot water.

Alina rolled her eyes. It was one of life's insoluble problems wherever you lived, at the palace of Craig Phádraig or in a swineherd's hovel. It certainly applied to nunneries and monasteries.

"Another bucket."

She would fast be running out of favours at the monastery kitchen. She sweetened it with a smile.

"I can carry them."

This went down better with the cook and his sweating assistant.

Easy. The Princess of Craig Phádraig and former

convent inhabitant suspended the buckets from their chain and slid the wooden yoke with practiced ease across her shoulders.

It was a good job it was not far to the dangerous invalid's chamber.

"I will be back for the others. Four more," she added in the voice that had directed innumerable banquets involving roast venison, quail dressed in its feathers, mead, wine, jugglers, singers, stuffed boar and jellied quince all in one evening.

They bowed.

Something unsavoury unravelled itself from the doorway.

"Give you a hand with that?"

"No, but you can fetch the rest." She eyed the disreputable shuffling heap of wool. It seemed to waver in the wind as though it hardly had the strength to stand upright. "Eight buckets."

"Eight?"

"You work it out using all the fingers on both hands minus the thumbs."

Something furtive moved amongst all that hair. She fancied she caught the gleam of remarkably well-kept teeth.

"I shall remember that."

THE SOUND OF THE DOOR woke him.

Brand had no idea how much later it was. He had a vague recollection of eating at some stage. He tried forcing his eyes open.

"So how did you get on with that Pictish viper?"

"Remarkably."

It was not Duda. It was that other Pictish viper.

His wife.

Or else it was a shape-shifter. You did not expect the Princess of Craig Phádraig to be carrying buckets.

But then you did not expect a princess to have work-roughened hands and an undernourished body when she was waiting in discreet seclusion for her lover. You did not expect her to lie about the fact she had spent a night and a day nursing you.

Above all, you did not expect to have married her without knowing it.

But then, he had not expected her to leave him.

It was more than time that the mysteries about Alina were laid bare.

She still wore the sack but had given up the hideous wimple. Her jet hair streamed down her back and over her shoulders in cascading falls. She set the buckets down with a graceful turn of her body that must be practiced, using all of her weight for balance.

But she was so slight, especially now.

"You should not be doing that. Is there no servant?" he demanded. Which was a really clever beginning and only went to show the dangerous chaos of his feverish brain.

"Someone else is bringing the rest."

She was not looking at him. Just as well, because he had made some instinctive move to offer help. At the moment it was not the most productive stratagem to move before you were prepared. Or to speak.

He had levered himself into some semblance of control when the door opened again to admit something carrying further buckets. It was either Duda or some other and less fastidious shape-shifter. He was followed by a retinue of servants who deposited more buckets.

The servants vanished. The buckets steamed gently. Duda remained, examining the wooden, iron-bound pails with distant curiosity. He and water had not always been the best of friends.

"Always good for a man to look his best."

It was a shape-shifter. It had to be. He committed the lethal folly of catching Alina's eye. She had been watching Duda with the gravity she might have accorded to one of her uncle's ambassadors. But then she did not have to make any obvious change of expression for him. He just knew.

She managed to turn the small break in that polite gravity into the sort of smile that turned people as pliable as beeswax. Duda retired in self-satisfied triumph.

It was perfectly done, and the real truth was that he did not know anything about her at all. Not what had gone amiss between her and Hun, not what she thought or what she did.

Not why she had ever gone with him in the first place.

The ache of that was unbearable and behind it was

the fury. The fury for what had been done to Athelwulf, to all of the people who had had to follow him into the penury and the danger of exile. The burning, white-hot, limitless rage for what had been done to his home.

And after all that had happened, she had chosen to follow the perpetrator.

"It is going to be a bath," she said and began tipping buckets. "I will help you."

The mind-blackening impulse to stop her at her game, to use force instead to bring whatever was in that beautifully poised head out into the light of day, was suppressed. There were other ways. Ways she might enjoy as much as she had seemed to enjoy them before.

He slid off the bed. Quite controlled, this time. Every life-giving thread of anger harnessed into a strength that was unreal, that had an existence far too powerful for the fever-ridden shell of his body.

"Then help me."

She turned that maddeningly graceful head. He expected the skilful smile that had slain Duda. She just stared at him and her breath forced its way past the soft curve of her lips in a startled gasp. As though he had shocked her in some way. Perhaps she had not expected that he would even be able to get to his feet. Perhaps she had expected, nay hoped, for a weakness greater than it was. She had no idea what was inside him.

"I have poured the water. There was not much but I can see if I can get more."

There was more than enough for anyone.

"It will do."

Her gaze slid slowly away from him, the dark lashes veiling her eyes. For all the world as though it were not his actions that had shocked her, but himself. As though she were some blushing virgin of fifteen winters. But that was too much after Hun.

"Then come and help me, Alina."

He had not meant the danger in his voice to be quite so plain. But he could no longer suppress that, and if she fled instead of coming near, then so be it. He would almost rather she did.

But she did not. As always, she took her own path, in her own time. She placed the last bucket neatly beside the others, and then she crossed the small space that divided them.

She touched him. That, he was not quite prepared for, despite the stone-hard anger inside him. The jolt seared through flesh and bone and all the fever-crazed recesses of his mind. It was sharper than the axe wound in his arm, the awareness of her, the violent need of her that had been one step removed from madness.

She made the same breathless sound of surprise that had escaped her lips before, a tiny helpless sound of shock. Her slender fingers tightened on his undamaged arm.

The reaction of his body slipped the reins of thought. He moved, obliterating the small space between them. His hands caught her, imprisoning her so that their bodies touched, melding for one breathless instant of time.

The fire inside him was not what he had counted on. The fierce desire of his body would be another betrayal if he let it. He would not. Betrayal would not happen again. He took a breath, but that only let the faint wood-rose scent of her deep inside him.

Their bodies moved together so that he could feel the coarse material of her nun's habit against his flesh, the roughness of it a sense-shatteringly erotic contrast to the imagined smoothness beneath.

He sought control. He was not clumsy enough to kiss her as she might have expected. But the possibility no longer existed that he would let her go. They stayed touching at every point in an intimacy that was nothing of the kind, that left every sense aware of all that it burned for and all that was forever denied.

He held her in that closeness, moving all that light fragility against him until he could feel every curve as she must feel the exposed naked planes of his body. He held her so until her thick black lashes fluttered and shivers crossed the exposed skin on her neck and the small buds of her nipples tightened from the touch of him.

He held her until he was rock-hard.

Until the swollen, blood-gorged jut of hardness of his own flesh was something that ached and burned against the softness of hers. Until the control that he had was something strained beyond the ability to endure.

But still he did no more. Until her eyes would no longer open and her fingers dug into his skin with a force that stung. He bent his head until he could feel the soft rapid pulse of her warm breath against his fever-dried lips, until he could feel the drag of her small weight against his shoulders and arms because she could no longer support that by herself.

Still he did not kiss her. Not until he heard what he wanted from her lips, his name, not Hun's. He moved, but as their breath mingled in that searing instant that presaged touch and denied it, he heard what he did not expect. The last of her breath left her lips, achingly soft and only faintly discernible against the coarse unshaven roughness of his face.

It was the sound that caught him. It held not only the sharply hidden passion he knew lived inside that fragile body, but the last thing he had expected. Fear.

He let her go, felt her stumble away from him as though she could not bear to be near him. Which was, must be, the truth.

What was true for him was that the desire that now terrified her and scored through the hard-won bands of his control was still there. Not lessened by what he had done, but magnified a thousandfold.

"Brand…"

He could not so much as bear to look on her face. The truth forced its way past his parched lips.

"Go, Alina, just go. There is no way that either of us can help the other."

WHAT HAD SHE DONE?

Alina's steps quickened, taking her in endless circles round the walled herb garden of the monastery. The hot afternoon sun beat at her. The scents of the plants teased sense, released where her heavy skirts brushed at them, where an unwary foot bruised leaves: comfrey, horehound, pennyroyal. They whirled past her in dizzying succession. Circular, endless, always the same wherever you turned. Like her life.

Why had she touched him?

Why had she started that dangerous stupidity with the bathwater? Reckless fool. Had she thought that because she had nursed him when he was senseless, slept with him when circumstances had constrained them from going farther, that she was safe? Had she been that stupid? That sure of her own power?

She did not have any. Not where he was concerned.

And he had done nothing to her. Nothing. Just held her in his arms. And that had been enough to dizzy her out of her mind with yearning, to fire her senses until her body melted with it, and the heat inside her was like a fire that consumed thought and will and her whole being.

It had taken away her control. But not his. That had been there in the way he had held her. In what he had chosen to do and what he had not. He was the kind of man who knew all about the power between men and women.

That was what she had wanted him to show her. She had wanted all that mysterious hidden passion to be unleashed, through the fierceness of his body moving on hers, inside her.

And yet she had not wanted it. What she had felt in the end had been tainted by fear. The shameful fear of what he would do, and the fear of how much she wanted him despite that.

Her feet bruised the leaves of white horehound, releasing scent in dizzying waves. Comfrey. Pennyroyal. She sat down on the wooden bench against the wall.

He had not wanted her in the end. She had betrayed him, and all she could do was stay away from him. And remain alone, the way she had always been. It was better so. She buried her head in her hands.

"Alina? What is it? Are you not well?" She was stiff with sitting when she heard it. The deep voice seemed part of her waking dream. The dream she often played out in her head: when her father spoke to her kindly, as though he loved her.

The most unreal dream you could have.

Only one person's voice mimicked the shape and the sound of her father's, *their* father's.

"I am perfectly well." She did not look up.

"Then what else ails you?" asked Cunan. His hand settled on her shoulder, lightly, as seeming-kind as his voice. Her very own brother. "It was not—the Northumbrian has not offered you insult?"

Her shoulders tightened under the softly placed hand. There was only one Northumbrian to Cunan. Just as there was only one to her. She kept her head lowered in case her half brother could see the remains of the disturbing sexual encounter written on her face, the brand mark of her lover's touch.

"Why should you think there is aught between us? I betrayed him, remember?"

"Betrayal." Cunan's voice hardened, just as her father's always had when they had talked statesmanship. "How is it possible to betray an enemy? In the end you did what was right."

"Did I?"

"Yes. It was Hun that Maol wished for you. Our father wanted you to have a man of purpose, not some lecherous kinsman of a usurper like—"

"Cenred is now King of Northumbria. Cenred holds our brother. I would have thought that—"

"King for how long?"

Something froze in her veins.

"What are you saying?"

"My dear sister, you should be thinking of the future, *your* future. There are others who would support better claimants to the Northumbrian crown, people more well disposed toward the Picts."

Her blood froze in her veins. "What others?"

"Those whose own futures are at stake. Goadel—"

"Goadel?"

She glanced round the garden, the high walls, the fruiting bushes, the gate. No one. No noise but their voices.

"He would still have you," said Cunan softly,

"Why not? Do you think it matters to a Saxon that you were his brother's? Hardly."

"No…" The word was out before she could stop it. The grip on her shoulder bit through flesh.

"Think of your duty to your birth kingdom."

Her spine straightened. "I tried. But my birth kingdom gave nothing to me. I have never belonged there. Never."

"And whose fault is that?"

Guilt, familiar as a second skin.

"My fault. My mother's. Do we not both know that, you and I? Have we not known it since we were children?" She would give anything to be free of the guilt.

The grip on her shoulder softened.

"Nay," said Cunan's voice, suddenly soft as the hand, full of the elusive tone of Pictland. "Not your fault, your opportunity. Think on it, Alina. What can that English lecher offer you? Do you fancy he loves you?"

The hand moved down her sleeve, scraping coarse wool against her skin. Cunan's hand—

"The Northumbrian is a creature of impulse. Solely. How many women do you think he has had? What would make you special, Alina? You were just one more amusement and a greater trouble to him than he ever expected. All he wants of you is revenge for that trouble."

No. But the word this time was only in her mind. It had no reality at all.

"There are other ways of releasing your brother from Cenred. Better ways than walking straight into the trap of Bamburgh in the keeping of the man you all but destroyed. Do you think he will have a care for your future? No. Only your countrymen can do that, your kindred. In the end, it is your true kin that you are bound to."

Cunan's hand caught hers, lean, hard fingers sliding over the scars that had been put there through her never-spoken longing for just such an impossible tie as that.

As Cunan knew.

"You should have seen the pain in our father's face when he thought for a second time that you were dead."

"I do not believe you."

"That is where your problem lies, Alina, you never believed."

"And you think I should have?"

"Yes." The expression in her brother's eyes stunned her. It might have been her own: the bitter, fathomless need for acceptance. Had she not realized? Not seen? It seemed like a common bond. And Cunan believed—

"You should believe. It was I who first found out that you were alive, not your Northumbrian. Did you know that? No, do not speak. I can read your face. I always could. After all, we are one blood, are we not?"

Cunan's hand tightened over hers. "Ask him, next

time you go to him, your clever light-minded lecher, ask him whether what I say is true." The wiry fingers covered hers, blotting out the scars underneath as though they were no longer there.

"Our needs are the same, Alina. I ask no more than your trust. You will see."

CHAPTER SIX

THERE WAS NOWHERE ELSE to go.

Not unless she wanted to sleep in the hall with the servants, or in the dormitory with the holy brothers.

She stepped over a haphazard drift of rags snoring quietly across the doorway. It did not object. She was its master's wife, after all. She let herself into her husband's chamber.

She had left it till it was well dark, long past the time even the most hale would be sleeping. She did not go near the bed. She hardly dared take two steps into the room in case she woke him. She settled herself on the floor, facing the glowing embers in the hearth.

It took a long time to sleep. All she was aware of in the night quiet was the soft sound of his breathing, more sensed than heard, the knowledge of his presence. The thickness of the surrounding dark.

She woke on a sob, choking it back into silence with the ruthlessness of practice. It was not one of her more pleasant dreams this time. It was a nightmare, the sort that she had had, off and on, since she had been taken back from Strath-Clòta to Pictland at the age of nine.

She had learned to make hardly a sound under such circumstances because it had not been to her advantage to wake either her nurse or any of her sisters. She had been the outsider, isolated by the years of living in another land with her mother, by barriers she had never fully understood. She had learned not to expect companionship or love, or the kind of indulgence her younger sisters still enjoyed at Craig Phádraig.

She lowered her head back onto the hard floor and stared with dream-blind eyes at the smoky thatch of the roof. There was silence except for the pounding of her heart.

She turned her face towards the wall.

"What in heaven's name are you doing on the floor?"

The gasp was unstoppable. Because he was there, right beside her, kneeling on the floor in the dark. The faint glow of the dying embers outlined his body in red-gold and black shadows.

How could he have moved so fast and without a sound in the small confines of the room? She had hardly dared to take a step through the betraying rustle of the rushes on the ground.

Then she saw the gleam of the *seax* in his hand. Her heart pounded faster than it had in her nightmare.

"At least you did not throw it this time."

"Just as well." The white glitter of his teeth was brighter than the blade.

"Yes. You might have been off your aim again."
Only then did she realize they were speaking in Celtic.
The way she had with Cunan. Except not so. She
shivered at memories of what Cunan had said.

"What would you know about my aim?" enquired
the voice that gave life to the brilliant sounds not of
Pictland, but of Strath-Clòta.

She bit her lip. He was so very assured, as always.
So close and so big in the darkness. She tried not to
look at naked skin, at the compressed muscle of his
thigh where he knelt beside her. At the blackly shadowed flesh that betokened his manhood. The shivering just got deeper inside. She saw his arm move, the
one without the *seax,* the damaged left one. His hand
touched her.

"You are shaking." But now she trembled because
she could feel the confident slide of his fingers across
the bare skin of her arm, a warm, effortless pressure
across her exposed flesh, seemingly careless. Not so
at all.

*How many women do you think he has had? What
would make you special?*

"Are you cold? You have only one cloak over you.
What were you doing on the floor?"

"Sleeping," she said through the dizzying beat of her
own blood in her ears. "Or I would be if people did not
keep asking questions and contemplating whether or
not to throw things. Besides, where else do you suggest I go?"

"Get in the bed."

"What?"

"You asked for suggestions."

"Yes, but—" The rest was lost as she was hauled to her feet. "I will not—"

The teeth gleamed, quite differently this time, like the invitation of a beast of prey.

"Neither will I. We are both safe from each other on that score. We have proved it, have we not?"

She could not reply. Because of the crippling tightness of her throat. And because she could see and guess the beast of prey's body in the dark: the way the muscle of his thigh moved when he stood and the straight gleaming line of his side. He held her and her bare feet scarcely touched the floor, even though he was wounded, even though he should not have had the strength to take her like that. Her feet lost the floor entirely.

The bed was still faintly warm from the weight of his body. There were a lot of heavy covers. He arranged them. She felt as though the cold had been blocked out. Instantly. Not from furs and wool but from him. Because he was close.

The fire's glow was faint, so that she could scarce see him at all. Just darkness and black shadows. But she knew he was there. One touch away from her skin. Lying beside her, outside the bedcovers.

She tried to find her voice, to regain some control.

"Now it is you who will be cold." She had to fight to keep her tone light, as seeming-careless as his touch.

"No. I have the cloak."

She fancied she could sense the dangerous edge of his breath whisper across her face and her throat. But it was only fancy. He was farther away than she had thought. Always.

"It is you who are ill," said her light voice. "You who should have the bed."

"If I choose to have you in my bed, what do you think should stop me?"

The chills started again, chasing in waves across her skin. Not from cold.

"Only honour," she said into the lightless dark.

"Only *what?*"

"Honour." She swallowed. "Not mine. Yours."

"What a cutting way with words you have. I had forgotten. But this time, it is you who have missed your aim. Any honour I had was the first thing to die when Hun brought the king's army down on my home."

And his brother had been the second.

"I did not intend what happened to Athelwulf."

The words blurted out without thought. Wildly inappropriate. Lethally dangerous. She heard the hiss of his breath and this time she did feel its touch when he breathed out, like ice vapour on the burning heat across her cheekbone.

"Did you not? Then there are two things we have in common—lack of honour and bootless intentions. My brother Athelwulf, of course, says it was his choice, but then his honour remains—"

"Athelwulf *what?*"

She sat up through the frightening darkness, every muscle in her body rigid with the shock.

"Surprised I should say that? Or would you disagree with me because your lover had my brother flogged and enslaved?"

The danger in that perfectly cultured voice was unmistakable to her. Her mouth worked. But she was so shocked that no sound came out, which was what saved her.

Because all that beat through her brain were the words *Hun did not kill Athelwulf* and then the burning thanks to Saint Dwyn that it was true. Even while the sane part of her brain, the one that had made the ruthless decision to part her from the man she had loved and damaged, screamed silent warnings that the words could not be said aloud.

She was supposed to be the despicable creature Hun's whore. She was supposed to know already what had truly happened to Brand's brother.

She heard the faint sound of Brand moving. She tried not to imagine the *seax* blade or what he must feel in his heart.

"Of course, the only thing you can not know is that I had found Wulf again, because that happened the day I killed Hun. You cannot know what happened after he had been flogged and sold in slavery to that Frisian Goadel found."

The bedclothes shifted across her body as his weight moved, intimate as a lover's caress, unfeeling as a stranger's touch.

"My brother made his way back to England. To Wessex. It must have been a shock to Hun when he found out. Your betrothed must have thought Athelwulf was safely away, over the sea. That is, if Hun had not injured him sufficiently for him to die anyway, slowly and in pain."

Some small sound did escape her then. She could not help it.

"Do you not care to face what we two have done? Did you push all that from your mind in the greater knowledge that you were back with what was then one of the most powerful men in Northumbria? That in spite of your little lapse with me, you had secured a triumph for yourself? And, of course, for Pictland? Or do you want to know the rest? How Wulf came to live and Hun to die?"

She forced her head to move on the stiffness of her neck. She could not speak.

"Yet I cannot tell you truly what effort it took for Athelwulf to survive because he would not tell me. No one but him will ever know. But it is not too difficult to guess the times he must have wished that he had died as I believed he had, rather than endure what he did."

The softly breathing darkness seemed so heavy around her, inside and out.

"When did you know he was still alive?" Her voice stretched thin. "How did you find him?"

The silence and the dark remained unbroken for so long that she thought he would not answer. Then she heard the faint rustle of movement as he turned, towards her or away, she did not know.

"He saw me and I—"

He had turned away from her. She could tell by the sound of his voice. The short, cut-off sentence shimmered in the darkness, out of her reach, like him, holding the key to so much that she wished to know about him, about what he felt.

The night air raised gooseflesh for no reason, except that she was still attuned to him in mind as much as body, with the very essence of what she was. And he had said not *I saw him,* but *he saw me.* Her skin prickled with a different awareness, the way it did sometimes near clear water, near those dangerous places where other worlds could break through.

"What do you mean? Where were you?"

"In Mercia, trying to disentangle myself from the panicked remnants of the late King Osred's personal guards. They were fleeing down the coast road after witnessing Osred's murder. They thought I might want to stop them. I did not."

"No." It was a statement of belief. She did not know whether he would accept it. But she took the next step anyway.

"And your brother?" Such a small question. Yet it was not. The air in the cramped chamber thrummed. She did not know whether he would answer. She thought the great shadow of his head, with its rough tangle of hair, was still turned away from her.

"In Wessex. Somewhere. There was a clearing

among trees and a great sheet of water, very still. The water was freezing."

The tension in him was palpable, even across the darkness that separated them.

"Water," she said with infinite care, "is very powerful."

She let that opening to the possibility of further speech hang between them. She did not ask directly how he had felt the coldness of this particular sheet of water when he had been many miles from it. She simply held her breath.

The bonds between Brand and his kin were unbreakable. Unlike the bond he had once had with her, a stranger. She bore the silence and waited.

"If he had not seen me, it is quite likely the axe that splintered my shield and hit my arm would have killed me."

She stared at the blackness of the steeply-pitched roof. The terror of near death blinded her mind, and with it came the urge to touch him through the dark. To know his wholeness, to forge a connection she could never have.

All she could do for him was speak, try to make him say what was in his thoughts. She shaped the next question.

"How did you find your brother?"

"I kept moving south. Once I knew he was alive I— The woman who now owned my brother had sent a man to seek me. I caught up with her messenger on the Icknield Way. That is how. Quite simple."

The silence was complete this time, not the slightest rustle of movement in the bated darkness. Not so much as the sound of her breath.

Quite simple.

Why had he told her so much?

The fierce, dazzling creature she had loved had been a warrior, first, last and always. Action had been the compass of his life, not dreams, not the unexplainable, nothing that could not be dealt with in practical terms.

Or so she had thought.

Yet even warriors had hearts, minds. They dreamed. Or they could not be human. They just…they did not admit it.

Why had he done so? Now? All he had needed to tell her was about the messenger sent to seek him, not what had gone before.

The tension in the strong, dark bulk of his body was finely wound, lethal. The forbidden urge to touch him, to take some of that tension from him and into herself, was more than she could bear.

If she could not touch him, she must find the words. But words were so clumsy to express what she felt: such helpless longing for the bond of understanding that had once sparked between them.

"It happened because your brother means so much to you. Love can make people—"

"What? What can love make people do?"

She heard the rustle of his movement, sensed the speed, and then she was looking into the white blur of his face, the feral eyes.

"Tell me, Alina, what love can make people do."

It can make people do that which they hate most.

"I cannot."

"Nay, I do not believe that you can."

If only she could not see his eyes. If only she could stop feeling. If only her own need for him had not been enough to make her believe that he could want any comfort from her.

What he had said concerned his brother. He had said it to underline the closeness of his tie to his kindred. He wanted her to know that that was indissoluble.

Kin ties.

It was I who first found out you were alive, not your Northumbrian... Ask him about that...

But she could not. She forced Cunan's voice out of her head. She knew Brand was not hers. She had always known.

She knew it to the depths of her soul.

He leaned over her, power locked in shadows, despite the traces of fever and exhaustion, despite the wound that would have taken his life but for his brother's love.

"Hear the ending. When I found Wulf, your lover had tried to buy him back. The request was refused. So Hun came, with all his followers, and with the wolf heads he had hired, so he could take my brother back by force."

The ending... She knew it beyond doubt.

"But you were there. You killed him, before he could harm your brother again."

The gleaming eyes never wavered.

"Yes."

She was not able to tell the man she loved that she was deeply, savagely glad that Hun's evil was gone.

"You have to know how things are. Your lover died at my hand, by the sword you held in that room at the nunnery. This time, I was there. This time I could save my brother. It was not revenge. It was justice. If there can be a difference."

"There can—" She stopped the words. She would not look at his eyes. He would see through her.

"What truly makes justice is the fact that after all that happened my brother found a happiness neither you nor I are capable of. He found someone who loved him."

She buried her face in her hands. But through all the pain of bitterness, ran the strand of fierce gladness—that something had been redeemed for the future, beyond any hope she had ever had, and beyond anything she had ever deserved.

The bitterness and the gladness seemed to fuse inside her, into a determination that would admit no boundaries. If such things could be redeemed out of the bleakness that filled the world, then it was proof that she had made the right choice.

The debt she had left to pay was the one that would assure the future.

Redemption.

"Can you understand that kind of justice?"

Yes. The word screamed in her head. Her hands

balled themselves into fists against her mouth. There
was silence of an intensity that penetrated through
flesh and bone while the ripples caused by that word
spread out, washing over both of them.

"Can you?"

She regathered the threads of her will. The only
possibility of redemption for Brand did not lie with
her. It was impossible to repay the boon that fate had
granted to one brother by damning the other to live
on through the nightmare.

Somewhere outside these walls was Goadel. He
wanted her. If she cast herself on Brand's mercy now,
he would protect her with his life, whatever she had
done to him. Because that was how he was. She could
not allow it. She had seen him almost die already.

"Tell me what goes on in that beautiful head of
yours, Alina. Did you fall out with Hun before he
died?"

She could feel the same bone-eating intensity in his
voice that had filled the silence. She forced her hands
away from her mouth, straightened her hunched
shoulders so that she might appear careless.

"No. It is your turn for disappointment. I had made
my choice and this time I was happy with it. I have
told you I regret what happened to your brother because he should have had no part in this. I am glad he
is…well. But do not flatter yourself that it changes
what I wanted."

"And just what, exactly, did you want?"

The great black shape of him was closer to her

now. She could feel it breathe. Feel the thinly stretched edges of the control that held all that limitless power in place. Her mind sought desperately for the right words to say, the words that would fill the terrifying dark and the silence. The words that would convince a mind that had more depths than she yet knew.

She fell back on fragments of truth.

"What I wanted was my place in life. And I wanted to please my father."

You should have seen the pain in our father's face when he thought for a second time that you were dead.

In the end, it is your true kin that you are bound to.

She swallowed. The fragments of truth hurt as much as the lies.

"You cannot know how it was at Craig Phádraig. My father…" Her mouth felt so dry. "My father and my mother hated each other." She made herself speak through the rawness in her throat. "I did not tell you that. There was a lot I did not tell you."

The truth fragments were like daggers. But they would pierce only her.

"There seems so little time to exchange confidences when you are fleeing pursuit. We did not know each other at all, did we?"

"No."

She could feel the attention beating at her like waves hitting the cliffs.

"My mother hated Craig Phádraig. She might have been brought there for marriage, but in her heart she was always a Briton. All she thought of was her home in Strath-Clòta. She was supposed to do the same as me—prop up a useful alliance between two kingdoms who were uneasy neighbours. You have a name for it in English."

"Frithuwebbe." Peace weaver. The deep-voiced Northumbrian word took shape in the darkness like something you could get hold of. But of course you could not. The web of peace was as fragile as gossamer.

"It is not an easy thing to do. My mother left my father for a while. She took Modan and me back to Strath-Clòta, to the great palace at Alcluyd. Just a visit to see her own family. I was four when she took me there. By the time my father finally forced her to come back, I was nine.

"You saw the beauty of Alcluyd before I met you." She took a breath. Brand had seen two years at a court where he had been in much the same position Modan was now in at Bamburgh. "I know you must have hated it there—"

"Because they wanted to hang me?"

He moved back, just slightly, control there, cloaking the fire beneath.

"No. I did not hate it."

She stared at the huge, shadowed shape. How could he not hate it? The way he must hate her.

"But how did you survive it? Knowing that your

life meant so little that it could be gone at any moment?"

The gold eyes glittered in reflected firelight.

"That is how I did survive it—by the moment. How does one survive anything?" His voice was fathoms dark and full of twisting shadows like the air.

"Besides, nothing is permanent. Sorrow and joy follow each other as hunger follows the feast. Even life is only lent."

That was what all the English believed in their hearts, but the way he said it made her own heart ache inside her chest.

"So many people have wanted to kill me over the years." The truth of that sent shivers coursing across her skin. So many—Osred, Hun and now Hun's brother outside these walls. And—*her* brother?

Kin ties...

She heard the tormented movement of a body that must ache both with physical pain and all the fires of fury. But when he spoke, his voice was lighter, the darkness pushed aside.

"At least the Britons of Strath-Clòta had a valid reason for wanting my life. In those days I was constrained to take my turn at representing the late King Osred. That would be enough to make anyone feel like hanging me."

The sudden lightness held a glimpse of what she longed for. The subtle paths of a mind that understood all the noble and dishonourable, selfless and selfish reasons that compelled people to act as they did. It was that understanding that had made her cast her fate into his hands without the slightest reserve.

It was that understanding she had to defeat now.

"I was so happy as a child at Strath-Clòta. I—" She paused. The truth had to be used sparingly now. She took a breath that swallowed the child's feelings.

"But unlike my mother, I knew where my destiny should lie. I would be a peace weaver. I would do all that I could for my father and my uncle and for Pictland. I would make a success where my mother had failed. I would have…" She could not think of a word that could fit with the monstrous image of Hun. She took a breath that almost choked her. "I would have wealth and security and…power."

The air froze. There was not a sound. She might have been the only person in the room, but she was not. She could feel him. She could feel him move closer. Without a sound.

"Is that what you wanted from Hun? Power?"

The thread of truth was broken. She held herself just as still as him.

"That is exactly what I wanted from Hun. That was what he could give me. I know that I temporarily lost sight of it when I was with you, and believe me, there is nothing I regret more deeply than that…." Her hands bunched themselves into fists. The remains of her nails dug against her palms.

"But in the end I came to my senses. In the end I suppose we both had to. I went back to Hun and all was well."

"All was well?"

His rough-smooth voice was the deepest whisper in the dark. Something felt with more senses than just hearing. He was so close that the loose, newly-washed fall of his hair brushed her throat, soft as the touch of an angel's wing. And over her, the shadow of his shape.

Her skin shivered.

"Was it so?"

The shadow of his form overwhelmed her and her mind was spinning out of control with her need for him. The hunger of the body, the hunger for completion he had taught her here in this room was tearing through flesh.

He was not hers. He could never be. She forced deadly words out into the breathlessly charged darkness of their shared bed.

"Yes, it was so." No need to try and make her voice harsh. It sounded like the croaking of the horn-beaked raven after battle. "All was well with Hun and with me and at last I was doing my duty to my father's land. And I would have my place in the world. Until you came. Just like last time. Only until you came."

The shadow above her gathered itself, changed shape. Cold air against her throat where there should have been the falling softness of his hair. But behind that coldness was the ice heat of him. She knew the anger was there, deep inside him. She knew all of its causes and she could only guess at its power.

If he had been Hun he would have killed her for

what she had done. She thought his body was stronger than Hun's. She knew it was. She had touched it too intimately. She had learned the beginnings of its power. The rest was a matter of instinct.

Of course there were other ways for men to take their revenge. She had wanted him before, when he had held her in his arms. Her body had shown him. But now there could be only hate in his heart.

Only hate. His body above her blocked out the light.

She thought of her father and her mother, and the blackness was tearing its way into her mind—

"Then sleep well, this time, Alina. You will need strength."

"What… Where are you going…"

There was air above her. Emptiness. Emptiness that would kill her soul.

"We leave for Bamburgh in five days. Tell your brother, the Strathclyde Hound. He needs to be ready. So do you."

CHAPTER SEVEN

HER CLOTHES WERE GONE.

Alina blinked in the half-light. The dark shapes spread out before the fire to dry after her unhandy attempt at washing were not there.

She sat up. The thick coverings of Brand's bed pooled round her and the cold struck her skin. She hugged her arms protectively around herself. But there was no one to see.

She slept alone.

She had scarce seen Brand for the last three days. She did not know where he was or what he did.

She stared at the space where the tattered shapes of her tunic and undergown should be and then she saw it. *Them.* A pair of saddlebags draped over the foot of her bed.

Her skin shivered with an awareness beyond cold. Recognition. Even though it was scarce light. Even though the fine leather bags with the silver buckles had had their existence in another life.

They were hers.

They held all the things she had taken with her on her mad flight from Hun. Her only possessions. She scrambled across the bed and ripped open the buckles. An expanse of fine, deep blue linen trimmed with silk ribbons spilled out. She stared at it. It shimmered in a mixture of dawn light and firelight from the hearth.

It was beautiful. It had made her look beautiful. Or so…people had said.

So she had kept it, her fine and costly dress, even though it was totally impractical for a dangerous journey into exile. It had been the first thing Brand had seen her in.

He had looked at her and the heat in his eyes had scorched inside her. No one had ever looked at her like that before. No one ever would again.

She buried her face in its soft folds. The silk from Byzantium was like cool gossamer against her face.

Why was it there? Why had he kept everything that was hers? Everything that she had been unable to take with her when she had fled from him into the south?

She delved deeper. It was all there: cloak and gowns, stockings and underlinen and even, unexpected blessing from heaven, a pair of shoes that would fit.

She put them on.

She did not dress herself in the silk, but in a fine wool tunic of forest-green over a gown of paler green. It was warm, soft against her skin.

Without the slightest regret for the wimple, she fastened a delicate linen head rail round her hair with a ribbon of twisted coloured thread.

There was no such thing as a mirror in a monastery, but… She realized what he had done.

He had forced her to recreate the person she had been before she had abandoned him to ride south. Perhaps even the person she had been before she had met him. She began to shake.

"Will you come, lady?"

Duda, pounding on the door fit to wake the dead. She cast one wild glance around the room as though she might still find the protection of her plain nun's clothing.

She would have to go out looking like this.

She opened the door. Duda stared. Then he turned away.

She followed him into the courtyard.

Brand was waiting for her. His eyes, when they lighted on the ghost of what had been, held the fire that had called her blood across the painted torchlit hall at Bamburgh. But this time it could only be from anger, not desire. Her hand went instinctively to the frivolous scrap of veil around her head, drawing its edges closer, as though she could hide her face from him.

"Ready to go?"

He was striding towards her. Her gaze took in the fine riding boots, the swirling folds of the dark cloak pinned with gold and garnets at his left shoulder. The decorated scabbard swinging from his jewelled belt—

"You cannot," she shouted, straight across the cold-tinged dawn air that divided them. "You cannot mean to go now. Today." Was he mad? He was not well enough yet. He would kill himself—

Behind him were his men, one holding the bridle of the great black horse he rode, another leading the smaller grey that had been hers on the ride here. Farther back, she caught the gaudy flash of Cunan's chequered cloak.

"Change of plan. It seems to be upsetting people." The bright gold eyes flicked carelessly from her to the press of men and horses. Bright red crossed with blue caught the sun.

We leave for Bamburgh in five days. Tell your brother, the Strathclyde Hound. He needs to be ready.

Her own gaze, guilt-studied reflex that she could have killed herself for, flew to the bright slash of colour. The disturbing encounter with her half brother in the herb garden was stinging at the back of her mind. She shut it out.

"Well?"

She could feel her face lose its colour, go stiff. She tried to find the mask that had always served to hide what she felt. Practice had made it second nature for her to do that. Easy. But not with him.

"Come. We have a long way to go."

He extended a gloved hand and someone tossed him the reins of her mount. He closed the small distance between them, dragging the skittish horse behind as though it were no more substantial than a spider's web. His feet in their heavy boots struck the hard-packed earth of the courtyard with dangerous precision.

She waited until he was so close that what she said would belong to the two of them. She said the only piece of truth she had behind her mask. Even though there was little chance of her being heeded.

"I meant only that it is too soon for you to travel. Because of the wound. You could cause damage, make yourself ill again—"

"You were thinking of me?"

She kept her gaze on him. She refused to look at the chequered cloak. She did not know whether the mask was not in place, or whether it was too well fixed, but his eyes had hardened into ice.

"You should be thinking of your brother."

"What?"

She could see the gaudy cloak advancing towards them out of the press. She thought of the secrets in its wearer's head.

"Cunan…"

"Who? Oh, I am sorry. Did I not clarify which brother? I meant Modan."

Bastard.

Cunan kept walking towards them. He would hear.

"I hope you have replenished the medicine bag with herbs."

The sweet scent of horehound in the monastery garden…

Cunan with his dangerous thoughts and his dangerous whiplash strength. Cunan with his terrible vulnerability.

"Did your brother help you?"

Cunan's footsteps came to a stop. "It is as well she has someone who cares for her welfare. She needs her kin. We have discussed that, have we not, Alina?"

Some detached part of her brain, the part that made calculations, told her that it was just as well if Brand believed her false. It was what she was trying to achieve. That part of her brain made her smile, in the way that had lashed her father and uncle into fury.

"Aye."

Cunan's smile held an exactly equal measure of warmth.

"So did you ask him?"

"No."

"Why not?"

Her heart began beating out of time. She tried to widen the smile so that neither of them would guess what was inside her. But she thought her eyes must hold the wildness of something hunted. She could not bear it. "I will not."

"Then I will—" Whatever Cunan would do was obliterated in a blur of grey. Brand caught the reins before Cunan could be trampled to death.

"Sorry. The horse is restive. Can I help you up?"

"Cunan…" She stepped between. Because she never learned. The instant of stillness she created gave Cunan the chance he needed.

"Ask him," screamed her brother, rolling in the mud of the stable yard. "Ask him for the truth." He got as far as his knees. "Ask the Northumbrian whether it was me who found out where you were when everyone else had given you up for lost. Ask him whether that is true."

Not a word would come out of her mouth.

"It is true." Bright gold, achingly clear, locked with her gaze.

"I told you—" Cunan had gained his feet, mud streaking the garishly dyed cloak. "It was me who knew. It was me who spoke to the traveller whose arm you healed. It was me who guessed. He described you."

The goldsmith. The man with the broken arm she had helped the abbess to set. His gratitude…

"He could have been describing any woman whose charms had witched sense. But there is one thing you can never disguise." Cunan was reaching towards her, his face alight with triumph. "The man saw your useless hand."

She snatched her left hand away before her brother could touch it, before his fingers could grasp the ugliness of badly-healed bones and scarred flesh.

She stepped backwards. Only one step. It was quite controlled. The mask of cold indifference was in place. But even so, her head turned.

Not towards Cunan.

"Is that how it was?" Useless question. He had already told her it was true. Brand was not a person who lied.

"It is true. I have told you. I believed you were dead." The eyes clear as melted gold, just as hot, held her.

"Besides, Cunan's sources of information are impeccable. Your injured goldsmith was selling his wares to Goadel."

"Goadel…"

She tore her gaze away. Her eyes sought her brother's, sought to find all the things he had not said to her.

You should believe.

She lurched away. Brand caught her before she slid into the mud like Cunan. His arm closed on her body, crumpling the soft folds of her dress, holding her. She heard the hiss of her brother's breath, sharp and dangerous. The hellhound. She tried to pull away, stumbled, then the air left her lungs as her body slammed full-length against the toughness of Brand's.

Cunan was right behind them. She saw his face. She saw his hand move.

"No! Let me go." She swore savagely in Celtic. But she did not know why she was pleading and cursing. Because of what Brand might do. Because she was afraid that Cunan would kill him. Because his hair dazzled her eyes like teased gold in the first light and the feel of him struck through her like glory.

Because they were nothing to each other. Just nothing. She struggled, but his grip tightened, so that she could feel all of the hard length of his body, the tension held back in each muscle.

It was not a strength she could combat. Yet her mind registered the breath that came slightly too fast, despite that harshly held control, the body warmth that burned through the touch of his hand just slightly more than it should.

She felt all of his anger.

Then her feet left the ground and she was tossed into the saddle, one hand clutching at the horse's mane, the other entangled in Brand's sleeve.

"Take care, Alina. We have a long way to go."

His eyes were unreadable. Somewhere below her Cunan's hand slid away from his left hip. Behind that was a slight flutter of ragged clothing.

"The journey has only just started."

His gaze was not on the hellhound of Strath-Clòta or on the slowly settling rags draping the faithful Duda. She realized what he was looking at. Her hand was clutching like a raven's claw at the richly woven cloth of his sleeve.

IT WAS SOMETHING AS SIMPLE as a blackbird's call that told her. She had gone aside, for what small amount of privacy she was allowed, and she heard the fast angry clacking of its voice. Blackbirds were the world's sentinels. They announced every disturbing presence.

She thought at first it was her own presence that had caused such indignation. But it was not. The bird was too far away, its attention directed elsewhere.

Duda, then. He was her watchdog. They both pretended this was not so, but no one had any illusions. She could not say he intruded, but if she was ever rash enough to consider a bolt for freedom, they both knew how it would end.

This time he had been spotted, if not by her. She allowed herself a smile. Over to the left a twig cracked and the blackbird screeched. There was a hasty rustling noise. Caught out—

Duda never rustled. In spite of waving rags and leaf-snarled hair, he never rustled.

The hairs on her forearms rose.

It was someone else, one of the others bound on the same errand as herself. Cunan? Cunan with his secrets.

She did not want to be alone with her brother again. She plunged back through the bushes towards the camp.

They were all there. Even Cunan. No one could have got back to the camp before she did. She had taken the most direct route. She sat down. There was food. She began chewing through the unlikely amount Brand expected her to eat.

Suppose it had been one of Goadel's men? Suppose he knew where she was already? Suppose Goadel was out there, now, just waiting for his chance?

Ridiculous.

It would have been some animal come to drink at the pool across the clearing, a fox, a stoat, an early evening badger.

Her gaze went to Brand. He sat, talking quietly to his men. One of them laughed softly. They seemed frighteningly relaxed.

Cunan was as tense as a hawk.

If it was Goadel's man... Goadel was death.

She had to warn Brand. The instinct was pure and unstoppable. She realized equally quickly that she could not. Her own deception had prevented her.

There was only one other way.

She waited until Duda had settled himself into an untidy drift beside a beech tree and wandered past. She threw him her saucy look that held a hint of mockery.

"You are losing your touch."

There was a furtive blink among the debris. She took this as a sign of interest. There was nothing else to go on.

"Just now, when you followed me. You startled a blackbird. I heard you."

"Not me."

The rags settled back into complacency. Or was that vacancy? She glared in irritation.

"Then it must have been someone else." She tried to turn the glare into an encouraging look. *If it was not you, you* wantwit, *then it must have been...*

"Nah. A fox, then. Or...just you."

She resisted the impulse to apply her foot sharply to where his brain seemed to be lodged.

"I do not think so. Do you never get nervous of what might be around us?"

"No."

Her foot twitched.

"New shoes pinching?"

She suddenly became aware that Cunan was

watching her across the fire. So was Brand. Whatever chance she had had was gone.

She settled her feet. "Not as much as they might, Duda, not nearly as much as they might."

"LET ME SEE the wound." There was always more than one way to achieve what you wanted. She would just rather it had not been this way.

"It is fine."

"I need to check it."

"Wifely duty?"

The eyes that held hers were as dangerous as knife blades.

"What else?" She hesitated. She could feel Cunan's eyes on her back. It was like being caught between two wolves snarling over the kill. "There is a pool through the trees. I may need water."

It was the thinnest of excuses and if he had seen the pool as she had, he would know the water in it was not clean enough. But if there was something wrong with the wound, if he was like to take ill again, she did not want Cunan to see. Not after what she had thought she had heard.

She tried not to flinch under the measuring look and Brand got to his feet, in one smooth movement that belied the day's weariness that dogged her own limbs, weariness that he must feel doubly.

Cunan's gaze remained riveted on her back until the trees swallowed her in shadows. Even after. She could feel what it said: *Traitor.*

"The water is useless."

"Is it? I did not realize. I will just use the salve." She had the wit not to look at his face. She fixed her attention instead on the swollen, jagged scar across his arm. She closed her eyes against one brief moment of sickness.

"The scar is pulling. You should not ride again tomorrow. You should not have ridden today. Did the monks not tell you? Delaying another two days could not have made that much difference—"

"That seems to distress you as much as it does Cunan—two days. I thought you would have been anxious to see Modan."

Brilliant beginning for the conspirator she was not. First stir up your opponent's suspicions and then try to deliver your warning.

She scooped salve out of the jar and touched his skin. It was warm, not feverish, just solid and heavy with the kind of warmth she had longed for all her life. She bit her lip. The urge to be done with a deceit she was not designed for, to blurt out the truth and the full measure of her longings, seared through to her heart.

Her fingers touched the violently distorted flesh of the wound and she knew she could not speak. She would rather die than see more harm come to him. Or to her brother.

"I do want to see Modan. You can believe that much, if nothing else. I will go with you to Bamburgh. So you are stuck with me, all of you, however much you might dislike me."

Her fingers, slick with salve, slid across the reddened, horribly ridged line of the scar. She tried to
keep from shaking. She tried to keep her touch fin-
gertip-light, so that she would not hurt him. So that
she would not feel the touch of his flesh, even the
scarred flesh, against hers.

"I have offended Duda already," she said in her
light voice. Idle chatter. Just noise to distract the patient's mind. Or her mind, because she did not particularly care for what she had to do.

"I heard him following me, you know." She added
a hint of triumph, a shade of resentment. She had
hold of Brand's arm to steady it while she worked and
she thought the thickness of muscle tightened. And
then she thought it did not.

"He would not admit I had caught him out, though.
Tried to claim it was just some small beast, like a fox,
that I had heard. I admit I did not actually see, but I
knew it was a person."

Brand would know that no one heard Duda when
he moved. Would he realize what she was saying?
Would he understand?

"It was just near here." She risked a glance at the
thick bushes shadowing the remains of last year's leaf
mould. "So I rushed back to the camp and everyone
was there, so it had to be Duda." Her voice crowed
with a fatuous triumph that would make even a
wantwit feel superior. Brand was not a *wantwit*. The
true meaning of what she had recounted would be as
plain as day.

"There. Finished." She let her breath out.

"I do not think so."

The jolt that went through her made her fingers catch on a jagged edge of reddened skin. She swore. It came out in Celtic.

"What are you about, Alina?" The words came out in the same language. The damaged arm moved. The hand pinned her wrist in a grip that made his muscles bulge.

She raised her head.

"You know very well what I am about—looking out for myself. I am good at it. You should take lessons from my single-mindedness, and then perhaps you would look after that wound."

"Why? So I can preserve my own hide, or so I can make up for lost time getting you to Bamburgh and your brother? Which one is all this about?"

She looked at the uncomfortable eyes that were never satisfied with less than everything. She looked at the sword-trained hand on her wrist.

"Both," she risked in half-truth. "I want to get to Bamburgh. I have said so. And of course I need you to get me there."

"And is that why you stayed with me when I was ill?"

Her hand jerked against his wrist. Useless, betraying movement. But she had not expected that. She had let herself believe he was not concerned about that, had not really known. Saint Dwyn, how much had the moth-eaten Duda told him? How much had he seen and understood?

"Answer me."

She could not move.

"Tell me." The strong, battle-scarred hand slid round until it held hers, not by mere force, but by something far stronger. She did not want to look at their hands together so, but she could not take her gaze away.

"You were ill. I know about healing."

"So does the infirmarian. Why did *you* stay?"

Because I did not want you to lose your life. Because you are the only person in the world who has ever made me feel alive and cherished, however briefly.

She stared at their joined hands. No, not joined. Her hand was balled uselessly under his, like a stone. Because that was all she could manage.

She lifted her shoulders in what, during some other lifetime, might have been a gracefully careless shrug.

"I have told you. I need you to get me back to my brother. It would hardly have been convenient for me if you had died."

"You did not need me. Duda would take you back to Bamburgh. I told you as much."

Trust Duda... He knows...

That had been his last thought in the morass of pain and fever. For her.

He had also said that Cunan would betray her. He would certainly betray Brand. She thought of the un-known watcher in the woods. It was like battling in one of those magic pools full of sea monsters. Wher-ever you turned there was a new threat.

"Did you say that about Duda? I suppose I forgot."

Through the small gap between her half-closed lashes she could see stray glimpses of him: the bright sun on his hair, the purple shadows of evening across the taut muscles of his arm.

"You forgot? Is that why you decided to say you were my wife?"

She kept her hand very, very still under his. So that the shivering inside her would not leach out through her skin.

"Oh, that. I thought that was particularly clever of me. It meant you would be stuck with me. You should have seen Duda's face. Well, what anyone can see of it—"

"Alina, why are you so afraid?"

The question came from nowhere. Or so she thought. And then she could see under her eyes the way her fingers had moved, despite her will, so that they turned upwards, threading their way through his like the tendrils of a vine seeking warmth. The trembling she had closed her mind to must be obvious to him. He had felt it.

His hand, the hand that had been tangled with hers, slid slowly across her arm. Just as it had before, when she had brought him the bathwater. Just as it had when he had taken her in his arms and made her feel all that she did not want to feel. All that she knew she was not capable of feeling.

"I am not afraid. Why should I be afraid?" Her voice trembled like her hand.

Under the inadequate protection of her lashes, she could see him: the black cloth strained darkly across his thighs, the bronze-gold fairness of his skin, the wide expanse of his chest with its deep-shadowed muscle, dark-gilded hairs. Male. With a beauty that was feral. Perfect. Yet not so. She could see the ugliness of the scar left by one of King Osred's men. Goadel was Osred's kin. Goadel was near, somewhere unknown. Had to be.

He leaned closer and the sense of his nearness was enough to drown her. Just like last time.

"It is you who should be afraid." Her voice flailed at him. Ugly. Harsh with the sum of all her fears. "It is you who are in danger."

"Why? Because Goadel will bring death to me, and will bring you all that you want?"

"Yes."

"But Goadel is not what you want, Alina. Just as Hun was not what you wanted. Not truly."

"How can you think that?"

He said nothing, but his hand slid from her arm, brushed the frail barrier of her veil aside, found the delicate exposed skin of her throat. Settled there. So that the slight column of her neck fitted into the hard curve of his palm.

He did not do anything else. His hand did not push lower, to the uptilted curve of her breast, only a breath away from the hard-muscled wall of his chest. The warmth of his skin. He just let her feel his presence, let her sense his closeness until her whole body trembled and her bones ached with it.

He had such life. He was like the sunlight made real. She could see him breathe and the way the light through the trees cast dancing shadows across his skin. Then she could not see him at all because she was too close. Her head leaned into his hand and the longing for him was tearing at her with beast's claws.

"Tell me now what you want."

"I cannot." The words were hard as stones scraping. Her breath touched him.

"Then I will show you."

She could feel the tautness in the hand on her skin. The weight of his body leaned over hers. He would touch her and there would be no defence for her. All that she had tried to do would be lost. There would be no way to stop him. There had never been any way. She had lost. The sordid heat of misery and helplessness mixed with the burning desire, and she wondered whether that was how her mother had felt. Just such helplessness.

"Alina—"

"You can do as you will. There is no way I may stop you."

BUT SHE COULD. Just by looking at him. Brand's muscles froze. The fear that he had sensed was hidden inside her, the fear he had glimpsed in her face the last time he had held her, lived in her eyes. She had denied it. She had said she had wanted Hun. She had said her actions had been guided entirely by choice.

Yet now she trembled, and her body burned to his

touch. The weight of her head lay helpless against his open palm.

He had expected anger, the echo of the bated fury that lived inside him. He knew with every drop of blood in his heated veins that there was a desire that matched his, because it was the other side of the same coin. That was how it was. Like an inescapable fate for them both.

But now there was her fear.

He wondered whether she hated him and whether that was stronger than anything. There had been so many times when he could believe he hated her. But the sight of her fear was something he could not bear.

Why had she stayed with him when he was ill? Duda had said that she had done all to make him well. That she would not leave him and had been jabbering at him in Pictish.

He could not remember that. All he had were fever dreams in which he could see the delicate perfection of her face, and she had told him she could not do without him and that they would abide together. But that much could not be true. She had said words like that before and then she had left him.

"What is it that lies hidden in your head, Alina?"

She said nothing, neither in pleading nor fury, and all her thought hoard remained locked behind the smoky darkness of her eyes.

For all the burning fire in him, he would not have constrained her if she had pulled away. But she did not. The sleek, dark head full of secrets lay against his flesh and then her hand moved. Her fingers fastened on the flesh of his arm, curving round the blood-thickened muscle that strained to... One of the fingers dragged.

It was the hand that had suffered a childhood damage never fully explained.

She had sought him out. She had made up some transparent nonsense about hearing Duda crashing around in the undergrowth when they both knew it could not have been him. That it must be Goadel's man, directed here by the half brother she cared so much about. Looking to take her just as Hun had.

Hun. The thought of the foulness of that creature having been near her turned the corded muscle under her lamed fingers to fire-hardened steel.

He realized she was trying not to weep.

The steel-hard muscle moved, with a force that would crush bones. He tried to loosen the strength of his grip. What he could not stop any longer was the recklessness of what he felt.

He knew she did not want this, and if she feared him as much as he thought, the tears would come. Or she would scream and claw at him with her damaged fingers.

But her arms fastened round his back in a grip that had as much power in its own way as his. And if it did not stop the tears, there could be no doubt of what she wanted in this moment.

A wanting that held its own destruction. He understood nothing of her and everything. All that he understood was compassed in the need with which she clung to him and the sobbing sound of her breath, and the soft touch of her skin.

Her lips found his mouth.

The unexpected force of her touch, the hunger in it, overcame reason. His response had no control. The bitter aching swell at his loins came to full blood-throbbing hardness in one breathless instant.

She did not draw back. The recklessness in her heart must match his, surpass it, because she had called forth the storm. The anger and the passion and the near hatred of the last months of his life were ignited.

CHAPTER EIGHT

SHE WOULD DIE.

She could fix on no other thought. She would die from the sheer force of him, and from the force of what she felt. His body pinned hers against the richness of the forest floor. She could smell the sharpness of flowering wood-meadow grass and crushed bracken and the hot human scent of him.

His mouth was bruising heat, his body bigger, fiercer than she had dreamed. More than she could control or comprehend.

She did not care. She wanted only what had for so long been denied.

She knew enough to understand that men did not give in such acts as this. They only took. But she would let all that fierceness have its course if only she could be with him. She had been told enough to know what she should expect and that—

She knew nothing at all. The terrifying force in him changed, or some other strand, unidentified, took shape in it. His mouth moulded itself over hers, expertly sure. The touch of his hands, inescapable and with a strength beyond her reckoning, was enchantment. Wildfire. It made her feel such things, things she wanted...

She wanted *this*. She wanted what he did to her. As much as she wanted what she did to him, the way her hands touched the hard planes of his body and the way she could feel all of his warmth and his power. The way she could feel her own power. Like something called up in answer.

And then the miracle happened and she was not being kissed. She was doing what she had first tried to do out of all the reckless need of her heart. She was kissing him.

His body moved, taking the weight of hers, moulding its hot strength over her slighter form, and she was moving with him, in a response she could not stop. Her mouth slid over his, pressed against it, moulding it in the same rhythm, so that she could not tell where one movement began and the other ended. Or even where one being began and the other ended. It was like merging with the other stronger, more powerful half of herself.

But so different. The warrior-tough planes of his body, the shape and the movement of it, were something unknown and strange. And infinitely, maddeningly, desirable. Nothing, no one, could ever feel like him.

Tendrils of delight coiled through her, sharp and potent. She let his body and the feel of him take her until her senses swam and her mind dizzied with it. She held him, her hands pressed against his skin, locking on the long line of his naked back, fingertips buried in springy flesh, thick flexible muscle. She held him with all of her strength, clung to him and if that had been all, if it were possible for loving to be like that, she would have stayed so. But it was not.

His body moved with a sureness and a knowledge she could no longer match, even as his mouth gentled over hers, his kiss deepened. Her lips parted against the dark, wet heat of him and she felt fierce shock as his tongue entered her mouth. His strong hand slid under her hair, cradling her head, turning it towards him so that his access to her mouth was complete.

Her mouth opened to the invasion of his because she could not help herself. His tongue tasted inside her, thrust deeper. He did not stop. She felt the breath quicken in the broad wall of his chest. Felt the heat of the desire in him through his skin, the way she had felt his fever heat. His body pressed against hers, forcing her back against the soft grassy bank at the pool's edge. She gasped, but the sound and her breath were lost against the heat of his mouth.

She could sense the weight of him, held back, as yet, carefully balanced so as not to crush her. But holding her with his nearness, with the heavy solid length of his thigh across hers. She could not move. Her body was spread out against the earth, open to his touch, to the way his hands moved across her, exploring every curve.

She felt so utterly vulnerable, yet her flesh thrilled to the feel of his hands through the smooth barrier of her finely-woven clothing. He could make her burn. She could not stop him.

She could not stop anything he did.

He touched her with an intimacy that made her skin tingle and her breath catch and left nothing of her that was not his. It was as though he wanted to learn through that touch who she was, to know her as time and grief and separation had never allowed.

"Brand?"

She could feel the half-shed tears stinging at her eyes and she wanted to touch him in the same way and she did not dare. Did not know how. Her hands flattened out. They were shaking. She slid her palms gently, tentatively across his back and felt muscle tighten, the sudden sharpness of his breath against her mouth. It was as though the urgency of the need inside him was so strong it would leach through his skin. The same need was in her. But she did not know how to express it, or what to do.

She wanted to speak. She did not know what to ask.

"Brand…" *Fire.*

His fingers were at the neck of her dress, tugging at the ties with insistence, parting the laces as though they were no barrier at all.

He touched her skin.

His hand palmed her breast and she cried out. Her body arched against him and the burst of feeling inside her was sharp as the claws of a predator ripping through her lower belly. His fingers brushed the tightened bud at the centre of her breast and that made the feeling sharper, but he just kept touching her.

His touch was soft now, carefully so, gentle. That should have made it better but it did not. It made the feeling worse, fiercer a thousandfold, so that she thought nothing could exceed the power of that. Then his lips found her skin and she felt the moist heat of him, the secret dark wetness. Then the shock as his tongue touched her, the way it had invaded her mouth, and the tightened sensitive peak of her breast was drawn into the dark heat inside him.

She thought her body would split in two. It writhed against his like a soul in torment, which was what she was. Her eyes were closed so tightly it hurt and she could see nothing, only blackness. The blackness would drag her down because her mind was so dizzy with it and her body was no longer hers to control.

She was afraid of that and the fear took the sense of her power away from her. *He* had taken it away with his touch and his mind-aching beauty. With his heat and his sureness and his skill.

That was his skill, seducing people.

There was no defence against it, especially not for a lamed creature like her. It was not only the raw measure of his strength which was to be feared, but that.

The terrifying thoughts came to her out of the blackness and a thin, biting coldness sliced its way through the dizziness of her head. Remembrance was forced further back, to the nightmare she could not free herself from.

Helplessness. Her mother cursing.

She was like her mother. Worse. She was more than helpless, she was trapped by herself. Because inside her burned the terrible need for Brand's touch and what he did.

What he would do.

She felt his hand slide across her leg, drawing her hips against him, so that the full potency of his body touched hers and she felt him as he was, the blood-gorged hardness of male flesh, the fierce pulse of life and the power. She knew the intimate movement of his body and the primitive directness of that brought hot, bright-edged sensation stabbing through her, as though she felt him inside her already.

She could not permit it. The small slice of fear in her brain widened. She could not permit it because she could not face what it was.

Because if the last act happened, some terrible barrier would be crossed and there would be no going back. The joining between them that had been there from the first moment they had seen each other would be completed. It would be irrevocable. And even through her fear, she knew that if she allowed that she would have failed him.

"Alina."

The sound never touched the whispering air of the glade. It filled her mouth, together with his breath and his warmth. It was only sensed, the sound of it born directly inside her, like spellcraft, binding the soul.

His body moved, sending feeling shooting through her skin, as though he were part of her already.

She could not let it happen. All the sacrifice of separation would be for nothing. She would not be able to protect him.

His touch was possession. He would have all of her and if he did, then all that she was could not be hidden. He would know her for what she was: emptiness where he was fire.

Her body tightened, her muscles pushed against the full measure of his unleashed strength. But it could not have the slightest effect. What she had said to him was so. He could do as he would.

TRUTH HAD HIDDEN FACES.

He could see Alina's truth. Even through the edge of madness. The control it took to stop was of his kind. Ruthless. The kind that sliced through pain. It was a skill honed in hell. That was the last place he would send Alina.

She was afraid of him, beyond the strength of desire or the power of what had once been shared. Beyond redemption.

He rolled back onto the grass, putting the coolness of distance between them. Emptiness filled the living, sense-burning air where she had been, frozen and dead like a wasteland. The evening breeze cut at the heat of his sweat-sheened skin, dead cold, as though winter's breath had come in a moment.

Nay, it was not the air, the death was in him. He

stared at the mind-aching arch of the sky, but his eyes were blind. He fought for breath but it was the ragged sound of her breathing that made him turn.

She lay just as he did, staring at the sky. Her fine clothes were a mess, rumpled, gaping off her body so that he could glimpse the small fineness of her underneath, thin skin and small bones exposed to the biting air. He had done that.

Her hands were white-knuckled fists locked at her sides, the fingers bunched round the thick summer grass and the stems of some flower-starred plant, tearing at it. She shuddered. The whole of her slight frame seemed racked by the need to gain life-giving breath.

Through the deadness inside stirred the familiar, aching threads of the protectiveness that had been so strong it had taken all, mind and duty and honour.

Honour. He did not know how she had managed to force that word past her throat when she had lain in his bed at the monastery. Honour was gone. For both of them.

He watched her fingers twist in the long-stemmed plant. Vervain, subject of endless old wives' tales. He could see the pale purple flower heads. Her fingers slipped, the knuckles white, uneven, shattered and without strength.

He did not even know how that had been done to her.

It was impossible to summon the rage that had sustained him for so long.

Just as it was impossible to call back lost honour. Impossible for anyone to live by it in this world.

If you admitted that—

"Alina."

She looked not at him but at the mangled plant in her hand.

If you admitted the truths you did not want to see—

He watched the averted head and the undernourished body of the woman he had failed to protect.

He sat up.

You had to deal with what was. Not with how you wanted things to be.

She had to know that she did not have to fear him again.

He took breath. The coldness of the air struck like ice in his lungs. But its sharp clearness spoke of the north, of home. *Lindwood.* He closed his mind against charred ruins. Not yet.

"Alina."

She flinched.

The cold air settled on his skin. It was not as cold as guilt.

"Alina, look at me."

She turned her head. But not before he had seen the struggle for control. It seemed the most bitter thing he had ever witnessed.

"I am sorry," she said.

"What?"

"I am sorry," said her voice again. "For…for all this." The long-broken hand made a sweeping, helpless gesture that seemed to encompass the entire world. The sum of all the things he did not understand about her or what she did.

The kind of understanding he wanted was far beyond his reach. It made no difference to what he had to say.

"Alina, what happened now was not your fault. It was mine. I was wrong in what I did. No." He stopped whatever she would say because the guilt would not allow it. "What was so wrong was to think that the past has any hold over the present that...that there was still something that bound us. It is over. The past is dead."

"Dead." Her voice sounded like the thinnest thread, one that would snap for breathing on it.

"Aye. The past is dead between us." he said again, as though chanting his way through some spell that would have the power to end what he could not. "All that was done is buried. I will not follow its path again and neither will I hang its weight on you like some endless burden."

"Dead."

Her hand ripped at the small pale flowers turning to seed. The lamed finger snagged uselessly at a thickened stem, unable to break it. His hand covered hers before she did herself harm. Impulsive, reckless gesture. But the impulsiveness seemed embedded in him where she was concerned, the urge to act with a speed that did not negate thought, but merely outstripped it.

Pain jarred down his injured arm and her hand

stiffened under his. She must not even want to suffer that much contact from him. But he knew what was right. She would cause damage to herself.

"Let go of the stem. You cannot break it."

"No." She stared at the crushed plant, at her hand, anywhere but at him. "I do not want to let it go." Her eyes fixed on the woody stem and the nondescript flower heads as though that provided her only anchor to the earth.

"Then just stay still." He kept his voice steady the way he would with a wild colt. The hand under his stopped moving. "That is better. Just stay still." He opened his hand when he was sure that she would not move. So that she could be free of him. "I will—"

She let go of the plant and caught his hand, still not looking at him, but moving fast. Her fingers scrabbling at his, clumsy and uncontrolled, like someone blind seeking their way by touch.

He watched her fingers, stunned, and then he realized why she would touch even him. She was so alone; her only kin the predatory creature Cunan, and she had such dangerous choices to make. Cunan would, of course, make her choices for her given the chance. But Cunan played for his own gain, not hers. Did she realize that? That her kin would betray her?

Cunan wanted to get her to Goadel. He would do it by stealth or by force if he could.

He stared at the fragile half-clothed form, the thin hand clutching at his. Her consent would be unnecessary to Cunan, her painfully made choices irrelevant.

She said she had chosen Modan's life. She must want to hold to that because she had also made the choice to warn him that their watcher was back. It seemed that in this she was true.

Life would be so much easier if she were true.

He heard it. With a hunter's training. Duda's teaching overlying an instinct that was deeper than thought's reach. He did not think it was Goadel's watcher who sought the chance to come on him unaware. Not this time.

There was no doubt who it was. He was already moving with casual speed when both parts of his mind furnished another truth, beyond what he could believe.

Alina did not know.

THEY WERE FOOLS.

Oblivious. The silence with which he had achieved his aim had been masterly. He had forced his way through the trees with a stealth even the disgusting dog-eared Saxon peasant set to guard him would not have been able to match. And he had found them.

The low sun showed him the Northumbrian. On his feet. Light caught skin. His sight could not take it in. The carved handle of the knife dug into his palm. But his hand was shaking so much he could not unsheathe the blade.

And then he saw. The man was still half-clothed. The last of the sun's rays picked out the whiteness of the fresh binding on his arm where the wound was.

Cunan forced his hand to relax. The woman was not even close to him.

There would be time enough to deal with the debaucher. Just let them cross the border into Northumbria.

She was sitting on the grass in her green riding dress. She was fully clothed but her dark gleaming hair streamed over her back, its abundance shamelessly uncovered before the Bernician.

She shifted in the shadows. For one moment of blackened rage he thought that she was adjusting her clothes. But then she turned and he realized she must have been repacking the saddlebag that held the cures.

He forced breath into his lungs. She was not looking at the lecher. In fact, she seemed to avoid it.

He let the breath go.

Alina was not like her mother with that show of untouchable coldness hiding secret debaucheries. She was frail, yes, foolish and in want of correction after what she had done. But there would be someone to do that. Soon. Someone who had the right.

And this time she would be loyal to her kin. He knew it.

She looked up even as the certainty formed in his head, as though his thought had called her. Her gaze seemed to drift over him and then away.

His own gaze followed Alina's.

The Northumbrian was throwing on his shirt.

Such an ordinary thing. But as the linen sheeted over the other man's flesh, he saw what lived in her eyes.

ALINA STARED at the dying embers of the fire and beyond it at the dark hunched shapes that were sleeping human forms: Cunan, Duda, the rest of Brand's men. She slept slightly apart from them. Near Brand. It might have looked like a sign of possession, of connection. To someone who did not know.

She huddled tighter, and the coldness and the isolation wrapped round her, familiar to her as her own skin, as inescapable. The fact that he was there, a hand's reach away from her only made the isolation more complete. She could not feel his warmth. Not now.

She closed her eyes and her body trembled. But not from the familiar cold. From what she had done with him. And what she had not done. What she could not do, and what she had wanted. And not wanted.

The thoughts would kill her, in the silently breathing dark. They were like madness.

He was not hers, the frightening, lethally beautiful creature lying beside her. The fierce, knowing body and the mind that was so ruthlessly direct, the heat and the anger and the terrifying gentleness were not for her. If they belonged to anything, it was to memory, to an image of a woman who was no longer her, who never truly had been her.

In four or five days, it would be over, this enforced closeness that was no such thing. She would be at Bamburgh and King Cenred would send her to Craig Phádraig. If she was lucky.

Brand would have the place that he belonged to, beside his king, with land and wealth once more at his back, and this time unthreatened. He would have peace. That was worth more than gold. Perhaps more than love.

Certainly more than the terrible kind of love she could offer.

He had said the past was over.

It was.

Her body ached for him.

DUDA WAS MISSING HIS leather jerkin.

Brand watched rags twitch and resettle as though their owner wished some other covering were there.

So did Brand.

He suppressed an urge to twitch on his own account, in case his half-dressed henchman saw it. Or anyone else who might be watching. Or not.

So far, his men had not trapped Goadel's spies. All he had were snatched words overheard in the dark. He had no idea whether the stolen words meant what he believed. But it was all he had, the only time anyone had got close to Goadel's men.

The unknowing was likely to drive him moon-mad. He was not made for it.

The horse lunged, answering instantly to the unconscious urging of his body.

Patience was not something he had.

He curbed the stallion, slid a hand over the thick neck, the quivering muscles. It was like fighting himself, the urge to release power dammed too long into action, pure, direct and unstoppable.

He watched Duda and, without the consciousness of thought or impulse, or even will, Alina.

Patience was something life forced on you.

Not yet— Something changed in the air. He was not even looking at the crowding shadows of the trees. Yet he knew.

It would happen. Now. After two days of uneventful riding. While they were still in Mercia, entering the narrow stretch of land between the high hills to the west and the marshlands of the east coast.

It was so clear that Brand could not understand the obliviousness of those around him. The air pulsed with the knowledge. Fate's web. He watched Alina and, more closely, Cunan. Nothing could be seen in either face. Or in the faces of his men.

Yet the danger was there, something tasted. His blood surged. The response instant, familiar, burning him with the need to take the danger head-on, conquer it.

The fierce, double-edged joy of the risk lured him, spoke in a siren voice to the place inside him that was empty, the part that sought danger before it came. Because life held nothing else, certainty least of all. But he never gave in to the lure completely. It was something to be used to slake the emptiness, but its power had to be controlled.

It would not master him. If it did, it would take all he had and it would be worse than death.

His men knew what to do. He had made sure of that.

He told Duda the jerkinless, with one flick of his eyes, caught the flash of irritation in return. He crushed the reckless grin. It was worth a purse of silver to know before Duda did.

Yet the knowledge was uncanny.

Duda worked with a hunter's senses that were more finely tuned than most men's. But Brand's knowing had sprung from something else. Something that he had not acknowledged before the moment he had been aware, without reason, that his brother was still alive.

His mount sidled, catching the fire from him. He steadied it one-handed.

Athelwulf had said what had happened had been *wyrd*. Destiny. Athelwulf, who worked only in the realms of intellect.

The web of fate, spinning out.

Alina.

He did not look at her, at the soft green gown that had come apart under his hands, at the maddeningly fluttering stream of her veil, the dark rippling mass of her hair beneath.

He watched, keeping his eyes fixed ahead.

Duda moved closer to Cunan. The man with the shield slung across his shoulder moved closer to where Alina would be. What shocked was the primitive force of the urge to knock that man aside and place himself next to the Princess of Craig Phádraig.

It is you who should be afraid. It is you who are in danger.

As ever, she was right.

The danger was to him, not her, and his closeness could only bring a threat to her that would not otherwise be there.

He forced his mount to drop farther back, slowing its pace and mastering its eagerness. He let himself droop slightly in the saddle as though he were weary and the wound still troubled him. The pretence was less difficult than he would like.

He curbed every impulse, both instinctive and trained, to fight, to seize the initiative, to defend if not attack. Even to move. He held still, kept to the sunlight where he could be seen. Looked ahead, where the threat would not come from.

Nothing happened. While he waited, like a pig for the spitting. His mind could feel it. The bite of fire-hardened iron penetrating his body, splitting muscle and sinew.

It was Duda who broke, turning his shaggy head to look at him. Brand cursed inside because it could have made Alina look. But she did not. She stared ahead, her spine rigid. But she was aware of him. He knew that without the slightest sign.

His gaze met Duda's, its meaning unmistakable: *look away.* He did not know what else was in his face, but one grubby hand made a sign of the cross, then more surreptitiously a sign against enchantment just to be doubly sure. He blocked the word *berserker* out of his head.

His blood pulsed. The risk goaded him. The rush

of that was so strong in him it would take all, mind and sense and the power to control thought.

If he let it.

Duda looked away.

He wished suddenly that he knew whether he was right. He wished Duda was wearing the protection of patched leather that smelled of horse and nameless years of accumulated sweat. He wished he could take the fates by the throat and ensure the life of every man here, and of every man who would ever give him the dues of fealty.

He wished he could pay all the debts that came with honour. He wished he could believe in a future.

Alina.

He turned the horse slightly. There was no room for the smallest error in what he did. Too many debts. He used only his knee to guide the restive stallion, keeping the reins loose.

The movement exposed his back fully. It was the perfect shot. Now. In the clearing, with sun beating on him, casting his shadow forward.

He did not know whether he heard it, or felt it on the tightened edge of awareness, the faint whirring disturbance of the still air. He twisted his body, even though there might not be time, hoping that the arrow would strike obliquely, that the head would stick, that open metal links would be sufficient protection. That he would not be disabled.

He could see even through the fractured second that was all he had, how Duda was already moving away, how the other man, the one he had to trust, had flung himself, shield in hand, at Alina.

The last, unbelievable thing that he saw before he fell was the surprise on Cunan's face.

The impact of the blow stunned. It was knife-sharp, greater than he had bargained for. It was not beyond his capacity to manage, could not be.

He slid forward across the horse's neck in a fall that was less controlled than he wanted, gripping with thighs and knees until the muscles strained. He forced his hand to let the reins go. He could feel the shock rippling through the powerful animal muscle underneath his body.

But the horse was trained. It responded. He stopped the fall, tried to control the horse's urge to bolt after the others who thundered past. He whispered the names of Northumbrian saints into its ear as he watched hooves disappear across the rough ground, moving with planned speed.

He added a further prayer to the full panoply of the saints of Britain that they found something.

The second shot had been harmless. He forced himself to wait until they were out of sight. He would not—Alina screamed.

He slid round, hitting the ground on balance, the jarring pain through his back scarce felt. She was struggling against the man he had set to hold her the way she had struggled against him in the nunnery, with the same complete and mindless force. Like a battle rage. Like the echo of the force inside himself.

It was the kind of force that took account of nothing outside itself.

Until later.

"Cease."

They saw him. Alina's body went dead still. Her face turned the colour of chalk. The face of the man, Eadric, was wild-eyed. He had hold of her arms.

"Let her go."

There was no point in holding her trapped. She could not get to Goadel's men now. Her chance was gone, stopped by the man he had sent to save her skin.

Besides, she would not move. He could see it. The wild rush of strength must have drained out of her with the knowledge that the moment was lost.

The rush of that terrible power still beat through him.

She just stood, like a creature of fine white stone, the sun outlining every pure and beautiful line of her form, her head tilted at that maddening angle that made him want to smash something. Or strangle her slender neck. Or finish what they had started regardless of whether she wished it or no.

She looked as brittle as glass. Something that had to be protected from breaking.

He thought the black weariness inside would kill him.

Eadric's grass-stained hands were still on her arms as though he thought she might shatter. His transparent eyes bright with all the useless unnecessary urge to protect that ran in mockery through his own veins.

"I said, let her go." He did not know what was in his voice, but something made Eadric drop instantly to his knees, head bowed.

"Lord, I meant no wrong but if I have done it you may punish me as you will."

The boy had seen scarce more than twenty winters and had an unspoilt heart. His face had turned the colour of ash. The tearing anger and the guilt turned inwards where they belonged, familiar as his own skin.

"Nay, you have done no wrong. I owe you a debt for saving the lady's—" Honour? Decency? Her beloved brother's neck? "For keeping her life."

He reached down to pull Eadric to his feet. Eadric looked up as his hand closed over an arm and he saw the expression in the fear-widened eyes had changed into the one thing he could not face, the loyalty that was no longer his due.

"I would not have harmed the lady." The words came out in a rush. "But you charged me with her safety and she would have gone to you and I knew, you told me, that the danger would be yours and that we… Lord?"

His hand had frozen, like rock covered in ice. It quite probably bit painfully through Eadric's hide. He could not tell.

"It is true," said the singing voice of Craig Phádraig behind him, equally nervous. "It is not your man's fault. It was mine. I thought you were… I thought you would be killed."

His sight vanished. Just for an instant, darkness

shot through with fire that had an uncanny edge, like something that belonged in another time. Such coldness all round him, dragging at him. And Alina's voice shouting.

He did not actually fall. He would not let himself and it was just a split instant, and then control was back.

"Lord, let me help you." It was Eadric, his transparent face creased in anxiety.

"No—"

"Please." Alina. Her black eyes were like twin pools of night in her white face. He could not look at her.

"No. Leave it. Just break the arrow shaft." The discomfort was bearable. The wound was not serious but if they removed the arrow there would be blood. He did not know how much and there was no time for that now. He could hear the sound of hoofbeats on the rough ground. His men returning.

"Lady, I can do it."

Eadric moved behind him. There was a brief tearing of his flesh as the arrow head dragged. Then nothing. He left Eadric to look after Alina. He could not look at her face because of what he might see there. Because of what he might believe.

He walked forward to meet his men.

They were out of luck. Two corpses: one had been killed in the fight, the other had been taken prisoner and should still have been alive.

"Then why—" It was Cunan who spoke. Brand

had placed him in the front rank of their discussions because he wanted to weigh his reactions.

There was a shuffling of feet before someone spoke. "The prisoner took his own life. We were not quick enough to stop him."

Brand looked from his men's faces to the face of the second corpse. It was one he recognized. He had seen this man with Goadel before. He was a Northumbrian. Not a hired mercenary. He had a wife and two sons who would grieve for him.

"Why?" He knew full well, but it now seemed possible that Cunan did not. If that look of surprise at the start of the attack had not been the wildness of imagination.

"Lord, he said that even King Cenred would not be enough to protect him if Goadel knew he had been caught. He said he would rather die quickly. He said that with the last man, the last one who left Goadel, they...they got him back and he lived for three days. They all heard the screaming and they saw what..."

The man's voice dropped and Brand let the silence hang. It spoke more truly than words could. It was broken by Cunan's snort of derision.

"Those are tales to frighten children, not warriors. Who is to say that you did not kill this man?"

"No." Brand stopped the rustling movement of half a dozen knife hands with a single gesture. There was no point harming Cunan. And besides, he had seen it: the small flicker of uncertainty, of distaste in the keen, houndlike eyes.

He let his men tell the rest of their story. It needed no embellishment. And he had what he wanted. Goadel would think him wounded. Goadel would believe he had what he so desperately wanted to take. Time.

Cunan was the only one who could tell him otherwise.

He refused to think about Alina.

CHAPTER NINE

CLEAR MOVING WATER HAD its own power, different from the life of a spring, or the deep stillness of well water. But just as strong. Alina listened to its voice.

People were wary of the secret power of water. Brand seemed to seek it out by instinct.

She paused in the shadow of the trees, soundless.

This was the second time she had come on him unawares, in just such a place beside clear running water. The second time she had sought him. Drawn by that power. The water's power and his.

If there was a third time, it might be fatal.

But she knew she would not be able to stay away from it.

He was very still. The hidden corselet of chain mail that had saved his life lay discarded on the sunlit grass, glittering with its own light, like something alive.

He had bathed in the water. His hair was wet. It hung in darkened rivulets down his back. He wore his tunic. The arrow wound was concealed. She did not know how deep it went or whether the chain mail had left the tears in his flesh that were more open to poison than the arrow's bite. It was not she who had dealt with the wound.

She had not been able approach him. Because he would not let her. Because she had not dared. Because she had made a terrible mistake this afternoon.

She had said words out loud that should never have been born.

She had to put things right.

And it was beyond her power to stay away from him.

He watched the water.

She could not see his face, only the water-darkened spread of his hair, the broad hand that could throw a knife blade faster than sight and stir magic out of her terrified body with an unknown mixture of power and tenderness. She wondered whether he would throw the blade at her this time. And whether this time he would want to split her heart with it.

He moved his shoulders as though they ached. The sun glinted on the torqued gold at his wrist, on the dark gold streaks in his hair. Light slid over him and he was alive.

"You made me think you were dead."

They were not the words she had meant to say. Her breath choked in her throat. He turned his head. That was it. No surprise, no sudden move wild with danger.

It was as though he knew she would be there. Even what she would say.

"You let me think the same when you left me after

I had taken you from Hun. You let me believe you were dead, killed by thieves on your flight south. How did you do it? Find that charred unrecognizable corpse of a woman?"

"It was chance."

"There is no such thing."

She started. Because the Brand she had known would never have said that. "Then it must have been something else that let my steps pass that place at that time. Your English fate, *Wyrd.*"

The fair head bent in acknowledgement of a word that was true for him. It was like watching a stranger in the familiar body.

"I came across her on the road south. Some poor woman set upon by outlaws. They had thrown her body on the fire when they had finished with her. You could not recognize the corpse. I paid quite dearly for the news to go north that it was me."

"So I would not follow you on your flight back to Hun."

"Yes." *I did pay. Dearly. I still pay.*

He straightened up and it was as though the wounds and fatigue and all the stress of what he had done did not exist. She could see his eyes.

"How could you think I would not follow Hun to the ends of Middle Earth after what he had done to my brother?"

"I thought… I do not know. You were exiled. You could not so much as set foot in Northumbria without being killed—"

"I could set foot in Wessex."

But it was so far, and I did not know King Osred would send Hun there as ambassador. I did not know because I was hiding from him as much as from you.

"I did not think—"

"I would have taken Hun if he had been seated at the foot of the throne at Bamburgh."

"Yes." She did not say anything else. No need. She walked forward. It was like approaching a wolf. But she did it.

"Aye. I think you do understand the kind of single-mindedness that will take all in its path whatever the odds."

"Yes." She stopped in front of him, light-footed, wary, like a creature poised for flight in any direction.

"That single-mindedness is in you, too."

She planted her feet on the flower-shot grass and she knew she would not move.

"Aye," she said in Northumbrian.

He turned away, watching the water. Reflected light danced across his face. She could see the way the taut skin stretched across the bones.

"What happened after I left? To you? To Lind-wood?" She had made her next mistake. Her words echoed through the air, back through time, to the high and brilliant beauty of Brand's home stretching out across the hills, under the wide arc of the Bernician sky.

She could no longer focus on the water and the small compass of the grass. Her eyes saw the hall at

Lindwood, its tapestries and its soaring high-pitched roof and the pillars painted green. Space and light balanced by shadows. The deep calmness like a forest. The rich movement of life.

"What happened to all the people?"

"We all survived."

That was it. No other word of the dangers and the loss, the constantly shifting threat to a small group of people in exile. The responsibility for all that would have been Brand's burden, his to bear. She had left him to it.

Sun shimmered over him, the way it had always lighted on the brilliant and high-hearted Prince of Bernicia. The planes of his face underneath the light were stark, bedrock strong.

"And Lindwood?"

"That will survive."

"Because you got it back before the harvest could be taken?"

"Because I got it back."

She could see the inner toughness that had been hidden before by the glamour. As though the reckless charm and the easy grace were a covering, like her mask of indifference.

He leaned back. The light shifted and grace was the only thing evident, the fluid lines and the aggressive perfection of his beauty.

She did not think he would say any more. Then she realized he had only leaned back, in that polished assumption of ease, because he wanted to see

her face and how she reacted to whatever he would
say next.

"Hun burnt the books when he took Lindwood, did
he tell you that?"

"Books?" She thought of the impossible cost that
could not be calculated by its equivalent weight in
gold or silver. She fought to find the mask.

"All the manuscripts that had been copied out by
the monks at Jarrow."

"Yours…" She would not have thought that he
cared for such things.

"Nay." His gold gaze caught her with the look that
meant he read the thoughts in her mind.

"What would someone like me do with books?"
The hot amber eyes watched her with their blank
brightness. "Such things are not for me. They get into
your head, like something permanent."

His voice gave nothing, poised and careless as the
leashed strength of his body. She saw straight past it,
the way he saw through her. He had wanted those
books even if he did not admit it to himself. He
wanted the books and…something else she could not
yet fathom. Hun had brought destruction to whatever
it was, the way he destroyed everything. The way she
did.

"They were Wulf's books. His favourite was *The
Consolation of Philosophy*. Do you know what it was
about? The permanent joys of the spirit, not the transience of this world." The cultured Northumbrian
voice dripped irony.

"Boethius?"

"I would not know. And now I cannot. Of course it was only the expendable things that your betrothed burnt—the outbuildings, the chapel with the books. He had the sense to leave all that would truly benefit him, the hall and the workshops, the storerooms. They still stand. They are mine now. I will not let them go again."

"No—" Her voice stopped, because the air thickened, the way it did before a storm.

"I am rich and I have power." The air took her breath, but he spoke through it. "Why did you turn towards me this afternoon, and not towards Goadel's men?"

There was a pause, its span timeless. The water hissed through the heavy air. Behind her the coolness and the dark, the shelter given by the trees, dragged at her.

She sat down in the slanting sun that exposed every leaf and every blade of grass.

"I have told you. I want to go to my brother."

She stared at the water just as he had done, trying to draw the power out of its rippling lights. Not looking at the lights that touched him. It could not matter what she said.

He would not believe her.

"It is love," said her voice, while her eyes stared at the moving water and the blinding light, and her body thrummed with awareness of him, not a hand's breadth away from her. "Love is that strong. It will make you strong enough to do anything."

Her words took the power of the water. Their truth shimmered in the moving currents of the breeze.

"And that is how you think of your brother?"

Yes.

But I was not thinking of my duty to Modan in that fractured instant of terror. Saint Dwyn forgive me, I was thinking of you. As I am now.

"As you think of Athelwulf, so I think of Modan."

She closed her eyes against the light on the water. All she could see was Brand's face: as it was now, full of a light that had nothing to do with the sun, full of shadows caused by the body's grief and the mind's. Then further back, as it had been at Bamburgh, full of life and a joy that had a fierce edge. As it was in a thousand guises that only she knew, that only she had seen.

Perhaps.

More truth slid out.

"Modan was the only one of my kin who valued me for what I was, not for what gain I would bring, or to strike out at someone else."

She paused. The images in her mind took everything. "It is a rare gift to be valued for what you are, to know you can value another person the same way. That is why I loved…above all."

"Above all?"

"Above all." She could see his face against her closed eyes. It was better than actually looking at him. Because the face she saw held the rare gift, just as it had before loss had taken everything.

"I loved that more than life or my duty to my country or my father. That is how I love. I cannot prevent it or change it. It is there. You accused me of single-mindedness and it is true."

She held the face in her mind but the pain of doing that was becoming more than she could bear and the tears were stinging at the insides of her eyes.

"So now you know what I will do." The tears stung even at her inner vision. "You know why I will follow you. As far as Bamburgh." She tried to hold on to the mind sight of him, but she could not because the power of the outside world, the death knell of what would happen after Bamburgh, the separation that would be permanent, were becoming too strong.

"You said you understood…." She did not know whether the words were directed at the vision in her mind or at the real man, beside her on the sunlit grass. She heard him move.

"There is nothing to understand. There is no other way to love."

The real man and the dream man began to merge. The tears blurring her inner vision spilled out into the outside world. He touched them with his fingers, real and warm, catching her dream tears. She turned her head, eyes dream-blind, tear-blind, seeking the real warmth and the dream warmth together. It was there. His lips found hers.

It was different from the way he had kissed her before. His touch was so gentle. And that was what she craved. At first it was like part of her dream. The way his mouth covered hers, the tenderness of his hands on her body, the way the warmth of him seeped through her clothing and her skin to find its place inside her.

Then it was not like her dream, it was real and she thought she would feel the fear, and she did, and yet not so. Because even though it was real, his touch was still tender. And that was not possible.

But that was what she felt, his tenderness. Her body dizzied with its magic and the blood came to slow singing life in her veins, and it was bliss.

But the aching need inside her, the desperateness that had grown in the dark, in the loss and the separation, had a strength beyond control. It was tearing at her. So that without her will, her body quickened and her hands tightened against the lithe, warrior-tough form that was real and full of power held back.

She closed her mind to that. To the strength in the turn of his back, the war-thick muscle in arm and leg and neck. She would not think of that or of nightmares further back in the past. Of the echoing hall of Craig Phádraig and how her mother had railed and cursed against men and their misbegotten power.

But even so, she felt his body tighten against the unmistakable signs of the need in hers, against the small uncontrolled movements she could not stop.

She would not let herself think of pain or consequences or power or betrayal. They were just a price to pay, and she had made her decision that she would pay it from the moment he had touched her tears. No, before that, from the moment she had told him how much she loved him without saying a single word for him.

Her body moved against his in a rhythm as old as time and she knew she had made her decision the moment she had seen him in the small close confines of the Wessex nunnery. The moment he had come back.

She let his hands take her body as they had before. Let them loosen her clothing, tumble it away from her. So that she was open to the touch of his mouth, the heat of his breath against her skin, the scorching wetness of his tongue against desperate flesh and pounding blood. She let his mouth know each curve, take the aching hardness at her breast, let his hands feel under her skirts.

Touch her where he must.

But she was not prepared for the shock that came with that.

The intimacy of his touch on the hidden place that made her a woman, the most vulnerable part of her, swept away all thought, all defence, all her being. So that she was lost. Helpless under the longing.

That touch had the power to open not just her body, but her mind. Leaving her exposed to everything it was possible to feel, even to the memories buried in her thoughts like the poisonous barbs of an arrow. Her mother's curses rang in her ears.

She twisted wildly, but that only made her feel the pulsing hardness of him pressing against her. She knew what he would do and she wanted to move, to tear herself away before it happened.

Yet his touch was so different from all that the nightmare in her mind told her to expect. She had not known, even guessed, that a man might touch a woman in that way, with such sensuous lingering intimacy.

His clever, sure, frighteningly skilled fingers glided across skin that was swollen with need, traced its complex sense-aching folds as though he touched her just for the pleasure of how she felt to him. Perhaps because that overwhelming, uncontrolled pleasure passed through the boundaries of her flesh into his, and that was what he wanted: to feel and know what his touch did to her.

It made her body shake in aching waves, trembling with fear, with longing, she did not know which. But he did not stop the terrifying, seductive magic of what he did. The dark heavy heat of him, the pulsing hardness, did not force itself upon her, blotting out all the magic. Not yet.

His fingers touched her somewhere that made her body arch and every muscle tighten and then his finger slid inside her. Inside the hot, wet tightness of her inner body. It was not that other deadly hardness, and yet it was such an invasion and so unexpected. She did not know why he would do it but there was no pause in the smooth, heat-slickened movement of his hand. Not the slightest hesitation. So that his very assurance made it become part of the pleasure. Of all that she wanted and did not want.

Like him. She wanted him and she did not. She was afraid. The feeling inside her was building and building with a force she could not stand. Because of him. The intimate touch of him against her skin.

He made her feel every heated nuance of his body. He made her own body writhe with yearnings she could not control. The power of it and the vulnerability would take her very self.

That was what men did. Took away yourself, so that all that was left was a used and bitter wreck with no life and no power of her own. Even Brand would do that to her, just by the things that he did. Because despite her fear she could not stop wanting him.

Her voice was moaning softly, as though it did not belong to her but only to the heated aching body that had forced itself against his like a creature beyond sanity. She thought she said his name.

Her hips thrust against that tormenting intimate touch because she could not stop herself. It was as though she wanted to bring him deeper, so deep inside her. But then there was the edge of pain and with it came terror. The shock made her cry out, and the sound tearing her throat took the shape of the fear beating inside her head.

"Don't—"

She shouted at him. She had to make him stop before the sum of her buried fears took life and the truth came out. She could not bear this and she was not right for it. Above all, she did not want Brand to be to her what her father had been to her mother. She could not face it.

But then it did stop, both the fear and the magic. She was left on her own on the grass beside the clearness of the moving stream utterly bereft, beyond helping. The tears inside her eyes were no longer dream tears but sobbing gasps, real, wrenching and ugly with pain. Without hope. Like her.

The coldness of the air cut at her exposed skin. There was no movement. The choking rasp of her breath cut off all sound. She was alone, just as she had always been, and he had left her.

Nay, she had left him. Just as she had before. Only worse. Because this time she had done it out of the measure of her fear, out of the shame and the lameness inside. There was no redemption. A man would never forgive a woman for what she had just done.

She was not a woman. She was a maimed being, crawling about on the grass like some sick animal.

He knew all that she was now, and he did not want her.

He was gone.

Her fingers blundered against the solid shape of his arm.

"Alina…"

"Do not let me go."

They were the only words she could get out of the pit of her mind.

THE SHIVERS THAT RACKED her body were like fever chills.

She lay against his warmth. Brand could feel how

fast her heart beat because she clung to him as though she had a she-wolf's claws. He could also feel how small she was, so seemingly...helpless. All the beauty of her and all the finely balanced pride marred beyond saving.

The press of feeling locked inside him was deadly. He did not want to touch her. He did not even want to see her.

His hand settled on her head.

His fingers curved round the shape of her skull, stayed there as though it were possible to touch what was inside it. She did not move. Nothing. Nothing but the harsh sound of their breath and her stillness.

It was not stillness. She was shaking.

His fault. It was not something that could be borne. He wanted to take the pain away from her.

At the same time he wanted to kill her with all the strength in his hands.

Everything she had ever said to him had been a lie. Every action. All that he had believed.

He dragged the crushed clothing across her naked skin, moving round so that the bulk of his body sheltered her from the cold wind. It made no difference to her shivering and when he moved, her small shaking hands clawed at his flesh, biting with the blindness of panic.

It was not the cold that caused her tremors. It was terror. He had utterly misunderstood the depth of her fears. He had wanted to have her. The driving need inside him had been to wipe out her last memory of

Hun's touch with his own. An act of possession that had been as desperate as it was futile. The body's betrayal had been complete, in more ways than he had counted on, its closeness a mockery.

But even if the act had been completed, it would not have brought him what he wanted. He had wanted to be inside her mind.

That was what had driven him beyond sanity. The need to know that what Eadric had said in the forest clearing, that what *she* had said was true. That when Goadel's men had shot at him, she had turned not towards his enemy, but towards him.

But there was no truth between them. There was no way to change that. He had known it, even through his desperation.

"Why did you lie?"

He had not meant to say it, to let her have the smallest power to guess at the writhing vulnerability inside him. Certainly he had meant to keep the lethal blackness of his heart out of his voice.

She flinched as though he had struck her.

"What do you mean?"

It was as impossible not to go on, as it was impossible to stop the punishing breath that scored his lungs.

"Why did you say you had been with Hun when you had not?"

"How...how do you... Why do you say—"

Her voice cut off under the sharp, uncontrolled movement of his body. He heard the frightened hiss of her breath. But he did not know what on Middle

Earth she expected. That she could lie her way even out of this?

"Why…" She stopped. Because there was naught she could say. Yet the thin line of her voice held none of the bravado he expected, only despair and…distance. As though her mind were filled with something else, something he could not guess at and he was forced back into the morass of unknowing. The sense of powerlessness ignited fury to a depth that appalled him.

He tried to hold every muscle still, using the fighter's discipline that had been forced on him since birth. "I know exactly what you have and have not done with that man."

He made not the slightest movement, yet each word struck like fire off steel.

"What I do not know is why you lied."

She did not look at him. All he could see was the nightfall of her hair, spilling through his motionless fingers in waves, rich and tangled from their loving that had been no such thing. It could not go on so. He had to see what lay in her eyes.

His hand moved. The thick fingers, scarred from a life spent sword fighting, slid across the fine silk of her hair, sought the soft curve where neck met skull. In a lightning-fast movement, she turned her face away, eluding him in one last graceful motion of defiance.

Her body curved tightly, rigid in every small muscle. His hand stopped. Suppose it was not defiance? Suppose it was only her terror? She looked as though she wanted to hide herself from his sight. Yet despite that, despite everything, she still clung to him.

Do not let me go.

That was what she had said.

She had nothing.

Because he had taken it all from her.

His mind, casting ahead to anticipate the next step, warrior trained, seemed to know what her words would be before she said them.

"I could see nothing ahead but danger and sorrow for—" Her hands gripped at him in that travesty of connection. She swallowed something back, something she would not say.

But then she said, "There was nothing else I could do."

The words had the power of a sword thrust. He tried to breathe through the pain.

"I could not stay with you."

"Because of what would happen?"

But the truth had already taken shape. He had been a fugitive. He had been able to offer her nothing, not even the protection that he owed her.

"Yes."

He kept breathing.

"You thought it would never stop, the pursuit and the exile."

She made some voiceless sound but his thoughts had run far ahead, seeking the truth that seemed now in his grasp, even if it meant the sword thrust in her words would be lethal.

An Important Message from the Editors

Dear Reader,

Because you've chosen to read one of our fine romance novels, we'd like to say "thank you!" And, as a **special** way to thank you, we've selected <u>two more</u> of the books you love so well **plus** an exciting Mystery Gift to send you — absolutely <u>FREE</u>!

Please enjoy them with our compliments...

Pam Powers

Lift here

Peel off seal and place inside...

How to validate your Editor's
"Thank You"
FREE GIFT

1. Peel off gift seal from front cover. Place it in space provided at right. This automatically entitles you to receive 2 FREE BOOKS and a fabulous mystery gift.

2. Send back this card and you'll get 2 brand-new *Romance* novels. These books have a cover price of $5.99 or more each in the U.S. and $6.99 or more each in Canada, but they are yours to keep absolutely free.

3. There's no catch. You're under no obligation to buy anything. We charge nothing—ZERO—for your first shipment. And you don't have to make any minimum number of purchases— not even one!

4. The fact is, thousands of readers enjoy receiving their books by mail from The Reader Service. They enjoy the convenience of home delivery...they like getting the best new novels at discount prices BEFORE they're available in stores... and they love their Heart to Heart subscriber newsletter featuring author news, horoscopes, recipes, book reviews and much more!

5. We hope that after receiving your free books you'll want to remain a subscriber. But the choice is yours— to continue or cancel, any time at all! So why not take us up on our invitation, with no risk of any kind. You'll be glad you did!

GET A Free *MYSTERY GIFT...*

*SURPRISE MYSTERY GIFT COULD BE YOURS **FREE** AS A SPECIAL "THANK YOU" FROM THE EDITORS*

The Editor's "Thank You" Free Gifts Include:

- *Two BRAND-NEW Romance novels!*
- *An exciting mystery gift!*

PLACE
FREE GIFT
SEAL
HERE

Yes!
I have placed my Editor's "Thank You" seal in the space provided above. Please send me 2 free books and a fabulous mystery gift. I understand I am under no obligation to purchase any books, as explained on the back and on the opposite page.

393 MDL DVFG   **193 MDL DVFF**

FIRST NAME	LAST NAME

ADDRESS

APT.#	CITY

STATE/PROV.	ZIP/POSTAL CODE

(PR-R-04)

Thank You!

▼ DETACH AND MAIL CARD TODAY! ▼

© 2003 HARLEQUIN ENTERPRISES LTD.
® and ™ are trademarks owned by Harlequin Enterprises Ltd.

The Reader Service — Here's How It Works:

Accepting your 2 free books and gift places you under no obligation to buy anything. You may keep the books and gift and return the shipping statement marked "cancel." If you do not cancel, about a month later we'll send you 3 additional books and bill you just $4.74 each in the U.S., or $5.24 each in Canada, plus 25¢ shipping & handling per book and applicable taxes if any.* That's the complete price and — compared to cover prices starting from $5.99 each in the U.S. and $6.99 each in Canada — it's quite a bargain! You may cancel at any time, but if you choose to continue, every month we'll send you 3 more books, which you may either purchase at the discount price or return to us and cancel your subscription.

*Terms and prices subject to change without notice. Sales tax applicable in N.Y. Canadian residents will be charged applicable provincial taxes and GST.

If offer card is missing write to: The Reader Service, 3010 Walden Ave., P.O. Box 1867, Buffalo, NY 14240-1867

BUSINESS REPLY MAIL

FIRST-CLASS MAIL   PERMIT NO. 717-003   BUFFALO, NY

POSTAGE WILL BE PAID BY ADDRESSEE

THE READER SERVICE
3010 WALDEN AVE
PO BOX 1341
BUFFALO NY 14240-8571

NO POSTAGE
NECESSARY
IF MAILED
IN THE
UNITED STATES

"There seemed nothing ahead but danger. Because Hun would not accept a debt payment from me. Because of who I was, Cenred's kinsman and always a threat to King Osred, Hun's master. We had to be brought down, my kinsmen and I."

And your fate became bound by mine: a sorrow and a danger that was endless. You were left with the fate of someone who promised much and gave nothing.

"You were alone."

"Yes."

His words had sprung straight from his thoughts. Yet her answer was instant, as though it were the key to everything.

Alone.

She must have felt alone even while she had been with him. He watched her averted face and the hands clutching at him.

Clutching at yet another man she did not want. The blade thrust home.

"You did not go back to Hun."

There was a silence deeper than the earth's fastness. But he did not need her to speak. His own voice gave life to the words.

"When you left me, you were alone and you stayed alone. You were alone all the time, all through that journey—" He saw with the eye of the mind the charred body of the unknown woman she had found on the way, the woman who had been attacked by outlaws. His heart went black.

"You were so desperate to get away that no risk would stop you."

She made the same small sound as before, as though she would speak. But his mind had outstripped that. He could see all that his bitterness had hidden before.

"You were alone afterwards. All the time."

The fear and the loathing he had seen in her eyes for her intended husband must have been every bit as real as he had believed. Stronger than her duty to her father and to Pictland, stronger than anything. Strong enough to make her take risks he could not even think on.

He looked at the head buried in his tunic and felt the shaking in the small body. She had said that she wanted her own place in the world. He had been just as unable to provide that as Hun had been. The sunlight glinted on the thick gold at his wrist. Anything he could have given had come too late.

He watched the thinness of her shoulders, the scratches fading on her hands. He thought of the privation of the small convent in a foreign land. She had preferred that to being with him. She had gone to extraordinary lengths to be free of him.

"I wish I could have given you what you desired."

She turned her head and looked at him.

"You did. I just could not take it."

The world pulled out of shape.

Her eyes were wide and dark. For the first time, he believed he could see all the way through to their clear deepness.

"What you offered me," she said, "I could not take. Like now. I could not…take what you offered me now, not because it was not what I desired, but…because I do not know how."

Her hand uncurled, slid down the stone-hard tension of his arm, settled on white-ridged bone.

"I wish I did know how."

The breeze lifted her hair away from the whiteness of her face. Her flesh fused with his, flattening out his fist, twining round it. Her fingers dragged, small, damaged, frighteningly fragile.

Fragile and a virgin.

The very freshness of the evening air choked him. What he had done in all its lust-driven madness beat against his eyes. He would have handled her so differently if he had only known. But his bitterness, the unquenchable fire inside him, had blinded him. His need had blinded him.

He had thought that they fought this battle on equal terms. They did not.

"Alina, if I had known I would not—"

"You do not have to tell me." The harshness of her voice cut across his words. "I know you would not. I know why you stopped. It is because of me." He felt the breath she took against his side. "It is because I am not a proper woman."

"Not a *what?*"

"A complete woman."

CHAPTER TEN

SHE STARED AT HIM, with her eyes blacker than the darkest night, while his body pulsed with wanting. Brand's breath caught in his throat. It was impossible to think of a woman more complete, a face or a body that could be more beautiful or inspire more rampant desire.

She knew, she must know, what she could do to people. To him. Even the thought was enough to stir his body to a pitch of need like pain. A need that would frighten her out of her wits. He tried to move away from her so she would not sense how he burned.

She had run away from him.

He kept his voice as calm and expressionless as he could, even though it shaped what to him were the words that had the power to lacerate bone.

"I do not understand."

He could not hold her gaze. Its deep clearness slid away from him. He thought he had lost. But then her thick, dark lashes fluttered and he felt the warmth of her breath on the exposed skin at his neck.

"It is because I am like my mother." The words were small, faint, so that he had to strain to hear them.

"My father used to say she was bespelled. He used to say that I was like her. Everyone did. He said she had tainted her children with her poison and that we would never be free of it."

My father and my mother hated each other... I did not tell you that. There was a lot I did not tell you.

The words sprang out of the warm darkness of a shuttered chamber, when she had lain just this close to him and he had had the first glimpse of who she was.

He felt her tension without seeing it because her body still pressed against his.

What kind of a life had she had at the palace of Craig Phádraig? *Who* was she, this maiden who had once had the soul out of him?

"You told me, that night at the monastery, that it was a difficult marriage but what—"

"I used to watch the way they dealt with each other. He used to shout at her, endlessly. He said she was not a complete woman. Not a proper one. My father would shout those words in the hall, in front of them all. He used to say her indifference was part of her curse."

His fingers fastened around the wounded hand because he could not help it.

"She just used to stare at him, with her head up, and not say a word. Until he could not shout anymore. She never let him see all the anger inside her, the things that Modan and I saw. But for all her anger, there was naught she could do against him. Even when she fled to Strath-Clòta with Modan and me, he made us all come back."

Her body shivered against him.

"Strath-Clòta was the only place I was ever truly happy. My father took us away from there because he would not let her alone. What he wanted was power over her."

The damaged hand shifted in his grip. So that he had to let it go. She would not want his touch. Would not want him.

"There were three more children, all girls. He said he wanted, no needed, another son, a warrior who would be true to the royal house of Craig Phádraig. That was what he cared for most of all, the power of Pictland, and he thought Modan was tainted by the time we had spent in Strath-Clòta, like me. She died of the last child. It was the son he wanted but it was stillborn. He said that was more of my mother's curse. He was like a madman when she died."

Brand swore without breath. The snatches of rumour he had heard at Alcluyd slid into place—Alina's mother, the headstrong British princess who, it was whispered, had taken her own path long before the constraints of a political alliance with a foreigner. But the marriage had still taken place. He could see it all unfolding as it did so often, the desperation on both sides and the bitterness life forced on people. The bitterness they forced on each other.

Alina.

But she was not looking at him. Her words tumbled onwards.

"Nothing could change what was. My mother's curse, the fault that he blamed her for, whatever it was that was missing from her, won in the end. Because despite all the power he had over her, he could not defeat that. She was never really his, never like other women."

Her broken fingers twisted, catching in his sleeve because they were still so close.

"But he would not keep from touching her. He would not stop trying to get whatever it was he wanted from her. Why did he not stop?"

"I do not know. So many things drive people into acts that are desperate." He turned his face, staring at the deepening blue of the sky, the light fading out of it, the edges of darkness that would overshadow it.

"Perhaps…perhaps he did not know what else to do. How he could ever be near her." His voice cut the silence of the glade with a harshness that was jarring and out of place. But it was only because of the desolation leaching through him like deadly bale, and he no longer knew who he was speaking of.

"My father was wrong if he hurt her."

"Aye. He was wrong. As I was. I never intended to hurt you, Alina. I did not—"

The strength and the suddenness of her movement took him by surprise. She sat up, her hands gripping the tight-coiled muscles of his arms, her eyes wide open, burning.

"You did not. Never. It was not that. I wanted you. It was my fault. Because I am cursed, like her. I bring bad fortune and I...I am not whole."

She was staring at him. All the lethal desolation that lived inside him was reflected in her night-dark eyes.

"I know it is true and so do you. That is why you pulled away from me. That is why you wish you could draw away from me now."

Her words stunned. He had not thought the power of their misunderstanding could be deepened. But it was.

"That is not why I stopped myself from—" He bit back on the raw intensity inside him. "I stopped because I knew you were still a maid, that you had not been with Hun as I thought. Because everything I believed I knew about you and what you had done was a lie."

Fright blossomed in her eyes. A different kind of fright. The look of someone who has been caught out in their deception. But he no longer cared about the fact that she had lied to him. He understood why, and it was impossible to blame her for his own failure, for the depth of Hun's malice. The only thing that filled his mind was the need to deal with the other fear before it killed her.

"That was the reason I stopped. You cannot believe that I did not want you."

Her face, so fair, brightly vivid with the passion of all that she felt, was turned towards him. She looked as though she wanted to believe what he said and did not dare.

"But I do not understand that. How would you know?"

"How—" Disbelief died under the frightened intensity of her eyes, replaced by a spurt of anger for the mother who had suffered through five children and an embittered brute of a husband and had not even told her daughter that much. It was not possible. But the truth was in front of him.

He just did not know what to do about it.

Such things belonged to a woman's world, or at best in a marriage bed. At worst, in the crude and frequent jests of fellow men. He could not think of one word that would not either humiliate her or rekindle the fears that haunted her mind.

He had never touched a virgin.

There had been those who had sometimes stepped into the emptiness. None who had stayed. He had not expected it, and it had never been offered.

Then there had been Alina, and all that he was had been ripped open.

Her hands slid across his flesh. "I knew the fault was mine."

All the life and the vividness seemed to drain out of her face.

"Alina, it was not because of you." His voice cracked like a whip and his hand gripped her arm with a force he could not quite control. "It is not so." He softened his grip, sought the words. "It is just…something of the body, the same for all women. Something I felt."

"When you touched me with your hand?" Her voice was stiff but her fingers found his, rested there, as though she trusted him.

"Yes." He did not look at her face, because of her pride.

"It is… That is why there is blood when…" Her voice trailed off.

He stared at the evening sky.

"Yes. For all women there is a barrier, inside, that must be broken the first time."

Her hand shuddered in his grip.

"The servants used to gossip in corners about whether there was blood or not. My mother always stopped them. She did not like such talk."

His gaze went to her face then. There seemed no consciousness of anything except the most superficial meaning of her words about her mother's reactions, yet he could not stop his hand tightening on hers. Or the useless surge of fury about the hellish upbringing she had had.

But he could not say more, even if gossip and whispers were true. It was not his place and he would not destroy any more of her life.

Her eyes were night pools and her fingers were laced with his.

"That is why?"

She did not let him go and he had to speak past the savage pain in his chest.

"Yes. But that is only the first time and after that there should be pleasure. There can be pleasure, Alina. That is what I wanted for you."

"Before…"

He watched the destructive canker of defeat in her eyes. "Still. Now. With all that I have."

He turned, his body twisting warrior-fast over hers. All the strength, and all the force of life that burned through him, was concentrated in that movement, so that he was afraid it would spark her fear. Her hands were fastened on the tensed mass of his arms. She stared at him, her head tipped back on the slender column of her throat.

"But suppose it is true after all, that I am… Suppose I am too afraid to let it happen. Or suppose there should be…suppose there should be a child."

He could see the rapid rise and fall of her breath. He was no longer fooled by the arrogant tilt of her head. Her fingers dug into his flesh.

Suppose all my mother's grief is repeated in me.

She did not say it. Yet the words hung in the clarity of the air, with a power that was real. The force inside him burned, not directionless, but honed into a single purpose, connected to her. That was unshakable. He knew he did not have her heart, but that was as it should be. He had no wish to make her captive this time. He wanted to set her free.

"It will not be so."

He felt, rather than heard, her breath quicken, because it was the mirror of his. Her hand was tight on his flesh and her skin was hot with the fires that stirred the soul with madness. Her eyes never flinched.

"How?"

"I will show you. And you will have the power of it. You will know. This time, this day, there will only be the pleasure. Naught else." The words damned him before they were spoken. But the force inside him took no account of that. Pain, old and new, was coiled in his heart. He blocked it out with the ruthlessness that had become second nature since childhood.

"I will show you how."

He could feel through the touch of her hands that the trembling was still there deep inside her. The rapidness of her breath tormented her body. It seemed made of equal parts of fear and need. The doubt of herself twisted through the wide darkness of her eyes. It should not be there. He would wipe it out. There was no cost that compared with that.

She watched him move, obliterating the small space of cold air between them. Their bodies touched. The fire in his blood leaped.

Life was made of moments. They had to be taken for what they were.

His mind knew that the pain lay in the future, waiting for him.

But it would be his pain, not hers.

She let him touch her. She did not draw back. But he had to be sure.

"If this is what you wish."

"Yes. More than anything in the world."

It would be the last time he would ever touch her so. The future and the present and the past collided. He would have welcomed the protection of the emptiness he had raged at before. It was not there.

HE WAS WHAT SHE WANTED more than life. She did not have words to tell him and she would never be able to show him. Because she was not capable.

Alina's hands tangled in the sleeve of his tunic so that he would never be able to remove them.

He did that by kissing them.

That was how it began. It took her by surprise. Like everything he did. He was so direct and yet...still gentle. Kind with her because he knew how useless she was, would be. She shut her eyes. Because she was frightened and she did not want him to know it.

His mouth was warm against the cold skin of her hand. She knew she ought to make some movement, some response, in case he thought she did not want him, in case he stopped. She could not move a muscle.

She felt the slight familiar ache of badly-healed bone.

He had her crushed hand.

He had all the ugliness of that and he was touching it. He must know. He could see. And yet he did not stop touching her. His lips moved across her skin. Warm breath against the cold like blessing and kindness all in one. And excitement. A man's breath, dark and rich and full of strength. The kind of strength that would bow to nothing it did not wish to do.

He must want that, his heat on her skin. His lips moved as though he wanted to taste her flesh, explore the shape of each finger. Her fingers curved round, seeking that deep, unexpected warmth, wanting more of it. She felt the rough-sleek flick of his tongue, tantalizing, moist and heady and wicked. Something he should not do. Then she felt his mouth.

He took her ruined and malformed fingers inside his mouth.

A sharp burst of feeling shot through her as her fingers entered his heat. Her eyes flew open and she could see his bent head. The way his supple lips curved round her fingertips. She could feel him.

Her body pulsed. Just from that. Just from the heat of him. Or from the sight of him. Or from the abandoned way his mouth moved.

Because he wanted her. She knew it as though she could see inside him. Even though his eyes were now closed as hers had been. She thought she could see behind that shadowed, richly curved skin, behind the deep gold lashes, how his eyes would look. So hot in their gold depths, hot as his mouth. She knew.

He looked up. She did not know at all, had not guessed at either the fire or the brightness. She gasped. But it was cut off. Because he took her mouth and she could feel the heavy weight of him. So strong. It would hold her and pin her down. But almost before his body could cover hers, it was withdrawn, held away, just beyond the clamouring reach of her senses. So that she longed to feel it again. So that she wanted what only seconds ago had been too much for her to take.

He touched her only with his mouth. So that all feeling was centred on that, on the heat and the fluid darkness that had just touched her hands. She wanted the heat and the secret darkness of him so much. She thought of how his tongue had felt against her flesh. She thought of his desire.

Her mouth moved against his, pressing against the lips she had seen enfold her with such flagrant wanting, opening underneath his heat, wanting him so much, fitting her lips against his, matching his movement, until her mouth moved with the same abandonment, the same triumph of need over restraint.

Her tongue touched the delicate underside of his lip. Touched inside his mouth. She felt the shudder that ripped through his powerful body and just for a moment, the coldness stirred inside her and then it was gone, obliterated. Because she had what she wanted: the feel of his tongue inside her, the utter wholeness of the way he kissed.

She let him do it. No, she did not let him. Her hand slid up over his frighteningly muscled shoulder, plunged into the tangled-soft wildness of his hair. Found his neck. She took from him, just as he took from her. And gave.

Her fingers sank into warm skin, tracing a line that was graceful, for all its strength. Dense flesh. Her hand explored its shape.

She could have kissed him like that for ever. Perhaps she did, because her head swam. But then he moved, past the confines of her hand. His strength. Unstoppable. His mouth found her throat. His touch was light. Everywhere on her skin so that it baffled her senses and made her whole body restless. So restless that when his hand went to the rumpled neckline of her dress she did not want to stop him. Her senses knew with a sureness beyond her mind that the teasing, restless craving would only find relief in more of him.

His fingers, direct and unhesitating as everything about him, parted the neck of her dress, undid her belt, so that the tunic and the underdress were freed. By the time he touched her breast she was so dizzied from him that she did not pull away from him. She only wanted more.

Cool air stung across her hot skin. It meant her breast was completely exposed so that he could touch it, as he had before. Only this time she could see what he did and her dress was truly gaping.

Her breath caught. Her skin shivered, and in that instant of consciousness, he stopped touching her. The unfamiliar, bated feelings inside her wound tighter. She could neither move nor breathe and then she saw what he was doing. He watched her, because he wanted to see the hidden curves of her body, know it with an intimacy that admitted no reserve. No defence. She was afraid of that. The vulnerability of it would kill her. But then she felt his breath against her naked skin.

"You are so beautiful."

But she could not take that.

"No. It is not so." Her hand moved instinctively to drag the cloth of her dress tighter to cover herself. But he was faster. His fingers caught hers. Her mouth formed a sound of protest, but it was never born. Because he had not used his formidable strength. His hand rested lightly against hers, so that she could have pulled her fingers out of his grasp if she wanted to. Almost as though he expected her to.

She would have done it if she had not seen his eyes. If she had not seen the shadows in the fire that were as familiar to her as her own skin. If he had not taken breath to speak.

Her heart beat out of time. If only he would not speak—

"Beautiful," said the well-remembered voice of Strath-Clòta, in the secret intimacy of her language, theirs. Just as they had always spoken when no one else was near and there was only them. She felt him take breath and the words came.

"You are formed for love."

It was the one thing she wanted to hear. She knew it was not true. But for all that she could not stop watching his face, the smooth arrogant curve of his neck as he bent his head.

His desire.

Her skin shivered in response to the complete assurance of him, and the coolness of the air and the heat of his gaze tightened her. So that when his mouth took her, she was quite different, taut and swollen with a wanting that filled his mouth. She felt his moist darkness mould her, taking her into its heat, drawing her deeper and deeper so that she was spiralling beyond control.

Her body would not keep still. It moved with a lightning-fierce need and an instinct that was pure and beyond doubt, because it was part of all that she felt for him. She arched towards him, her hands and her body seeking his, desperate for everything she was afraid of, for the firmness and the sheer size of his body, wanting the closeness and the knowledge of that.

He would not allow what she wanted at first. His effortless strength held her. The touch of his mouth and his tongue was light, smoothly expert, teasing her. It ignited the heat inside her. Dizzying waves of it coursed across her skin wherever he touched. She wanted that, but she wanted more. She wanted him.

But he would not know that, had no way of knowing unless she told him. She could not say it, because she could not get the terrifying words out of her mouth.

The shadows came crowding into her mind. But they were not her shadows. They were his, pressing against her heart, the remnants of the past pain that claimed their place in his eyes behind the brightness of the fire. There was so much to atone for and so much she could not say.

She could at least say this. She could not bear him not to know what she felt in this moment.

"Hold me closer…please. I want you to."

The words were no more than a whisper in her mother's tongue, words her mother would never have said. She thought he might not have heard them, but he did. She knew by the sudden tightening in his body, the unexpectedly clumsy movement of his hand.

Her eyes sought his so that she caught the surprise before he could hide it, and then it was followed by something else, something so fierce, so predatory that it sent a jolt through her veins. And then she could not see because he was holding her. Far too tightly. Small tingling gouts of fear surfaced in her mind. But she could not let him see her fear, for so many reasons, more than she could explain, even to herself.

She put her arms around him, even though that meant she could feel all the harshness of moving muscle and the roughness of his breathing. He held her the way you held something you would never let escape. Her breath choked in her throat and then it was all right because he was holding her just the way he had touched her before, with such lightness, all the strength underneath hidden.

But they both knew it was there.

She was afraid to see what was in his eyes now, so she buried her head in his neck. Because then she could breathe in his scent. The brightness of his hair blurred the edges of her vision and she could feel the tangled softness of it where it threaded over his skin.

It was he who had the beauty, feral and wild-edged.

It was part of her fear, but also of her longing. Her mind was already dizzied with it before his hands moved over her body, brushing aside the fullness of her skirts, finding her flesh.

She was so sensitized to his touch that her skin shivered and the tightness inside her would kill her unless he...what? She did not know. And then she did. His hand touched her again where it had before. When— She would not let memories, *any* memories, intrude. Otherwise he would reject her and she could not bear that again. She—

He whispered her name. "Alina."

Her eyes opened, startled. She did not want to see him. She did not want— His eyes were pure light. He smiled at her.

He should not have done that. She could not cope with it. There was all she had wished and all she had ever dreamed of in that smile: reassurance and the tenderness that had been in his touch and the bright traces of the wildness that found its frightening echo coiled somewhere deep inside her. And behind all that lay his strength.

She could not move. Her breath hurt her throat. She wondered if he could see all the confusion that lived in her eyes, the fear. And...the desire. Because all the time her body burned and her blood pulsed like a madwoman's.

"Rest your head against my shoulder the way you did before. That is all you have to do."

She let him draw her to him, half sitting, leaning

against the bank, so that the scent of crushed grass and the sound of the clear water touched her. Her head rested against the golden threads of his hair and her heart beat and her blood raced and she ached, ached where he touched her. She did not want him to stop. Some instinct told her she had gone past the point where she herself could stop.

"What will you do?" Her breath came in small snatches, not enough for the wild beating of her heart. "Will you—"

"No. I promised you the pleasure. That is all there will be. It is all I can give you."

Her throat tightened and she wanted to hold him the way she had before but she could not. He was not hers. She could see his hand, covering her, broad, deep bronze against the whiteness of her thigh. She could feel the warm weight of it.

"What must I do?"

"Trust me. Trust what I will do."

The brightness of his eyes was more than she could bear. She had broken every possibility of trust. She turned her head away, her lashes hiding her shame.

She felt his breath against her skin. It was very warm. It was full of life and the strength grounded in the fierce virile body that touched her, in his mind. Yet what she felt seemed overlain by despair. The noise of the running water seemed suddenly too loud and she had to strain to catch his words when he spoke, even though his mouth was against her hair.

"Then if there is naught else, trust only this moment,

Alina. It is all that exists now. The past and the future have their own claims but they cannot touch this moment."

"No..." But the noise of the stream cut off her words as though it had its own voice, as though she should be able to understand what it said, but she could not. Her need was too great and his hand was moving against her flesh.

It was like nothing she had ever experienced. His touch brought to life with a blinding intensity all the fierce, tightly coiled expectation he had made her feel, heightening the arousal of her senses, making her body pulse and dizzy with the rush of blood through her veins.

He could make her burn. The fire that lived in him had taken its place inside her. The touch of his hand was like a brand on her skin. The broad tips of his fingers slid across her swollen flesh, scorched inside her, not deep this time, but tasting her heat, the aching unexpected moistness inside her. Touching and withdrawing in a rhythm that was calculated to send her mad. Frantic.

The fingers withdrew and she was mad then, not from fear of him or the mysterious power he might take away from her, but from the possibility of the loss of him.

His arm tightened round her, holding her still because she was clawing at him, and his fingers found some part of her that must hold the secret of all that he did, the secret of all that she had not known. Because as his fingers, slick and heated with her own moistness, glided across her skin every sensation that she had, every maddening sense that he had aroused in her, became centred on that smooth touch.

Her body moved in a rhythm that matched his in a wild and primitive surge. She was lost, beyond thought or fear or any constraint, beyond any control that she had. But he knew; he knew just how to touch her so that all the sensations gathered together and then disintegrated in light. And the shock was that she felt joy, deep and abiding and totally bound up in him, and all the fierce, shining pleasure it was possible to believe in.

CHAPTER ELEVEN

SHE WAS CRYING. The sound of it cut through him. Her dark head was buried in his shoulder. He could see the rapid rise and fall of her side.

The last thing he could take was her tears.

"Alina—"

"Do not let me go." That was all she said, just as before. So he held her while his heart beat as it did in the rush of battle and the blood still ran like unslaked fire in his veins. He fought to master his own breath, to control muscle and sinew and the desire in his mind that was one step from utter madness.

All he knew was that he could not place that burden on her. It was not fit, the depths of what he felt for her. There was too much pain in it and it was too absolute. It was not what she could want, not what he had wished to show her. He wanted her to see only the light.

She moved, stirring against his overheated body. Her finely curved softness brushed against engorged hardened flesh, sending a jolt of desire through him that was barbaric. He stilled her body, stopping her maddening inadvertent touching. Control, with her, was a matchless trial. Yet he still kept his arms around her because it was the only thing she had asked of him.

Her slight weight moved again, curving round him in a movement as blatantly sensual as it was naive. She had not the slightest consciousness of what she did. She was so easy to wound and yet so dangerously set in purpose. He still could not think on what she had done after she had left him and what might have happened to her.

She was moving against him with small sounds of desperation and he gave in and held that delicate slender body as it was meant to be held. And then because that was no longer enough he took her again with his hands and his mouth until she shuddered against him and cried out for the release his skill could give her. All that he had...

"Let me know you in the same way."

The words came out of the fever dream of her nearness and her wild secret heat and the searing touch of her body.

"Nay, that is not what—"

She moved herself against him, just as she had before, taking control past bearing, and this time it was not inadvertence. She knew what she did.

But yet she did not.

He trapped her gaze. Her eyes held his. But their directness was an act of will. He could see it because he could read anyone's eyes before battle and weigh the exact measure of their determination. And the exact measure of their fear.

"No. There is no need. That was not part of our bargain."

"Yes. It was. Always. Together."

"No." The word was violent. Beyond what was permissible. But he could not help that. Because the long-dead bargain she referred to was beyond even the limits of pain.

He saw the finely held balance in her eyes change, darkening their deep brown depths to blackness, and the regret for that burned with all the other regrets. Too many to count.

"Leave it, Alina. Let me take you back now. Let us keep at least what we have."

"No." Her word was equally strong and he realized that the balance had turned the other way. That what he saw in the darkness of her eyes was not fear, but the determination that had sent her four hundred miles south into a land she did not know.

"Please." She hated saying that. She would not unless constrained. Yet the fear that lapped at the edges of the impossible determination in her eyes seemed not of him, but of being bereft. Of being alone if he left her. Her hands clutched at him in a wrenching mixture of her determination and her fears.

"I will always keep what I have. What you have shown me that I did not know. Your gift. But I need the other half of it. I need to know that— Will you give me that much?"

She asked something impossible. If she had not

mattered to him, there would have been no more than he had promised for her: naught but the pleasure.

But she was the measure of all that his life had been and all that it would be. She asked more than he could give.

He sought for the words. Her hand touched the heavy gilded buckle at his hips. He saw that her fingers were unsteady. He saw that the fear still held equal measure with her determination. He knew the shadows that lay at the back of her mind. Because he could see so much, his mind made the only choice there was.

She could not get the buckle undone, so that he had to do it for her. His hands brushed hers aside, unfastened the jewelled clasp, removed all that he wore, quite slowly because he could remember the look in her eyes when she had tried to prepare a bath for him. She watched him. Every move that he made.

He could have killed that dangerous self-absorbed braggart, her father, for the look in her eyes.

He glanced away before she saw the anger, but the low sunlight reflecting off the water dazzled him. The muscles of his sword arm tightened, trained reflex mirroring instinct, as though in response to danger, as though the blade with the elk-sedge rune were in his hand and the power of death in it. His skin shivered like a presage of the future. But the future had no existence in this glade. He would not allow it.

He held out his hand to Alina. She took it without hesitation and then she laid her head against his shoulder as she had before, which made the breath choke off in his throat because he could not bear the full measure of her trust.

She did no more, as though she needed time to gather her courage. Her fingers tangled in the thin band of linen strapped round his chest.

"I could kill you for doing that to me. For letting me think that the arrow had found its mark."

That was so like Alina, confounding him with her words, unexpected, yet always so very much to the point. He could feel the laughter wake inside him and the echo of the joy that had been there when he had first known her. If only that joy could have survived. If it could lighten her heart now.

"The arrow did find its mark," he said. "You should see the size of the dent it made between my shoulders." He pitched his voice deep with indignation so that for a moment she was caught by it. But only for a moment. Her head assumed its most infuriating tilt and her hair spread in night waves across the heat of his skin.

"Empty boaster. You mean the dent in the meshed steel you were wearing."

"Steel? That was a mere token. You did not see what really saved my hide."

"What?"

"Over there." He raised her head so she could see the dark shape beside his corselet. His hands slid deep in her hair, feeling the hidden silk warmth of her neck.

"That?" she said dubiously. "I thought it was leaf mould."

"Leaf mould? That is Duda's leather jerkin." He surveyed the dark mound. "I have his word on it."

"And you wore it?"

"It was a gift."

"A rare gift."

The weight of that kind of gift pressed.

"Aye." Nothing showed in his voice. For this moment, there would only be the light. He shrugged, as though that would push the weight aside. The searing heat of Alina's body moved with him.

"Duda assured me it was fail proof. Or was that foolproof? It was one or the other."

She considered this while her arm slid round his rib cage for balance and she must have been able to feel the parched unevenness of his breath.

"Then I must be persuaded by Duda's superior knowledge. How many patches does it have?"

"One less than it needs right now. But he says there is a lot of wear left in it. Providing people have the wit to look after it properly." The feel of her against his bared skin, the knowledge of the discreetly full curves he had just loved were enough to drive him out of his senses. "It might be repairable. Were you keen on sewing?"

The maddening tilt of her head intensified. So that the heat in his blood would take all. He could not let it.

"Only gold work."

"Shame. I cannot really see Duda in gold thread." The suppressed laughter vibrated through her body, through his. Except it was more than laughter. He saw her eyes. Just as her hand moved. It landed in the hollow of his neck, in the wild mess of his hair where it meshed with the smoothness of hers.

"I have a taste for gold." Her fingers twisted, just lightly, tugging the thick strands against his scalp with small teasing movements as though she were the most accomplished *hor-cwen*. It was her courage that was splitting something inside him into pieces, the way she looked at him as though he would never betray her gifts when he already had.

"It is a high-price taste. Sometimes the cost of things can be more than a person should pay."

She could turn away, even now. In two days or three, they need never see each other again.

"Aye. That is why we can only afford moments." Her eyes were very clear. So clear he could see all the courage and the determination, all the past grief and the present fears, the longing for such things to be overcome.

"If we want such moments."

"Yes."

Her fingers slid down again, across the linen but he caught her hand and placed it higher, as if she could feel through his heart what there were no words for, even no thoughts for.

Her hand pressed against his skin. The rush of aliveness, of merciless desire took his body. He sensed its echo shudder through her as her hand fused with the wild heat of his flesh. She touched him with a firmness that surprised. Her touch was like no other, so that however he tried to close his mind, he could feel it through more than blindly aching flesh.

He turned thought aside. Nothing existed for them except the moment. The shadows of the past were shades to be overcome. He would leave no shadows on her future.

Her breath sighed across his skin. Her hands moved over the aching, white-hot planes of his body, downwards, seeking the desire-hardened, blood-hot sex.

"Let me touch you...."

No words existed, only the fierce unslaked hunger, the elemental needs of the senses. He showed her how to touch and where the pleasure lay. He kept control, and there was nothing he would allow her to fear.

And when control was no longer possible, she had no fear at all, not of his merciless desire nor his wildness, so that the desperate heat and the harshly-held need shattered at last against the touch of her lamed hand.

NO ONE IN THE ORDINARY WORLD could guess. They were safe.

Alina lay wrapped in her cloak, three paces away from the person who held her soul. None of the men gathered round the fire, no one, could know what had happened to her. That she had changed utterly and beyond the possibility of return.

It was hidden from the everyday world and yet it lived inside her, with a strength and an aliveness nothing in this world or the next could mar. She rearranged Brand's spare cloak over hers, hugging it around her body as though its touch against her skin could be his.

The night air caressed her face, but she was not cold. She would never be cold again, nor so frightened, nor so bitter about herself.

All the problems of the future remained. They waited for her in the dark, outside the small circle of light cast by the flames. She knew that. But her courage to face them had grown. Because of him.

And so had her power. It was so unexpected, but it was true. She had expected loss, but it had not been so. It was like a gift. One she did not deserve, but which was there.

Her heart twisted. Loss, true loss, lay ahead. She could not contemplate that. The shimmering light of the flames danced before her eyes. Flames, pure gold, like Brand. Nay, not as strong, not as hot.

She watched her lover's hands as he ate.

He was her lover now. That had been sealed irrevocably, by the acts of the body and the mind. Even if she never saw him again.

The man, Eadric, sat next to him. Brand was talking to him about something or other. She saw the gleam of Eadric's smile.

Duda was stretched out at their feet, trailing through the grass like a piece of frayed rope. Unconscious. Doubtless dreaming of how to restore his leather jerkin to a state of unblemished finery.

Everyone else slept. Even Cunan.

Her tired mind drifted and her body seemed to float, pleasurably aching, still full of secret warmth. Her eyes drifted shut and the floating feeling intensified. She gave in to it. It was odd to feel so...safe. She was caught in the middle of a journey from one form of exile into another and now there was this...release. Rest. She could not find the word for it.

Brand's face drifted into her mind, the way it had looked when he had slept after the fever.

Peace.

She buried her head in the folds of his spare cloak.

THE PAYMENT WOULD BE DEATH.

Cunan stared at a night so dense it robbed sight. That did not matter because what he saw was in the mind: the Northumbrian and the whore's daughter who paraded herself as his sister. How could she have done it? After all that he had said to her. He, and all of her kindred, meant nothing to her.

It had always been so, all their lives. None of them had been good enough for her.

His hand caressed the knife hilt concealed in his bedroll.

It was done now, beyond his keeping. The lecher had taken his chance, and she had fallen. Willingly. He had guessed that much just by looking at her face. And because he knew the blood that ran in her veins.

But the house of Maol would not be dishonoured again. He would see to that. It was his right. The slate would be wiped clean and all that he had planned would still come to fruition.

His gaze bored through the dark, seeking out the Northumbrian's shape. The knife hilt dug into his flesh. The frustration of not being able to use it yet was unbearable.

If only the man had died today. But Goadel had bungled that. Fool. He had not been supposed to act alone. That was what they had agreed. The attack had been too risky, too open to chance, too— It might have succeeded but for the Northumbrian's fore-thought.

It was strange. He would not have considered such a man capable of forethought. Or that kind of courage.

Goadel did not know the mistake he had made. He would think he had bought himself time that he did not have.

And if the reckless attack had succeeded what would then have become of Alina? His breath hissed through the dark. She was not for Goadel's keeping. Not yet. Her rightful keeper was coming. He would be this side of the high western hills by now.

Tomorrow, they would cross the River Humber into Deira, southern half of the English Kingdom of Northumbria. Deira. The Northumbrian would think he was safe, in his own land. There would be no fore-thought when they reached what was familiar to him, only the high heart of the man's natural recklessness. Then the trap would spring.

He slept with the knife unsheathed.

BRAND'S BLOOD SURGED. He knew the lie of every wood and every fold of land that marked the wide-open face of Deira. Beyond it lay Bernicia and the true north, all the wild riches of its soul hidden in blue mist. His heart sang. It sought home. Every instinct drove forward. Yet he paused at the crossroads marked with the ancient Roman milestone.

Crossroads connected not only human pathways, but paths of the spirit. *Wyrd* was there, waiting, so much more discernible where the barriers that separated Middle Earth from the other realms were thinner. His eyes sought Alina instantly. She was quite safe on the patient grey gelding, looking ahead as he had been.

This time the parting from her would be absolute. More final than when he had believed her dead. More deeply entrenched inside him. He had made it so.

All of her lived in his mind, the warmth of her skin, its fineness, the gasp of her breath. The way her eyes darkened. The deepness that lived in the heat of her gaze.

He would have looked away. But in that moment, she turned. Their gazes met, held in the bright sunlight. Then split apart as Cunan's heavy roan shouldered through.

Brand turned his own mount with a knee, leading

them off the exposed line of the road, toward the shade cast by the trees. It would hide them. It was home. Every sinuous line of the land, every tree and every blade of grass, seemed different, bathed in the subtle light of the north.

The brightness shifted, then was cut off by the black depths of the forest's shade. Like all that was inside him. This time the pain that lay ahead seemed greater than the instinct to live.

He did not have any regrets.

He quickened the pace, like someone rushing headlong to meet their doom, impatient to feel the fell weight of its hand.

The others followed.

"Alina."

She turned her head. They had stopped for a brief respite. Doubtless for her benefit. But she could ride now at a pace she would not have believed possible only days ago. It was probably the amount of food Brand made her eat. She was twice as strong and her clothes fitted.

It was more than that. It was the sparking of the life force inside her. Released by him. It seemed unconquerable.

If she did not look to the future.

She glanced up from the shade she had found, narrowing her eyes at the taut male figure looming black against the low sun.

"Cunan."

"Who did you expect?"

He stood like a jailer, his hand resting on the knife hilt at his hip. He had not been private with her since the day she had fled to the monastery herb garden, trying to hide from her feelings for Brand.

She suppressed the thought, lest he could read it. But her heart knew, with the sixth sense that women have, that Cunan had guessed what had happened since beside the clear water. She wondered whether he hated her for it.

She did not care. She was no longer a child to be bullied by an older brother, angered by the condemnation in his eyes. Hurt—

"What is it you wish, brother?"

"To know what is in your thoughts."

She tilted her chin.

"No one ever knows that. It is part of my charm."

Cunan's hand clenched on the well-worn hilt of polished bone.

"Like mother, like daughter. I will take a bet even your...*friend* does not know what goes on in your head."

She found her mask smile.

"No, he does not."

"He just has his uses, is that right? Oh come, Alina, we are no longer children. You have your needs, I do not doubt it." He must have seen her stiffen because he squatted down beside her, the hand that had rested on the knife hilt held out like a token of peace. His hound eyes watched her.

"I cannot blame you for that. In fact I am sure your

Northumbrian has fulfilled those needs most satisfactorily. I hear that is his defining talent. Seduction. And he always gets what he wants."

How many women do you think he has had? You were just one more amusement and a greater trouble to him than he ever expected.

"You hear so many things, do you not?" Her hands clenched, unseen.

She tried to make her fingers uncurl. It had not been just a heartless amusement, what had happened between her and Brand. It had not been just a meaningless satisfaction of the flesh.

...there will only be the pleasure. Naught else.

Her skin tingled. Such pleasure. He had known it could happen. She had not. It had overwhelmed her. Even now, the memory of his hands and his mouth on her could make her burn. She had given in to the pleasure completely, with all that she was. She had not been able to do anything else.

Seduction. Such an expert touch... Her face, her whole body, seemed to go rigid.

"So? I can see that you, at least, are not so light-minded, Alina." Her brother's gaze held hers, his hand, wide and sword-calloused like Brand's, stayed extended towards her. She looked at it. Her heart beat out of time.

Cunan was right.

She was not light-minded. She loved. Even if her love could not be returned.

And she owed debts.

The hand dropped.

"Come. You have more sense than that. Just what do you think will happen if you cast in your lot with that heedless fool?"

"I think that our…" She paused, getting her voice under control. She said it again. "I think that *our* brother Modan will survive."

And there was Cunan's face as it truly was, pared down to the bones and the twisting sinew.

"*Modan.* Modan will be safe enough, I have told you. Your duty lies in loyalty to our father's wishes. It is due to the interests of—"

"May I join you? Or is this a family discussion?"

Her fast-beating heart thudded at the sound of the English words. She had not heard him approach. He must move as quietly as Duda who was standing beside him. Cunan's face darkened with anger. She thought that hers must be whiter than chalk.

She did not know how long Brand and Duda had been there. Cunan did not move.

"Yes, it is a family discussion and therefore none of your concern. Or of your…slave's."

Brand settled on his heels like Cunan, hands carelessly resting on his knees. It was like watching a wolf ready itself to spring. Cunan's hand moved towards the bone handle of his knife. It fumbled, just slightly.

Brand's gaze missed nothing at all.

"I think we share some of your concerns."

There was not even a rustle as Duda settled himself on the grass. Cunan shot him a glance of contempt.

"Do you expect me to speak in front of that slave—"

"Duda is free."

"Want to know why I am free?"

The faint flicker in Brand's eyes told her that Duda's question was not part of whatever Brand had planned to say. Duda's gaze flicked from his lord to Cunan and then just as suddenly it was on her.

"Perhaps the lady princess would like to know." The sharp, crinkled eyes held hers and she knew that there was nothing irrelevant about what Duda would say at all. Cunan was seething. She could feel the wolf's tension in Brand, that awful focus that never stopped before it had…all that it wanted.

There might be blood if she said *yes.* There might be more blood if she said *no.* The sunlight rippled the way it did on moving water.

"Tell me."

"I would have been enslaved because I could not pay my compensation for theft. Brand paid my *wergild.*"

"A thief," spat Cunan.

"Aye. I used to steal to eat. I have no kin. They are dead. I have no home. I lost it years ago. It was burnt in a dispute between two noble thanes over who owned it."

"And you were not on the winning side?" Cunan's voice still mocked but she could hear the edge that it took when dislike, that strange self-dislike, crept through him.

She wondered whether the poised wolf beside her could sense it. Whether Duda could.

"Aye. It was not me who was on the winning side. It was Goadel."

Oh, they could sense it. They knew, her wolf and his running companion. Hunters so fell could always sense the kill.

She looked at Duda's rags. She thought of the desperation that lay hidden in the heart of a fugitive. She had had her own experience of that. She wondered whether the gnarled hand concealed in fraying wool was curved round a knife hilt with the same force as Cunan's.

Cunan looked at no one. "Disputes of a personal nature—"

"Are exactly what you were discussing, were they not? Is that not what you said?"

She glanced at the bright gold eyes. They held nothing but enquiry, and the unspoken challenge that had sent Cunan's hand to the knife hilt.

But he knew everything, her ruthless hunter. He knew all that had been said between her and her brother because he understood their language. Cunan was oblivious to that.

She had the power to explain it to her half brother. Kin loyalty.

She kept her eyes on the knife. Cunan's knuckles were white.

"That does not concern—"

"Yes, it does. You and I share the same concern, if you remember—to see that your sister is safe, that she reaches Bamburgh, and King Nechtán's ambassador."

The look Cunan gave held defiance. It also held secrets. She knew that with childhood's knowledge. She had grown up with power plays and secrets.

"There is nothing to discuss with you, Northumbrian. Some aspects of our family's interests are not shared. Just as some loyalties and some duties are not."

The wolf rearranged each lethal sinew, gathered for the next strike, the one that would come with the rending of teeth and heavy, tearing claws.

"Which duty would that be? The one that charges a man to protect those of his kindred who need it? The one that demands thought and a conscience?"

"What would you know about thought?" demanded Cunan. "You acted without it."

"No. I thought."

The strike caught her utterly off balance. But it was not a hunter's strike, or it was one so rash it had exposed far more vulnerability than it should. The reckless, gold-bright eyes had become transparent.

She could not believe what he had said, or even that he had said it. What he had done when he had abducted her from Hun had been the mad impulse of a moment for him, no more and no less.

Her eyes sought that bright gold transparency in desperation, to read what was truly there. He was not looking at her. His gaze was fixed on Cunan and she realized the battle was not over. It had just reached a new level she did not understand. Brand did not turn to her, but she knew he was utterly aware of her.

The sudden change brought its own confusion in Cunan's lean face, an instant when he believed those briefly spoken words. And then the belief was snuffed out by an effort of will.

"*Thought*. It is easy enough to confuse thoughts with…certain sudden impulses. But thoughts take into account the future. That truth applies to us all, from common men to kings."

"Aye." The gold gaze never left her half brother's face and she knew the transparency of it, the directness were a risk that had been calculated to a hair's breadth.

"Kings should always look to the future. That is their first duty." The words came steadily, no hesitation, as though he had worked out exactly what Cunan would say and why. It was like watching a death struggle from the outside and yet being involved in it intimately, with the same risk of being annihilated.

"And the duty to think should be the same for those who would try to make or unmake their king."

"That is one thing you may be sure of," spat Cunan.

The gold eyes flickered, as though the breach in her brother's defences, still invisible to her, had been found and the risk, however great, would be pursued to the end.

"I am glad you are thinking. No one can calculate

how long Cenred will hold the throne of Northumbria.
But what anyone capable of thought can calculate is
that the late King Osred's brother will not have
enough strength to hold such a throne either. Goadel's
support will not be enough to make the difference.
Neither would a temporary intervention from King
Nechtán of the Picts be, even if that was truly his
will."

Did she see Cunan flinch at that, or did she just
imagine it?

"The only way anyone will hold the throne at Bamburgh is not through deeds of battle, but through
something that takes thought and quite a different
sort of courage—finding an alliance and a compromise and holding it."

Cunan's mouth worked. It was as though he had
expected endless swordplay and had been hit with a
thrusting spear. He swallowed air. The thin discon-
tented lips twisted.

"You mean a compromise as long as your kindred
comes out best, with you in a king-making role."

"No. I do not care for king-making. What I care for
is the consequences. I care for what is mine and I care
for Bernicia. A man like Goadel cares only for himself and what he can gain, not for his country, nor even
for an alliance to benefit Pictland. Only a fool would
trust him. I believe you would be the last to say King
Nechtán of the Picts was a fool. You should have a
proper care for what is yours."

He did not even see the effect of the death blow because he was no longer looking at Cunan, his opponent. He was looking at her. The bright gold eyes were naked. Deliberately so. At what cost to do that before his enemy and before the woman who had betrayed his trust, she could not tell. You could see all that he felt, all that he believed, the incalculable depth of what he had called single-mindedness and probably should better be called courage.

His gaze caught hers, held it, changed. But lost none of its truth.

Truth did not allow mercy. She had seen that look before without recognizing it. Memory filled her ears with the clear sound of running water, his touch shivered across her skin, giving her new life. She had been so foolish, so reckless, even though she had known she would have to pay. She could read what filled her lover's eyes now, beside the pity he felt for her.

It was valediction.

That was how you bid farewell.

"CAN YOU NOT SLEEP?"

Rags flapped at her, appearing like a ghost's trappings in the starlight.

"Duda, I wish you would not do that."

"I wish you would sleep. Then I could."

"Why do you not? Or are you obliged to follow me in case I make a bolt for Pictland in the dark?"

"Aye."

There was nothing you could do with Duda. Northern English directness, subtle as an axe blow. Or a spear's thrust. She tried not to think of the two skilled hunters circling Cunan. Or of what Cunan might do. Playing deadly games with kingdoms' futures. And hers.

She had not quite appreciated the scope of Cunan's plans. Brand had, all the time. He had seen so much more than her. And yet not as much. He had not seen the effect when the death blow fell. She had. Cunan had looked lost. Utterly. Afraid.

"Well, why does it not just happen, then?" she hissed though the dark, even though she scarce knew what she was asking. They were in Bernicia, now. Tomorrow they would be in striking distance of Bamburgh. One more day and it would all be over. One way or another.

"It will. You had best make sure you are not in a position to regret it when it does. What are you planning?"

"Me? Nothing! It is everyone else who is planning."

"Aye. Must say I am keen to get myself into a position where I can stick a knife through Goadel."

"Goadel? What makes you think Goadel will be here?"

"What makes you think it? Cold, are you? You are shivering."

Alina dragged the thick warmth of her cloak closer round her with impatient fingers. Duda twitched rags.

"I suppose you want to avenge your losses, too."

"Aye. There is my dead family to think about, and then Goadel's man made a right mess of my jerkin. I do not allow that."

"Your *jerkin?*"

"Aye." She could see the fierce gleam of his eyes through the mass of unkempt hair and beard.

...Duda's leather jerkin...a gift. He told me it was fail proof...

Duda was not talking about the damage done to leather. She took a large steadying breath. It was not enough for the measure of her fears and her loss and her confusion. She took a stab at Northumbrian directness.

"I would not see such damage happen again. You...you know I would have gone to him then."

"Aye. Well."

"Ask Eadric to show you his scratch marks."

"Must be awkward for you, though, all these brothers."

She fixed her gaze on the stars. "All I have to do is get to Bamburgh and then it is over."

"Is that how you see it?"

"It will be over for me." She could not see anything, really, not even the stars she knew were there. She used her own axe blow of directness. "It will be over for Brand as well. It is already. What happened with us was a mistake, a wrong impulse, even if it had...the right intentions."

"One thing I have learned over the years about Brand, he is not as good at being impulsive as he likes to believe he is."

I thought.

"What?"

"Do you know what else he and I have in common?
No parents. But at least I know what happened to
mine. He does not. Never will. Could have been bad
food that made them scream in agony until they died.
Could have been poison. No way to tell."

"I—" Her voice choked. She did not know it had
been like that. She had no idea. He had never said—

"Difficult age, twelve winters. Not a boy, not a
man."

"Is that how old he was when they died?" All the
things they did not know about each other. All the
things there had never been time to say. All the things,
known and perilously unknown, that divided them—

"Makes it difficult to believe things can be permanent when something like that happens. Much better to take things as they come, especially if you are
an *Atheling*."

*That is how I did survive it: by the moment. How
does one survive anything?*

An Atheling. Throne-worthy and under threat for
the rest of his life. Hated by King Osred the vicious,
related to the royal house of Cenred. Poison. Twelve
years old and no parents. Not even angry and un-
happy ones.

"Thought you were permanent, though."

"Did he...did he think that?"

She had not understood. Had not been able to believe that. Still could not.

...nothing is permanent... And the bitterness in his voice, the terrible acceptance. Her heart felt as though it would break inside her.

What if it had been true all the time? What if he had felt as she had? What if...what if it had just been she who had not been able to believe?

She had killed more than she had known when she had left him.

But it could change nothing. She could not stay with him.

"Aye. He thought that. Bit of a problem was it?"

She thought of loss and flight and exile and cruelty.

"Yes. Something of a problem."

"Still is?"

She thought of Goadel's malice. King Cenred's precarious hold on the throne. The malice of the two rival kingdoms of Pictland and Northumbria.

"Yes."

"Pity. But just be sure, tomorrow, you make the right decision."

CHAPTER TWELVE

THERE WAS ONLY ONE decision to be made, right for whom she did not know.

"I will not go with you."

"Oh, you will. Did you think I would leave it to your choice?" The intensity in the harsh face chilled her bones.

"You are mad to ask it."

"No. You are the one who is mad, Alina."

But she doubted that. The mid-morning light showed her the keen eyes fixed on hers. They blazed with an intensity that frightened her soul.

"You must be mad for letting that Northumbrian anywhere near you, for crawling after his every footstep like a dog. Or like a bitch in heat."

She took a step backwards, even though he was her brother, even though he was her own flesh and blood.

"Cunan, did you not hear what he said? It will not work. Goadel is not enough. What you are planning will fail."

"What *he* said. Would you believe him over your own brother?" He was walking towards her, his feet cracking twigs in half, tearing the first turning of the autumn leaves.

"I believe what makes sense." Her back jarred against the thick trunk of an oak tree. She glanced round but there was no one, nothing on the edge of the woodland that could help her. He was between her and the camp.

"What makes sense for whom? Do you forget who you are, Alina? Do you even know? Is it true what they say? Is that why you always hated my father? Hated me?"

She did not know what he was talking about. The light in his eyes was something she had not seen before. Where was Duda, her guard dog? Anyone?

Brand.

"Cunan, listen to me. I do not hate my father, or you. I would not cause you harm—"

"Then do as I say."

She saw it, or she thought she did: the faintest movement caught out of the corner of her eye. Duda. Must be. But Cunan was so very close.

"Then let me think. Give me a moment."

"If you were as loyal to your family as you say, you would not even need a moment."

It was a shadow, moving. She must not look at it. Must not let Cunan realize— But perhaps her gaze flickered towards the shadow because Cunan's tightly sprung body tensed. The feral eyes widened.

"You are right," she lied, her eyes holding his, knowing she was betraying him but that she could not do otherwise. "I will come with you."

The shadow on the edge of her vision blurred, took another shape. Cunan's face vanished. The struggle was brief and without the slightest mercy. She could not watch it.

"Do not kill him!"

Her gaze skittered over the crumpled figure pinned under Brand's weight.

"Don't." The word was torn out of her throat.

He did not reply. Did not so much as look at her. The bright gold eyes sought her brother's. They held no mercy, just as his hands had not.

"Where is Goadel?"

Cunan spat, spittle mixed with blood.

"I have no idea—"

"Please do not…" The words were scarce formed, no more than a sound of horror. She did not even know why she pleaded. Cunan had showed her no pity. He would show none to Brand, and if Brand heard her, it made not the slightest difference. She cringed, as though the blow would fall on her, but it did not. It did not fall at all.

She read her brother's eyes. Behind the streak of animal fear there was something more chilling: a kind of triumph that had nothing to do with the terror of the present struggle, but with something unguessed at.

"You heedless fool," said Brand. "It is true then. He is here. And you did not turn him back, even when I warned you."

She realized the clearing was full of men, Duda, Eadric, the others, a man she did not recognize who wore brightly burnished ring mail and a heavy leather baldric painted with a device that looked like a red boar.

The house of Cenred.

Brand's gaze flicked to the king's man and then back to Cunan. "Tell him. Repeat to this benighted, self-serving creature what your message is."

The mail-clad man's eyes flickered.

"Lord, the message was for you, the king's kinsman."

"Aye, and if this *nithing* does not hear it from your lips he will hear it from mine. Get up."

The words had more force than the blow she had been expecting. Cunan was hauled to his feet. Brand's large hands released him. They were not steady. Not out of the kind of fear that lived in Cunan's eyes but from the force of what was held back.

"Go. Go and stand beside your sister while you listen to what this man has to say. Move."

Cunan crossed the four paces that separated them. He did not look at her. His gaze moved from Brand to the king's man, fixed there.

"The message my lord has sent is that he has confirmed the conditions of the peace treaty made with the king of the Picts—that the lord Nechtán has agreed, and that any man soever who breaks this peace shall be accounted a *nithing* and a traitor in both lands."

She stared at Cunan. The secret triumph in his eyes was gone, leaving the coldly seeping horror of the helpless. Or the guilty.

"Cunan... Why do you look like that? What does it mean? What have you done?"

He did not say a word. His face, white, suddenly as terrified as hers, began to fade in consuming brightness. There was a strange noise in her ears. She was half-aware of Brand leading her away, somewhere quiet, somewhere where there was only the two of them and no other.

She breathed in deep jerking gasps, trying to slow the dizziness in her head, fend it off; and she would have turned into his arms then. She would have sought the primal safety of touching him. But she could not. He was changed, utterly.

He did not touch her.

There was a wasteland of silence.

"I do not understand."

"Do you not? Did you think he would have taken you to Goadel after all? Or not? Did you think that he would have taken you somewhere safe out of family loyalty, so that you could be amongst your kin?"

"I did not... I just..."

"If you thought that, you were right. He would have done that for you, Alina. He would have taken you to your kin. But you would not have been safe."

"I do not understand what you are saying. What... How..." Her voice broke off. Fear struck ice through her, fear of what was in Brand's eyes. Not the brightness of the anger he tried to hide, not the lingering traces of the battle will that had defeated Cunan in a few fiercely honed seconds, but the pity.

"Cunan was going to take you to your father."

"My *father?* To Maol? No—" But she could see the answer in the carefully controlled eyes. "Then…it is my father who is here. *He* is the one Cunan should have turned back and did not."

"Yes."

"And you knew?"

"No. I did not know. Not until that last moment. Yet nothing else made sense. Cunan was sending messages to someone. Someone was shadowing us. Yet the attack made on me was a complete surprise to Cunan. He should have known what Goadel's men were doing but he did not. Yet even so, I could not believe it. That Cunan, or your father, would risk so much openness, knowing what was in King Nechtán's mind, calculating, surely, what would be the likely outcome of the treaty being negotiated at Bamburgh."

But her father had always believed he knew better than his brother the king. Cunan believed whatever her father believed. She had known that. She should have understood.

Her legs gave way. She sat down, the skirts of her fine riding dress snagging on brambles. She looked at the thorns. There was a tiny spot of blood on her thumb.

"My father is trapped, is he not? He has over-reached himself by coming south. King Nechtán, his own brother, has taken quite a different decision. Nechtán has thrown in his lot with your King Cenred, and now my father can no longer throw in his with

Goadel. He cannot win. It would be suicide. Point-less."

"Yes."

Her mind made the next step. "But Goadel is committed to what he planned. If my father tries to withdraw his support from Goadel, Goadel will kill him."

This time the matter-of-fact English voice did not say *yes*. It did not need to. She stared at the small trickle of blood on her hand. If she could just wash it off in the stream… But there was no stream, not here. She did not know why she thought she had heard it.

"What can I do?"

"Go to Bamburgh."

"Bamburgh? No. I have to go to my father now. I have to—"

"It is your king's decision you have to keep faith with. And your brother Modan."

She looked up. The blankness of his eyes, the tightly reined strength of his body were implacable. It was impossible to believe that he had ever held her in his arms with such passion or such…kindness. Or that he had ever let her touch him.

"There is no time to lose, Alina, not for Modan or for you."

She swallowed bile. Her hands fisted at her sides.

"I cannot leave—"

"You will. It is no longer your choice. Or mine." Ice-bright gold beat against her gaze, broke it. "Your fate is not my responsibility anymore. It belongs to

King Cenred's men. This is the moment when it is over, Alina. Finished."

She felt as though he had hit her with one of those large capable hands held so loosely at his sides. She felt as though he had betrayed her utterly. Even though he was right. Even though there was nothing else she could expect.

"Come. There is not one moment to be lost." He held out one of those lethal hands towards her. She could not take it.

"Suppose I will not go."

"Then you will be constrained."

"What? You—"

"Not I, Alina. I have told you. It is no longer my responsibility. That belongs to the king's men and king's men are not…scrupulous if someone resists their orders. I think you have learned that already. Besides, you gave your word. You have pledged it to Modan as truly as though you had spoken it in his hearing. He has nothing, not even a retinue of Pictish rebels. Will you break your word again?"

She got to her feet. Unaided. He turned away from her, striding towards the trees, towards the men with the expensive armour and the bright red blazons. She watched his back.

"And you, Brand, what will you do?"

"I will do what I have always wished. I will pay what I owe to Northumbria."

He did not turn. She should not expect it. She realized what her heart had refused to acknowledge yesterday when Cunan had turned away from the truth.

The leave-taking she had seen in Brand's face had been absolute.

THE KING'S MEN FETCHED her horse and allowed her to gather her things. There were three of them. They wore armour of hand-linked steel and helms adorned with flashes of enameled red. They knew exactly what they were doing.

Duda was waiting for them on the road.

"Duda? Where are…the others?" She could not bring herself to say *Brand*.

"Where do you think?"

There had not been one moment to lose. "Halfway to Bamburgh?" It was dishonourable to be bitter, achingly unfair.

Duda's shapeless form twitched.

"That is where we should be."

"Aye. Naught to hold us back."

"Right decision?"

Not mine. Like everything in my life. She wanted to yell it at him, at his cold, ferocious little eyes. But she could not. She did not have the breath. They were already riding. Fast.

Besides, it was only half-true. It was not a decision forced without will. In the end, Brand's ruthless assessment was also hers.

She kept riding. But despite the fact that she knew no other decision had been possible, her mind was split so that she thought she would die of the pain of it. Ahead was her brother. Behind her was her father, caught in a trap made of his son's relentless, misguided zeal, and of his own overbearing will.

She did not have much reason to care. Her father had taken no account of her wishes when he had sold her to Hun. He would not have deviated one hair's breadth from his course if Goadel's brother had beaten her senseless daily. The minor inconvenience of that would have been subsumed in the greater good to Pictland.

Just as the pain of what she was doing now would be subsumed by the greater good of rescuing Modan. It was only her misfortune that the pain inside her had the power to kill. She had no reason to feel torn between the two of them, father and brother. And what would she achieve anyway? She looked at the mail coats woven by master smiths, at the brightly coloured shields picked out in red and white slung across metal-clad shoulders.

She was hardly a warrior.

Not like them.

Not like Brand.

He was the loss that would really kill her. Even while her mind made the same sharp, clear judgment as his, her heart would not allow it. Her heart would admit nothing but the course of love.

She had tried to say that. She had tried to explain to Brand what lay so deeply buried inside her. But that had had no purpose. And in truth, she had not been able to explain anything. All that she had tried to say had perished in the gulf between them.

That gulf was now unbridgeable.

The speed of their flight was something she could not have endured even days ago. Now she could. So fast, and every pace of the muscular horse across the open ground a step closer to the end.

"Will we catch them up?" She shouted it. Stupid question but she could not help it. Just one glimpse of him before they reached the gilded prison walls of Bamburgh.

A red-flecked helm turned. She caught a brief look of incomprehension before the man mouthed something at her, the words snatched away on the power of the east wind. The earth thundered past her and the moving air of Bernicia plundered her lungs. She could smell the sea.

It was like the last time; fleeing toward the sea, turning west at the last minute to evade pursuit and the trap waiting for them on the coast road. Except that then Brand had been with her and she had felt that she could endure anything.

She had not known all that lay ahead, all the things she could not endure: damage to Brand, damage to his brother who had pretended to go on ahead and had really gone back in order to save their necks.

Who had pretended to go on ahead.

She wheeled the labouring horse round, so abruptly it nearly fell, nearly threw her. She clung on, fighting for balance, for control, for the speed she needed to evade three mail-clad men and Duda.

She was so much lighter than them. Her horse was

good, fresh. Fresher than theirs. She could ride like the devil now. She would need to.

She had no idea where she was going, only that it must be to the west and perhaps south. Only that she had to do it.

If one of them drew bow, or throwing spear, she was dead.

It was Duda who caught her, cutting her off from the refuge of the trees, forcing her to ride wide so that the others had time to complete the circle.

She looked at the swords and the bow on string. She looked at Duda's eyes.

"Made the right decision, have you?" she enquired through the heaving of her breath. His eyes snapped but he, at least, sheathed his blade. She turned her attention to the small ring of steel surrounding her. Everything was honed down to what she did next, what she said, whether she won.

"Perhaps we should have a careful think about decisions. Which one of you three would like to report to King Cenred that you left his kinsman to face death at the hands of a band of Picts and rebels when I could have prevented it?"

OF COURSE, she had no way of preventing it. The thought ate through her mind as they rode west and perhaps south. But the others did not know what was in her head. No one ever did. Even Duda must not know, because he managed to find Eadric for her. How, she could not contemplate.

"It is a difficult situation, lady." Eadric's eyes would not meet hers. "There was a dispute." *Oh, you fool, Maol of the Picts.* "The lord, your father, brought only a small number of men." *Doubtless because his brother Nechtán did not know or did not approve of what he was doing.* She gritted her teeth.

"Of course, when we arrived it helped. Brand could have taken Goadel, but we could not force the issue because…" Eadric became fascinated by a small patch of moss. "Goadel has the lord Maol."

"I see," she said through the freezing emptiness where heart and mind had been. "And the lord Cunan?"

"Rescued." She would have left him to his fate. Her hands clenched against the soft wool of her skirts and it was Duda who asked the next question. The one she could not force through the deadening emptiness.

"Brand?"

"He…he is in discussion with Goadel. Goadel wants safe passage to Ireland. Do not worry, lady," added Eadric, as though her voice had actually been strong enough to ask the question. "He will not let Goadel kill the lord Maol."

She could not imagine why not. He would have to, out of the most basic duty to his kinsman on an uncertain throne.

Or Goadel would kill him.

"Why did you have to come here?" The words were one long hiss of pain. She scarce knew who she was speaking of, Brand or her overweening father. Or

her crazed half brother. But she knew the answer: duty, twisted or pure. It was the wellspring of men's lives. Her father thought he knew better than Nechtán what suited Pictland. Cunan would die a thousand deaths to fulfil his father's wishes. Brand would not let Goadel go free to wreak rebellion.

She understood now. Brand's love was for Northumbria, beyond even the strength of kin ties to Cenred. Beyond anything she could give.

She crept forward so that she could see.

HE HAD TO KEEP MOVING, otherwise the damage to his ribs would seize up and he would be no use if it came back to fighting.

Goadel yelled and spat foam.

When it came back to fighting. Brand paced, tossing the hilt of his sword and catching it so that he could keep his arms moving. The sight of the blade sparking sunlight irritated all hell out of Goadel.

"I will not loose the prisoner until I reach the coast—"

Somewhere behind him he could hear Cunan reeling off curses in Pictish. He wished one of his men would have the sense to belt him over the head. He could not believe anything quite so ham-fisted had happened. He should have left Cunan to Goadel, not dragged him away and got his ribs knocked out in the process.

"...the coast..." bellowed Goadel. "Ireland..."

Brand spared one glance for the prisoner staked out

on the ground. Duty dictated he should be left to the consequences of treason.

"No," he yelled in turn and tried not to think how much his refusal might have to do with the unhealed wounds of what had been done to his brother by Goadel's kin.

Or to do with Alina.

He could not let his mind focus on Alina. The thought of her would take all that he had.

The prisoner stifled a groan. He could not imagine why, after the life she had lived, Alina would still care about her criminally arrogant father. But that she did was indisputable. Just as she cared for the other Pictish idiot, Cunan.

He transferred his gaze to the brother of the man he had killed.

"What I propose…" screamed Goadel. Something moved behind him. There was a small scuffle and a bitten-off curse. Someone had clouted Cunan after all? He risked a glance over his shoulder, swallowing the curse that rose to his own lips because of the jarring pain in his side.

"I have come for my father," said the Lady Alina.

The curse escaped. He could not believe she was real. Duda and the three king's men should have taken death rather than allowed this.

The princess of the Picts stared at them. Behind her a bloodied remnant crawled its way up off the ground. It appeared to have a broken nose. The princess rubbed her elbow as though it might have bruises.

"Take her away." They were the only words he could get out of his mouth. As a bellow, it was louder than Goadel's. "Now." There must be some of his men who would not be outfought by a woman.

"No. Do not do that." The voice, suddenly smooth, was Goadel's. The white heat in Brand's blood seemed to freeze. "I said, leave the lady be."

At a sign from Goadel, a small sound of shock issued from his helpless prisoner on the ground and was just as abruptly cut off. Brand saw how it happened. Bile rose in his throat and he knew the heat of the fury inside him was not extinguished, it was just held, under a thin ice-crust of frozen coldness, waiting its target.

Some things were not permitted. People should know that.

"I think the Lord Maol would like to hear his daughter's offer," said Goadel.

Brand quietened his own men with a gesture, hoping the prisoner on the ground would have enough sense to keep silent this time, because there was nothing that could be done. Yet.

He could see the small deadly glimmer of the knife held above the prisoner. So could Alina. Her face was chalk-white, her eyes twin wells of the pain he had never wanted to see in them again. He kept near her in his restless pacing, knowing what she would feel driven to say. Knowing that with those words, the choices, precious few at best, would narrow down into one.

"I will go with you instead," said Alina to the brother of the man she had been betrothed to. "It is what you wished, if you remember. Would that not be a more...agreeable solution?"

Goadel's laughter made her hands clench. But she did not back down. Just stared at him.

"Do you believe I am still so much enamoured of your charms?" Goadel's gaze lingered on her with the kind of look that must cut straight through one with her fears. Brand's hand tightened on the sword hilt. But the ice stopped him. It was deadly, as deadly as what lay beneath.

Goadel spat.

"Wait—" It was the infernal prisoner's voice, wire thin, but everyone heard it. Behind him Brand heard Cunan surge to his feet.

He knew what would be said. It was both suicidal and held more selflessness than he had thought Maol capable of. The pinned body twisted, the mouth formed the words that would damn Alina. "She is not as you think. She is—"

"Worth less as a hostage than Maol would be." He yelled it. Before the words *a bastard,* true or not, could hit the air. Because if Goadel thought his dead brother Hun had been offered tainted goods he would kill Maol outright. The man should have calculated that. He stepped straight in front of Alina.

"But that is hardly going to matter to you, is it, Goadel, because I will not let either of the Picts go. And besides," he said, not even looking at the knife suspended over Maol, not even looking at Alina. "There is something else that you want more, is there not? Vengeance."

The word obliterated every other thought shifting through Goadel's eyes, as he had known it would. He saw all the thwarted fury that must twist through the blackness of that greedy soul begin to burn.

He stopped, close enough, taunting, the sword held with deceptive looseness in his hand.

"Would you like to know what I did to your brother Hun before I killed him? Would you like to know what he said? How I could force him to plead like a frightened child? How I could make him crawl and beg for mercy I would not give? Go on begging—"

The black fury ignited. The only recognizable word in the stream of abuse was *liar*, which was unfortunately true because Hun's death had been instant, a matter of defence as much as vengeance. But at least he had driven Goadel beyond reason. He swung the sword.

"*No...*" It was Alina's voice. The shocking desperation in it made him break the self-imposed rule and look at her. Turn his head. The change in the air warned him more than Duda's immediate shout. He twisted, forgetting about the pain in his side. Goadel's blade missed. He jumped back through the blackening mist, avoided the slashing backhand follow-through aimed at the knee by instinct.

He swatted his sword, flat-bladed, at Goadel as his body came back round in one fiercely balanced arc.

The blade missed Goadel's face by inches, striking his shoulder, deflected by the mail, slashing sparks. But it was not a blow meant to maim. It was an insult. Goadel screamed under the weight of the men holding him back.

Brand stood still while everyone got over the shock and rearranged themselves. His gaze sought Alina.

She was still struggling against Duda, who was trying to hold her back without using too much of the kind of weasel strength that killed people. She looked almost as wild as she had with Eadric.

Could she not understand what he was doing? That he was not going to abandon her or her father?

His own men closed round him as Goadel screamed a string of curses that ended in the words he wanted to hear.

"I will kill you."

"Then try it." His voice overrode everything. He flung off Eadric's restraining hand, striding forward into the clear space between the opposing sides. So that all could see him. So that all could hear.

"Do you listen, Goadel? My life or yours. The winner walks free. With whatever he wants to take with him, Pict or Northumbrian, man or woman, Cenred's retainers or yours. Those are the terms. My word."

CHAPTER THIRTEEN

THE MEN YELLED, on both sides, because it was the only way out without starting an indiscriminate bloodbath. They pressed back, clearing the space for the fight. Somewhere beside him, Eadric was holding his shield strap. The blackness in front of his eyes held for a moment, with a sensation of numbing cold, the way it had happened after the arrow attack.

But this time he recognized it.

It was like drowning.

He forced the memory back. Controlled it. Controlled everything. He did not look at Alina, but turned his face towards the sun, so that the bright light almost blinded him. The blackness faded like mist and he moved his shoulders, his back, forcing life into muscles tightening inexorably from the last fight. The weight of the chain mail dragged at aching flesh.

He glanced across at Goadel being manhandled into some semblance of order by his companions. Goadel's eyes held death. It was in the air, like a dancing shadow.

He forced his concentration back to what had to be

done. He did not want to think of fate pricking the hairs at the nape of his neck.

Duda, you ham-fisted lackwit, look at me.

He saw the shaggy head turn, as though in response to the unspoken thought. One glance told him that Alina, standing next to Duda, was totally still. He turned his gaze away from her. He could not look on so much as the dark fall of her half-hidden hair.

He glanced at Duda. Duda shuffled his feet.

Just explain it to her, you fool. Tell her that whatever the outcome of this, even if I die, her father's men will not let Goadel take her. They will not be bound by my word.

He could see Duda bend his head to speak softly. He knew that Alina watched him across the space that separated them from each other. He could sense her nearness, the tightly held stillness of her. He could sense her grief.

The madness he felt for her made him look at her eyes, as though he could convey across a distance of ten paces the power of the living pledge in his heart. Her night-deep gaze held his and then he could feel it slipping away.

Duda spoke to her, shaking her arm. She looked at her father, at Cunan.

It was not ten paces of Northumbrian soil that separated him from her. It was a whole country. It was grief and loss and blood and the inescapable ties of other loyalties and other cares.

Insuperable.

He had known that.

He took the shield off Eadric. Light spiralled off the painted sun wheel in Cenred's white and red colours. He set his hand to the well-worn iron grip, adjusted the leather strap. The weight of the shield settled over his forearm, the linden-wood panels strengthened with curving iron bands, the rim bound with hardened leather fastened with iron nails. Familiar as a second skin.

The sword was eager in his hand. Sunlight reflected off the rune-blade a thousand times more brightly than from the shield. The blade moved in his grip, as though its will merged with his. That was how it always began.

The dangerous exhilaration of the battle rush took his body, obliterating the pain. For now. But the pain was still there. It would break through the consuming fires later, and if it did, that would be Goadel's opportunity.

It was an opportunity that should not be granted.

This moment would be stronger. His blood surged. The power of that was something that should be controlled, always, for the future's sake. But not this time.

His future did not exist.

Only Alina's.

He let the wildness that was both his strength and his bane take his mind.

"HE CANNOT MEAN TO DO IT. He cannot. We have to stop him."

Alina's feet paced the green earth, flattening grass,

moss, the last of summer's flowers. The small circles of her steps dizzied her.

"If you know how anyone can stop Brand from what he wants to do, I would be interested to learn," said Duda. Then, and more urgently, "If you are going to swoon, save it for later. You do not have time now."

Duda's voice seemed to come from a vast distance, even though he was standing next to her. She felt something catch her arm. The feral stiffness of her fingers fastened on what might have been a bony wrist under all the coverings.

"I am not… I will not…" But she could not even get the word *swoon* out of the dryness of her mouth. Because if she said that, she might do it. Right there and then while there was not time.

"What have I been telling you about what will happen, eh? Repeat it to me. Wench!" The English word, offensive to her rank, scarce penetrated. Duda's claw-like hands shook at her arm. "Unless, of course, you want to make what he is doing worthless."

That got through. She blinked her eyes against the otherworldly tinge to the sunlight. The light was so fierce she did not understand how it could be so cold. She tried to shake off the grip of that coldness, to concentrate.

"What did I say?" demanded the creature attached to her arm.

"That whoever—" *whoever is killed* "—whichever

way it goes, there will be confusion at the end, and that is when—"

Brand moved. Light caught a thousand woven silver rings, then shattered under his power. She had never imagined so much ferocity. Goadel staggered back. There was blood.

An inarticulate sound from Duda drew her attention. What she could see of his face was without colour.

"*You* cannot swoon," she snarled. "You have not got time." But her hand slid under the grubby rags where his arm might be. "It is all right. He hit Goadel. Duda?"

There was the sickening sound of rending wood. She looked back. Goadel's shield. Brand's weight behind it. Goadel staggered. Almost fell. Twisted aside. Caught his balance. The next blow almost cut through to his neck.

"Duda?"

She could not turn her head.

She heard curses, then, "Tell me the rest of your instructions." As though she were some bondswoman.

"As it finishes—" She watched Goadel's massive frame collect itself, drive forward suddenly with the strength of thick muscle and the unslaked thirst for vengeance. With all the malice that had left her father bound to the torture of the knife.

"Well," snapped Duda.

"The Picts." *Your people,* Duda had called them. *Her people.* Her gaze took in the contorted figure bound at bleeding wrist and ankle with rope, then across the clearing, the helpless fury in Cunan's face. "My people," she said, "will free my father and—"

Goadel lunged. Brand caught the return blow on the brightly coloured shield. The edge held. He twisted as Goadel had done before, regaining balance. But slower, surely? No, it had been imagination. The shield edge caught Goadel's arm, nearly sending the sword spinning. Goadel leaped back as Brand's blade slashed at his legs.

"My father's men will protect me." She watched the moving bright-gold fall of Brand's hair, the sparking light as fire-tempered steel met its equal match. "And after that—" She watched his body twist away from the blow as before, a fierce, subtly woven glitter of silver and gold. *After that…nothing. Because I will not be able to leave you.* "After that—" She was suddenly aware of the effort in that lightning-fast movement, as though she felt it.

"Duda, what—"

Brand was back on the attack but as he twisted a second time, Goadel's sword hit. It was so quick, she did not at first know what her eyes had seen. She would have thought sight deceived her because it made not the slightest difference to the driving attack of Brand's body.

But she could see the blood blossoming just above the braided sleeve edge.

"Duda…" It was not really a sound because the word could not escape the tightness of her breath, the sick dizziness that would kill her. She could hear Duda's curses. There was not the slightest alteration in Brand's movement.

"All the saints," said Duda. "He did not feel it."

"What?"

"He did not feel it. Perhaps he does not even know. I cannot imagine. I have never seen him do this. He has never let himself."

"Do what?" She stared at the blood.

"It is just…there is such fire in him. I used to tease him about being a berserker. Only of course he could not be, not with his heart. But I always said if he wanted, he would…"

"Be able to do that."

"Yes."

They did not feel their wounds, those fell Northern creatures. They just went on fighting with a spirit unquenched, whatever happened to them, until they died.

"Why would he do such a thing now? Why—"

"Maybe you can answer that better than I can."

Her heart seemed to catch in the painful tightness of her chest. But Duda did not realize how things were. He seemed to think, to believe, all sorts of things that were wrong. Because he did not understand what had happened in the past.

It could not be for her.

I will do what I have always wished. I will pay what I owe to Northumbria… Your fate is not my responsibility anymore.

"No…" She closed her eyes against the blood and the fierce, untiring movement of the wounded body, and asked the only question left.

"Will he live?"

There was a small silence that seemed to hold the two of them, while outside it was the sound of steel and wood and the primeval yelling from the throats of a score of blood-crazed warriors.

"I do not know. That was not a crippling wound, though it is awkward. The blood will make the sword hard to hold and the loss will tire him even if he cannot feel it. If that had been the first wound—"

"What do you mean?"

"Eadric said he was hurt rescuing your brother. Did you not know?"

No. The word was like a silent scream in her mind. There seemed no limit to what her family could do: her half brother, her father. Herself. She fought to breathe.

"And what about Goadel?"

"Scatheless. Before this."

"And is he…very good?"

"He was always good. Brand's made him angry."

"I see." She looked for one brief instant at Duda's face and she could see the reflection of her own fears, the terrible tie of friendship, the unredeemable bond to someone you owed more than your life to. "Thank…thank you."

"For what?"

"Telling me. Letting me understand. I…I am sorry I hit you."

Duda snorted through his swollen nose. She heard him sniff. "Girl's hit, that. Watch this."

She opened her eyes.

"And for pity's sake do not start crying. You have got a job to do when this is over."

"Yes." The tears faded and with their going, her mind became clear as ice water.

"I know."

IT WAS ACTUALLY POSSIBLE to see his orders being carried out. Brand's hand flexed round the sword hilt, bettering his grip. It was as though some part of his thought hoard remained, ice-clear and remote, unsullied by the mad desperation of his body.

That part of his brain could discern the pattern in the seemingly random movement of the yelling blood lust that surrounded them, the careful placement of his own men. And the Picts. Even Cunan, now closest of all to Maol, dangerously close. The guilt of failed plans. How familiar that was. None of it would be atoned. Ever. Unless Alina was safe.

He struck, forcing Goadel to retreat, watching the fury grow in the pale, malice-filled eyes of Hun's brother, goading it, waiting for that fury to cause an error that would be fatal.

The blade came back at him, high, cutting for his face. He parried with the shield, training that had become instinct angling the board to take the blow against the metal boss, the lunge of his own blade in response instant. Yet not so. The blade slipped again in his grip. The palm of his hand must be sweat damp. The power of the blow was deflected.

Goadel sensed the weakness. The greedy rage in the pale, narrow eyes had blunted under the fatigue that came with the unrelenting ferocity of the attack. Now the greed became sharper, eager for its reward of death. And all that would follow.

Brand's gaze flickered over the seething press of men around them, straining to see whether the preparations were complete. He had so little time left. The clear part of his mind knew it. His left arm blocked the slashing blow of Goadel's blade. The shield cracked. Wood splinters flew, striking his face. He shook stinging wetness out of his eyes.

It should be his left arm that was numbing from the force of the blow over the older wound, slowing him, but it was not. It was his right. He could not understand why.

He saw that his men were there, high on the grassy slope beside Maol. Every man of Goadel's watched the fight, heedless. It was time.

Just as he moved, he thought he saw the darker swirling green of Alina's dress at the foot of the rise. His hand gripped the slippery hilt. Duda would stop her. He would not let her be so near to where the danger would be. Not again. The single fast glance that he could spare showed her still moving.

It was now. Had to be. Before she got too close.

He stepped inside the next blow, striking out with what was left of the shield. His blade sought the gap the splintered wood created. Goadel saw it coming. The bale-filled eyes widened. The mouth stretched.

"Kill—" The voice screamed. He struck. Before the name of the helpless prisoner could be loosed into the air, ordering the death that would plunge both sides into carnage. Before Alina's fragile body could move up the slope.

The rune blade flashed, just as Goadel struck with his own sword, crashing forward, overbalanced, the full weight of him falling. The blades clashed, steel ripping along steel. The ground slammed into his ribs.

HE ROLLED, hearing already damaged bones scrape without feeling it, twisting his body to free it of the crushing weight. He clawed half-upright, seeing the writhing mass of men around the staked-out body resolve itself into order at the sound of Eadric's voice yelling orders.

He could not see Alina.

Or Duda.

He could not move. The weight seemed to cling to him. And then he saw her. Not pushing upwards through the brief skirmish on the hill slope but on the other side of him, with Duda. She was turned towards him. They both were.

He saw what was behind them.

His sword was gone, the hilt out of his reach, useless anyway, because he could not move. He kicked at the weight that held him trapped. It seemed to move with him like a death grip. He clawed free enough to get a hand to the *seax* hilt at his belt.

He had not the slightest consciousness of moving after that, only of the faint glint of shining metal cleaving the air. Then Alina's scream and Duda's curse as they turned. Behind them Goadel's man, the one who had been set to cut pieces out of the prisoner, collapsed, the bloodied knife spiralling out of his hand.

He expected Duda to stop, then, to at least make sure the man was dead. But he did not. He charged, holding his own *seax* in one outstretched claw. Then he felt movement in the dead weight, saw the brief flash of steel.

He struck out backhanded, with all the strength of his arm, just as Duda dived. The double impact took his breath, Duda's weight adding to the other in a bone-jarring thud. Then nothing.

He levered himself up out of the mess.

"Is he really dead?" But it was not his voice that asked the question.

He turned his head and saw Alina. His sword was in her hand, in a warrior's grip, with her thumb all the way round the gilded wood of the hilt. Her face was death pale. But she was whole.

"Aye, the creature's dead now," said Duda. "Give me that sword, woman, before you do some damage." Duda was dragging the weight off his lower body.

"Dead all right," muttered Duda. "Would not have

lasted five minutes anyway after that sword thrust. I only gave him a flea bite. But it was worth it."

Once he was free of the weight, he could get to his feet. Duda and Alina were staring at him. Horrors lived in Alina's eyes. The instinct that tore through him was to crush her in his arms and take her head against his shoulder, the way he had before. To tell her that she was safe, that no one would harm her. That she was his.

His feet took the first step towards her, even though he could say none of the things bursting against the walls of his heart. She did not move. Just stared at him with that look he could not describe.

He held out his hand, not knowing what he could say, or what he could do, but unable to turn away from her, unable to stop just looking at what he had so nearly lost. To Goadel's malice.

Her stricken gaze moved slowly from his face to his hand. He realized it was covered in blood. She would hate that. She loathed such sights. She was too tenderhearted for that.

He snatched his hand back, feeling suddenly and utterly disoriented, like a sleepwalker who had stumbled unknowing into the world of those who were awake: an unwelcome creature out of someone's nightmare.

He stared at the blood. At his sleeve sticking to the uneven surface of a gash.

"The knife blade must have caught me after all." But there was too much blood, some of it drying.

"Nay," said Duda in the kind of voice you would use when you did not want to provoke a wild animal. Or a savage. "It happened before. It is a sword cut. Goadel's blade."

He had no memory of it. The implications of that were something he could not bear. He took a step backwards. He stared at the blood on his arm, still welling sluggishly. He could not feel anything.

He took another step. At the edge of his vision he could see the fluttering movement of Alina's skirts, the narrow shape of her bronze-buckled shoe. It moved towards him. Not away.

Of course she would not turn away. That was the other side of her tender heart. Its strength. She had such pity.

He realized he was utterly covered in blood: Goadel's, his. It clung to his body. It must be mired over his face from the splinter cut. He could not let her touch that, could not let her anywhere near him. Not just because of that, but because of what must be on the inside.

He was a creature of nightmare.

"Brand—"

He spoke across her, to Duda. "What of my orders? The prisoner?"

"Safe enough." Duda's answer was quick, as one should answer a commander. At least that much was still his, still real. He looked across the vast distance of two paces that separated them.

"And?"

"Most of them surrendered without striking a blow. You did not leave them much of a choice."

"Cunan?"

"With his father. Where else?"

Not with his sister who had nearly been cut down by the man who served as Goadel's executioner. Of course not. He tried to focus his thought on what still had to be done.

"I will see Maol."

"I will come with you." The ridiculously small feet in their expensive shoes moved.

"Not now." He looked up, met Duda's sudden frown, then the disbelief in Alina's gaze swiftly succeeded by anger. He shook his head.

"No." The force in the word was vicious. It made her flinch but he could not help that. He had no breath to explain, and he did not know whether Maol would look as bad as him. He did not want her to see another image that would haunt her mind.

Besides, there were things to be sorted out with Maol the Pict. Now. While the evidence of what the man had done was still before his eyes.

He turned away from the masked hurt in the night-dark eyes that was all too visible to him, the incomprehension of what he was and what he had done. What he had turned into.

At a gesture, Duda handed him the sword. The blade was covered in blood. Dirt crusted it from where it had hit the ground. It was his match. He did not clean the blade.

He climbed the slope. The blade hummed in his hand as though the power of the elk-sedge rune hidden beneath the dirt were something living. Such dangerous force. He did not need to be able to see it. He could feel it.

They fell back to let him pass, his men, the Picts, even Goadel's men. He could see the same expression in all of their eyes, like men who saw one of the *hellkinn*. The other word he would not name, not even in his mind.

They had cut the man's bonds, but it was not a sight Alina should see. He knelt down.

"Did you give him water? Mead? Fetch him my cloak."

He laid the ringing blade across his knees and waited. There was silence. Of a kind. It seemed impossible no one else could hear the sword's voice.

He studied the man before him while they covered the body and gave him aid. There were only surface wounds. The man must have the devil's own luck.

The Pict turned his head. Brand watched the eyes. They were quite clear. They saw the blade first. Then they focused on him, with an intensity that was sudden. The Pict's gaze held the shades of what he had read in the eyes of the others around him. In Alina's gaze.

The sword sang.

"What will you do?" His accent was pure Pictish, no soft overtones of Strath-Clòta. He watched the blade. His eyes were like Alina's. Not so much in their colour, which was lighter and more like Cunan's, but in something else.

Perhaps the man was her father.

Perhaps no one knew.

Brand let the silence stretch.

"So it is you and your King Cenred who now own the price of my life."

"Yes. It is." His voice cut across the sword's, merged with it, so that the clarity of it split the air. He missed nothing, not the moment's surprise in Eadric's face over his uncompromising assertion, not Cunan's tightened lips, not the small flicker of fire in the eyes so like Alina's.

"And my daughter?"

So he had remembered Alina. That was good. And he kept on with his acknowledgement of her as his seed.

"Safe enough. Now."

"You mean safe with you?" The words dripped with the accusation of what he had done when he had taken Alina from her intended husband.

"Yes. She owes me her life as well. Did they tell you that? Cunan?" He turned his head and the shift in attention was as fast and as disconcerting as he had meant it to be. The lean face on the other side of Maol's body darkened. "So? Do I tell the truth?" The question was sharp, Pictish.

Cunan's eyes widened, blanked off with the realization of how much he knew. There was a pause that lasted an age of time.

"It is true," said Cunan in the same speech, with more directness than he expected. "I saw it. When the fight ended she tried to get to the Northumbrian. One of Goadel's men went after her. He…he would have killed her. The Northumbrian knifed him."

It was succinct. He kept his face blank. Maol kept eyeing him, and the blood that covered him. He had forced himself to hide nothing of that, or of the remains of whatever less material horrors clung to him.

"You have the price of two lives. What do you want?"

"Two *wergilds*."

Maol would understand the Anglian term for a life-price, he had no doubt.

"Riches in compensation?" The sloe-shaped eyes sparked, just like Alina's.

"Nay. Greater things."

"What?"

The bloodied wreck seemed to gather itself. He watched, forcing his mind to assess, choosing the measure of his words. The sword was quite still, the fork shape of the rune invisible, the protective curves of the serpents felt beneath his hand.

"The first payment is that I want no impediments to the peace your king has pledged with mine. If you have your own ambitions, you can exercise them north of the border, not south, and to prove your faith, you will come to Bamburgh. To your other son."

The blood-streaked head bowed. But it was easy enough to accede to that. Nechtán was likely to make it difficult for him to do otherwise, and he did have another of his expendable children at stake.

"Do you want to know the second payment?"

The power of the blade.

"I am sure you will tell me, Northumbrian."

The words waited in the shadows of what was to come. He fought to give them shape, out of his power and the sword's.

"I want your daughter's future."

CHAPTER FOURTEEN

THE WATER WAS SWIFT. So cold it stopped the blood almost immediately.

He would have to go back, soon. He knew that. To have the wound bound if not stitched. To relieve Eadric and Duda and Cenred's men of the burden of organizing the dangerous rabble of uneasy Bernicians and sullen Picts back on the road to Bamburgh.

He would.

He would do all that, but first he wanted, needed, to feel real.

No one had dared to follow him.

The water dragged at his clothes, its pure clearness streaked rust-brown. Its coolness seemed blessed, filled with strange memories, or future glimpses.

It had been clear water that had let him know that his brother still lived.

It had been clear water that had nearly given him the peace from life he had craved.

Drowning.

But he had been a child then. A child whose parents had died, screaming. That time was gone. There were responsibilities to fulfill, as there were always.

Perhaps even as a child he had sensed that, if not fully understood.

But if only he could feel again, even the pain. Quite ordinary, human pain.

But then he would feel everything.

He thought of Alina, of the way her eyes had looked at him after Goadel's death.

He stepped farther out into the water.

In the end, it ran clearly.

Just as his mind did. Clear as that small part of it that had been untouched by what he had let himself become with Goadel.

All he had to do was hold to that. And to his decision.

He had done right in his request to Maol.

But he had to make sure of that, make sure that the Pict kept to his word, make sure that Cenred did. And that the tormented creature Cunan realized what true loyalty was.

Choices.

He turned back towards the stream bank. The weight of his sodden clothes, the weight of a thousand links of handcrafted metal, dragged at him. The weight of the water. He did not think he could climb the riverbank alone.

Alone.

The pain hit him. Pain that was real.

But the unreality was still there, like the waking dream in the forest clearing. When he moved, his senses swam in darkness shot though with fire. Not fire. There was such coldness. Ice cold. He pushed through it.

His mind heard Alina's voice, shouting.

BAMBURGH WAS DEADLY.

Alina knew both its faces: the palace whose secret inner beauty was a richness beyond price, and the fortress that breathed power in every unyielding line.

It was the place where her destiny had begun and now would end. It watched her in its brilliant pride, rising skyward on its massive rock, guarded on three sides by the vast, power-seething expanse of the North Sea.

So many different lives had played out their heart-stopping risks here, felt the same desperation. Perhaps the hidden beauty of the palace locked behind walls understood that. Its own life had felt the same risks. It had been fought over many times, almost burned to the ground by the pagan King Penda of Mercia, saved only by a saint's prayers turning the wind.

The kinship she felt as the high walls closed round her was unexpected. Her hand fastened on a painted column in the inner chamber. The strength that lay beneath the sense-stealing beauty seemed to flow inside her from the wood.

You are not a prison, she thought, only a creature who has to fight to survive. Like me. I did not realize before. Sometimes your battles are fought outside the walls with spear and shield, sometimes inside, with guile or an assassin's knife. Yet you know you will survive your span of time.

Even life is only lent.

Do not let all we have fought for end now....

The thoughts in her frightened mind tumbled over each other, all centred round a blank, expressionless face.

Protect your prince. The words came carefully into her head, in English so that the living, breathing palace would understand.

I would give him to you if it would save him.

Eadric was calling to her. He sounded terrified.

She let go of the column.

SHE HAD A COMPANION in her vigil. Night-dark eyes, the mirror image of her own, kept moving from her face to that of the ice-cold warrior in the tapestried bed.

"I still cannot believe this."

Alina's hand tightened on one that was utterly lifeless and felt nothing.

"Which bit can you not believe? Father acting as though he has more power than King Nechtán? Cunan leading him into stupidity? Both of them willing to sell me off first to one hell fiend and then to his brother? Or perhaps it is the fact that they would have left your fate to a hangman's noose until they got round to remembering you existed?"

The dark head shook in negation.

"You. You and this Englishman." Modan's glance flickered. "They say he fought like a savage, like a...berserker. Does that make no difference to you?"

"No."

"But—"

She looked up. "The difference it made was to you. If he had not fought, you would be dead. If Goadel had begun his rebellion with Father's support, King Cenred would have hanged you."

"But...that would be nothing to an Englishman."

"Of course, I forgot. You know how he thinks. Have you worked out who else would have been dead if he had not *fought like a berserker?* Me. Cunan. Your father and all of his men, and a few other unnecessary Englishmen."

"Yes." The intelligent face flushed dark. "But Alina, the man abducted you by force. Twice."

"Really? What makes you, or my father, think he needed force?"

Her brother surged to his feet.

"By all the saints, you...you are in love with him. That is why you will not leave his side now, not even to go to your own father."

She looked not at Modan's shocked eyes but at the white face cleaned of every last trace of blood.

"Yes."

After that, people came and went. King Cenred and an array of courtiers. All of Brand's men.

Everyone except Cunan and her father.

The ones who had stayed longest had been those from Lindwood. People whom she did not know, who had come to Bamburgh because they knew their master would return there. One of them had been near seventy. She thought he would have wept if she had not been there, a stranger.

They loved Brand. It seemed to make no difference to the ice-locked face.

King Cenred's personal physician hovered, unwilling to report to his master that every remedy he had tried was useless. The table was littered with herbs and potions. She sent him away. When nightfall came, she thought they might leave her alone.

The door opened. It was someone from Lindwood. Or it was Modan. He did not like to leave her alone, so he sat with her, watching her with his grave dark eyes. She knew he went to see their father as well. Divided loyalties. It was the way she used to feel. Before her heart snapped.

She was standing by the table, sifting through the herbs as though she could do something the physician could not. She turned.

"Modan, did you—"

It was a king's man, one she did not recognize. Cenred's retinue of hearth companions seemed endless. She could not cope with them.

"You can go away," she said in weariness. "There is nothing new to tell your master."

He came farther into the room, a neat figure, like all of them, hair cleanly cut about his neck, beard well trimmed...an unusually large nose. He kept walking. Persistent.

"There is no point—" He sat down without invitation, which was an offence to her rank. "You may go."

The man unsheathed a *seax* and began sharpening it.

"So may you. I believe we have had this argument before."

She stared at the swollen nose.

"Duda?"

"You told me last time we sat like this that you screeched very well. I now believe it."

"What have you—" She controlled her voice. Stared. Silver flashed in the candlelight. "Where did you get…"

"The clothes? The arm ring?"

"The face."

"Ah. Like the trimmed look do you? I hear it appeals to the ladies."

"Very…very winsome."

Duda preened.

"And the rest of it?"

"Him."

The coldness of the room and the shadows beyond the light pooling across the bed closed in on her. Outside was the sound of the sea. It never stopped here.

"Feeling cold? You do a lot of shivering for someone who comes from up north."

"Aye. I do." She stared at the ice-cold remoteness of Brand's face.

"He gave me the silver and the clothes. You know, like Athelings do for their retainers, as though I were a proper thane with rank and honour and all that sort of thing. I decided not to wear any of it until I had vengeance on Goadel and his kin for what they had done to mine. Like a matter of honour."

"Duda…"

"That is what thanes do, and Athelings. Have honour."

The eyes that had once been concealed in so much hair and other things pinned her.

She looked away.

"It was not that much blood. Was it?"

"Yes. And the bruised ribs. Two of the bones might be cracked, the physician thought, perhaps three." Her hands shredded dried herbs off the table. Duda kept sharpening the knife.

"Duda, if you make any more use of that oilstone, there will be no blade left."

"Does not matter. Done its job now. Too late, like as not. Wish I had had the chance to stab him earlier."

"There would have been carnage."

"Aye. Well. Cracked ribs?"

"So they say." But just like last time, the wound was not the problem. She was glad Duda did not realize it.

"Why do you not you try jabbering at him in your funny language again?" *The tongue of poets, not ignorant Northumbrians.* "Worked last time."

Duda saw too much.

She stared at the white face and took a breath that scorched her throat.

"This time, there is nothing to say."

She realized what was in her hands. Vervain. The shredded leaves fell on the bedcovers.

Later, when it was truly dark and there were only the rare and costly wax candles to give light to the tapestried walls and the painted wooden columns, when she was the only one left, she crawled into bed with him.

But she could not speak.

The sound of the sea, and behind it the silence that could defeat the tongues of two kingdoms, beat against her ears.

SHE WAS THERE. At first that made him believe he had not truly woken, that he was still trapped in the world of unquiet dreams.

He could sense her breathing, feel the soft fragile line of her body fitted against him. Her hair spilled over his skin like a deeper layer of darkness, smooth as Byzantine silk.

She was asleep.

The blackness was very thick, and then he became aware of flickering light, somewhere. Dim, but still enough to stab through his aching eyes when he turned his head towards it. That movement, so slight and insignificant, brought a pain that could make him scream. Years of merciless training stopped that. The same training kicked what was left of his brain into action. But the scenes that it presented to him were chaotic, disjointed, the stuff of the nightmares that had held him in thrall for he knew not how long.

The only tangible fact that his mind could grasp was that Alina was with him, that she was whole and safe.

Mayhap.

He stared round at the blinding dark with its flitter-ing fire edges. Nothing moved. There was such si-lence, the kind of silence that belonged only to somewhere vast when the deepest hours of the night claimed it for their own. Above the silence was the restless beat of the sea.

There was no one else near them. He knew that much by instinct. There was no danger in the room at all.

He closed his eyes.

When he opened them again, the pain was instant. But the darkness was no longer complete. It was fad-ing before dim silver cloud light, the grey light that only existed in a Bernician dawn, clear, laced with the deep-seeking tendrils of coldness and the awareness of the wind and the ocean outside.

He knew where he was.

Alina's hand was tangled in his hair, her arm flung across his side. He drew breath and even that small movement brought sparks of fire behind his opened eyes. The small, almost imperceptible weight of her arm across his ribs was like lying under an iron band. Mayhap the ribs were cracked, not just bruised. But just like the gash in his arm, it had made no difference to him.

Because he had not been human.

He woke Alina.

"YOU ARE BACK."

She looked at the opaque frozen ice of his eyes.

Of all the things she could have said: *You are well, you are conscious, you are not dead,* or *thanks be to the saints,* she had chosen the worst.

He would know that she could see all that went beyond battle wounds: the fact that he had slipped into another world, another shape.

Why could she not have said, *If you had died, I would have, too. Because that is how much I love you.*

The ice eyes were impenetrable.

"You should not be here."

He pulled away from her, to sit up. To escape her touch. He did not know how hurt he was.

"Do not," she said frantically. "Wait." She slid across the bed with a speed that cared for nothing, out of it, reaching for the draught the king's physician had prepared.

Vervain.

"Just stay still. Take this." She turned, with a precious glass beaker in her hand. "Do not move."

He was lying quite still.

"What did you think I was going to do? Run amok and murder every inhabitant of the palace?"

He watched her with an expression she had never seen. She forced herself not to look away.

"Of course not. I just… The physician prepared a draught for you, the king's physician. He wanted me to give it to you as soon as you woke. It will heal…your body's hurts and help the pain."

He did not move.

"Will you not take it?"

"No."

"But you must." She could see, even in the thin dawn light spreading past the glow of the guttering candles, how the shadows clung round his eyes, the way the skin seemed stretched and thinner over the strong bones of his face.

"You must. Please."

"Is this where you ask me to do this for your sake?"

Her hand tightened on the glass with the memory of that night in the forest and her fear, and the first touch of his body. How she had yearned for him, despite their separation. He had taken her fear and released her from it. As he had released her from all the bonds of her past.

She looked at the price of that in his eyes.

"No. I will not ask such a thing of you again. Not for my sake."

The icy cold struck through her rumpled clothes. It had to be that which made her shake inside. Not the ice in his eyes. Because there was naught else she could expect, after what had happened.

What she wanted to do was to set him free of his bonds the way he had freed her. She wanted it to be over for him. But it was not. The nightmares still had their place inside the shadows of his eyes. Vervain slopped over the bedcovers.

She turned away.

"There is wine if you would rather have that." She found the silver-chased flask, picked up a pale green glass goblet decorated with blue tracery and poured. "It is Frankish." She turned back to the bed.

He took the glass out of her hand. The strong fingers bruised from the battle did not touch hers.

"There is food, too, if you could—"

"No."

The linen tied round his forearm and the strapping across his ribs caught the light.

She sat down on the wall bench. The cold in the room would kill her.

"King Cenred came to see you. They all came. The whole palace, I think. Modan. Your people—" *Not my father. Not Cunan.*

The words burning her mind forced their way out of her mouth. "I thought you would drown in the water."

"Aye."

That was all he said. No explanation and no denial. The coldness in the room was lethal.

"Why did you not drown?"

"It was not finished."

Her hands twisted. "And now it is?"

"Yes."

She looked round at the richly furnished bower, glowing in the firelight and the pearly dawn. It was not cold at all, not really, it was just her.

This was his place, everything, the English tapestries that hung on the walls, the English shapes of the carving on the cushioned wooden chair, the serpents etched in niello on the oil lamp, the Northumbrian air, all that was his: what he belonged to.

Give him your strength. The vast palace seemed to breathe round them like the sound of the sea. This was like his home. He still had possession of his home. If it, in turn, possessed him and all his thoughts instead of loss and treachery, then perhaps, just perhaps, he might find the peace that should always have been his.

Lindwood. Named not only for the linden trees in its woodlands but also because it meant a warrior's shield.

She stood up. Her fingers traced the intricate curving lines carved into the bedpost. She tried to smile.

"The king will give you a victory feast, and rewards, as you should have. You will need extra horses to carry home all your honour—What is it? What is the matter?"

"Naught."

She stared at the strained mask of his face.

"Let me call the physician—" But his eyes stopped her.

"What of your father?"

Her hands tightened on the carved wood until the chiselled edges dug into her flesh. She raised her head. Her eyes met the frozen waste of his and her voice took on the shape of the only weapon it had left, the bright-steel edge of irony she had learned from Brand.

"They are holding a mass for his deliverance tomorrow. King Cenred will be there. The king wants to give thanks that his ally was saved from the traitor Goadel who tried to kill him when he refused to aid the rebellion. It is a very good tale and everyone pretends to believe it. If you were well enough, they would ask you to go."

"I will go."

"What? How can you say that?"

"Because I would not have all that has happened be for naught."

"Oh, it will not be for naught. My father always survives. Cenred will let him go back to Pictland because it is too difficult to do otherwise. Because he wants to keep the peace treaty with Nechtán while he sorts out his own kingdom. Maol of the Picts will win. He can do nothing else."

"Not exactly. He is not going to try forcing Nechtán's hand again in a hurry."

"You do not know what he is."

"Alina, he has paid. The man nearly died."

She kept her gaze on the linen strapping, the bruised hands.

"So did you. He acted on his own choice, you did not."

"My decisions are my own. Always. Besides, I did not die."

Yes, you did. I can see it in your eyes. He made you do something you loathed and it haunts you with the power of hell-cræft, Hell's power.

"Where is he?"

"Maol? I know not, neither do I care." The wood scraped against her hand.

"You have not spoken to him at all?"

"I have naught to say."

The cold, fiercely-wrought face turned stone hard.

"Find him. Bring him here."

"What?" How could he ask that? How could he expect that of her? How could he not know what was in her thoughts? "Nay, that I will not."

"Then I will."

He moved, making her cry out with all the suppressed fear and bitterness in her heart.

"You cannot—"

The deep hidden currents below the ice in his eyes were suddenly and shockingly visible.

"Nay. That word no longer has meaning. It is no longer possible to say what I cannot do."

She turned, eyes blind, heart blind with the rage inside her. She wrenched open the door, blundered against someone coming in. He caught her, hands clutching at her flailing arms. She saw the bright gold ring with the stag-shaped device of the house of Nechtán, hands as bruised and cut as Brand's.

"You bastard."

"Daughter—"

"Do not call me that. Not after what you have done. I am no child of yours."

"No. Perhaps you are not."

The hands set her on her feet. It was the restraint of that gesture as much as the words that got through the wall of her fury.

"What…what do you mean?"

"That I know not whether you are of my getting or no. Is that something your mother did not tell you among the many things she said?"

The world shifted out of shape. She took a step

backwards, then another, all the way back across the room until her spine jarred against the wall. She stared at the arrogant, familiar, brown-bearded face. Her father.

"I do not believe you." She looked away, turned her head, primitive instinct, toward the one source of comfort there had ever been in her life.

Brand knew. Even though she had not. She could see it in the edge of pity that lapped at the coldness of his eyes. If he knew, then it was true. But he had no way of knowing.

Unless he had only guessed. The way he could see through people's inmost hearts to all the things about themselves they were too afraid to show. The things he must see in her face now.

"Alina."

His voice. His fierce body, heavy with muscle, the stuff of remembered dreams, moving across the bed in a tangle of finely woven wool and linen. He would come to her. He would touch her, and if she had his touch then somehow all would be well.

But the outstretched hand did not come to her. It reached across the small table to pour wine for her out of the silver-chased flask.

"I will do that." A broad hand with the Pictish emblem snaked forward to land on the flask. She had not even heard her father, Maol of the Picts, move.

The air in the bower suddenly seemed to vibrate, tingling with the primitive challenge that flared with the speed of lightning between men.

She had seen enough of such sudden volatile confrontations in her father's hall. Always, before, her father had stopped them, not begun them. Because for all his bullying, he was never reckless. Except when her mother—a small strangled sound escaped her throat. Both men turned.

It was Brand's hand that withdrew.

The sound of the rich wine filling the costly glass was like the clear running water of the stream.

"Take it," said her father.

"No."

"Alina! You will take it. You will drink it," shouted Maol of the Picts, blustering in his accustomed way, browbeating everyone to his will. "You will listen." The harsh voice choked on something. "Please."

The wine burned her throat, but nothing scorched through her mind like that single unfamiliar word. She turned her head, watching the stranger who had said it pace up and down the bower, awkwardly because of yesterday's stiffening hurts. His fault. Her mind screamed it. But she still watched him.

Yet now he had her attention and he knew it, he said nothing. The pacing stopped in a swirl of decorated wool.

"It was her fault," began Maol, dropping into Celtic. "My wife betrayed me, the—"

"Nay. Remember to whom you speak, and why." The same language, lightened by the tones of Strath-Clòta and tinged with Bernician, cut off the word. The voice held as much cracking ice as the blank-gold eyes. The challenge that had been there before stretched the air until it was unbreathable. Maol stepped backwards like someone who had taken a body blow.

"Tell me." Her voice hardly found substance in the dangerously thin air. "Tell me whether I am your child."

"I do not know." The air split.

CHAPTER FIFTEEN

SOMEONE WAS HOLDING HER HAND. She was still sitting on the bench and nothing had changed, not really. Things were just as they had always been. It was only that she had not understood their shapes before.

She blinked away the humiliating dark spots that had formed before her eyes. Weakness because she was so weary.

The heaviness of the hand curved around hers.

"Brand..." The thick gold ring engraved with the stag's mask bit into her skin. Not Brand's hand. Of course not. Brand's warmth was gone. She had no right to it.

"Alina."

She looked at her father's hand. No, not her father's. Probably. No one quite knew. Maol's hand. She did not know what to call him.

"Finish the wine."

This time it did not scorch her throat. She could not feel anything.

"I have to tell you. I have to make you know how it was. I should never have married your mother," said Maol. "But...it had to be done."

"For Pictland." She tried to keep nineteen years of bitterness out of her voice, but she could not. It made the hand vanish. Her last human contact.

"Yes."

She heard him get up. The terrible restless pacing resumed.

"For Pictland. We needed an alliance with the Britons and so it was made in all honour. Even though your mother's maidenhead was gone long before I bedded her. Even though she was already breeding when the vows were taken."

"Modan?"

"Yes." The first son. Her beloved brother. Mayhap.

"Then who—"

"Who had got him on my wife's body? Morcant. Need you ask it?"

A dark, lean face, arrogant laughing eyes jarred in her memory. Morcant of Strath-Clòta had been in her mother's train since she could remember. It had been he who had taken her mother back to Alcluyd with her two small children. He had always been there.

Until that last day when her mother had been forced to return to Pictland with the tears of hysteria streaming down her face.

"She must have loved him and—" She cut the shocked words off. Across the width of the room, the slow, heavy tread faltered, picked up again.

"Did you hate her?"

The heavy feet stopped.

"Is that the question of a child or a fool?" The man

called Maol turned round so that she could see his face. "I loved your mother to the depths of my soul. But she would have none of it."

The fine Rhenish glass slid out of her fingers. The faint musical sound as it shattered caught her senses, like the echo of her shattered world.

She had understood nothing of it at all.

"I would not let her make a fool out of me. I made sure, when she came back, that she never saw that whoremongering Briton again. She was my wife. It was me she was going to think of. Me who was going to be in her bed, and only me," spat the proud, arrogant, invincible Prince of the Picts. But the desperation in his face was visible.

Her unsteady feet scuffed the rushes as she stood, but he had already turned away.

"But whatever I said, whatever I did, made no difference. She was never mine. Just like Modan. Just like you. The only one who ever truly belonged to me was my bastard, Cunan."

The blood pulsed in her head.

"You married me into a kindred of savageness. You left Modan here to die."

He swung round.

"I made an advantageous match for you. I would have come for Modan."

"It would have been too late. Modan would have been dead. Just as I died inside when you gave me to Hun."

"No. It was only that you did not understand—"

"Oh, I understood. I understood full well that you did not love me. Even though I wanted you to love me the way I loved you. So much that I—" She cut the words off. Her damaged hand throbbed in the cold air where she held it out, a dumb, maimed witness to damage.

So much damage. Not just to her.

"I understand now why you cannot love me."

"No. It is not true—" The booted feet stumbled in their restless path, failed to right themselves. Then with horrifying suddenness, the figure in its fine Pictish clothes collapsed.

Her own feet crossed the chamber with a swiftness that was completely sure, even as the shock and disbelief blanked her mind. She dropped to her knees, her hand fastening on an outflung arm. His hand, buried in the sweet-smelling rushes, was coiled into a fist.

"Father—" He did not move. She stared at the bruised hand, the cut skin where Goadel had tied him. "Father."

She began shaking his arm like a madwoman, her damaged fingers sliding off his flesh. Then there was someone beside her, another presence, large, shadowing her. Her frantic hand was caught up, swallowed up by equally bruised fingers. The warrior berserker's hand. It was utterly safe.

"Brand."

He was there and he would help her with this, as with everything. Always. She forced the breath into her lungs.

"I cannot move him. He is too heavy." *Like you when I thought you were dead.*

"It is all right."

She let herself feel the living warmth of his presence beside her, drink in the incomparable steadiness of his voice. His free hand reached past the knot of their joined fingers towards her father's unmoving form, feeling for breath, for the life warmth.

"He is all right. It is just weakness. He lost blood yesterday and—"

"Like you."

"Fetch the bolster from the bed for his head and cloth and the water bowl, and some of the wine for when he wakes."

She did what he said, the numbness of body and mind responding to what had to be done.

She turned with the luxurious feather-stuffed pillow in her hands and looked at the helpless, sprawled-out figure. Then at Brand's bent head, the wide, muscular line of back and shoulder, the sure confident movement of his hands loosening the ties at the neck of her father's tunic. Maol's tunic.

Her father's.

She brought the bolster, kneeling down on the floor.

"I will lift his head and his shoulders."

"But you—"

"It is all right." Competent hands lifted the heaviness she would have dragged at. She slid the feather pillow under her father's head.

"Find the cloth."

"I do not know why you would help him. He almost caused your death. He would have deposed your king."

"Get me the wine."

The precious flask slipped in her left hand. He caught it, set the flask down. But her fingers remained trapped in his.

"How did you damage your hand?"

He had seen. He had guessed.

"A riding accident."

That was what she always said. It was the truth. And then she always... She found Brand's eyes.

"I took...Maol's horse."

She had said it and the world was still there. She kept speaking. "He had a new one. He wanted to try it out." Brand kept hold of her hand. "He took Cunan with him. He was going to let Cunan ride it. He would not take me. He never did."

She did not know why she said this. Now. When it could no longer matter. Because she was not Maol's daughter.

"I took the stallion he had left in the stables. I was ten winters old. I wanted to show I could ride. I wanted to go after them. After *him*. I wanted it so much that—"

The only thing she could feel was Brand's hand, his presence, the fact that he was there. That was how it always was. Even in the confines of the Wessex nunnery she had imagined he was there.

"I could not manage the horse, so it threw me. I did not die and it was actually Maol who found me. I thought things would change. I was only ten. But nothing changed. Only this."

She turned the crushed fingers on the steadiness of his palm.

"He had to apologize for the damage when he arranged my marriage with Goadel. He complained that it lessened the size of the morning gift Goadel would offer. I hated him for that." Her breath shivered.

"But you still wanted his love."

She could not even say the word *yes*. But Brand would know it. The way he always saw such things and understood. She felt the kind of acceptance that stopped people from turning mad with shame and grief and all the miserable hurts that life inflicted.

She watched her flesh lying against his and she thought of the way he had kissed her, taken her damaged fingers inside the passionate heat that was his, as though she were not hideous but something to be valued.

In a moment of time that had no future.

The heat surged through her again and her twisted fingers tangled with his, held there, and it was as though the power of the moment still had life, recaptured, and she was desired, deeply. Valued. Wanted in the way she had only ever known from him. She thought she felt the power of that vibrate through his skin.

But then his hand was moving, sliding away from

hers, placing the broken fingers on Maol's crumpled sleeve.

He poured water from the pitcher into the brass bowl and she found the linen, dipped it in, let the water flood over her hand.

"Why are you doing this? Helping him?" She tried not to tremble, just because he had touched her. Her hand pressed the damp cloth lightly against a brow etched with lines of high temper, the thinner skin at the temple.

"You have told me yourself. Cenred is having mass said for him. It is not for me to choose."

"I do not believe that is the reason."

"Then call it a debt payment."

Her eyes sought his.

"A—"

"He is waking."

Her gaze turned to the white face and the eyes the colour of Cunan's.

"Alina."

"Father." The word was past her lips before it had time to form in her head. But she did not call it back. Sometimes there were no choices.

The thin lips in the bloodless face moved with an effort that pained.

"I am sorry…for what I have done to you." The temper-harsh voice choked and she knew that the pain had not only been physical.

"It is all right."

"It will be." He levered himself upright and then

she was lost in his arms. The shock took her breath. He had never, never done that since she was the smallest child. She did not even know what his touch was like. Her hands lighted awkwardly on heavy shoulders bowed with more than forty winters of bitterness.

"It will be all right, my daughter. You have my promise. I will let you go where you wish. To Strath-Clòta."

Her hands on the unfamiliar shoulders shook.

"To *Strath-Clòta?*"

"I have said so. Did you think I would go back on a promise made in return for my life?"

"A promise? A promise to whom?" The coldness of the air choked off her words. The coldness of the room. Emptiness.

"It is my debt payment. The Northumbrian...the Northumbrian holds my word."

THE DARKNESS WAS COMPLETE, starless. Alina could not see the waves, only hear them surge against the rocks, like the voice of some ravenous beast. It was so restless, this Northumbrian sea. So unlike the deep waters of Alcluyd, the jewel of Strath-Clòta. She could see that other palace in its high place, bright with the gilding of childhood memories. *Alcluyd.*

He wanted her gone.

He had taken a life-price to make her father agree.

He could have died.

She did not have to turn to look at Northumbrian Bamburgh to see the light that burned in his chamber.

She wondered whether his kinsman, King Cenred, was still there. Or his people from Lindwood. Or Duda flashing silver like a real thane. That was his life. It was not hers.

He had given her freedom.

It was what she had wished since she had been a small child: freedom and her place in life. Now they were hers. A gift beyond price.

She turned, blind in the dark, her feet slipping on wet rock.

"What the devil do you think you are doing?"

The shape, blacker than the starless night, seemed to grow out of the rock as though it were not human.

Perhaps it was not.

It was the hellhound.

"Cunan."

He steadied her arm, so that she could regain her balance. But when she would have pulled away, he did not let go.

"Why are you not with him?" The bite in his voice was sharp, familiar.

"I have been. Why did you not come to him? He is your father—"

"Maol? Ah. It has been a family gathering, has it? Nay, my father will not want me when you and Modan are by. I never crowd family gatherings. You know that. Did you wish me to let you go?"

He released her, so abruptly she almost staggered again as he brushed past her, swaggering the way he always did, all but forcing her feet off the rock ledge.

She watched his back. The wind tore at her and then she saw it. It was as though the scales of misunderstanding that had fallen from her view of her father had cleared her sight of her half brother, too.

"Cunan."

She scrambled after him. The impossibly vulnerable figure stopped, but did not turn. She could not see his face in the blackness, not with her body's eyes. But she could with her mind.

"He has told me." The words struck against the wind. "He has told me what you knew all the time— that Modan and I may well be no more to him than you are. Less. Because at least there is no doubt you are of his blood."

The man who might or might not be her brother turned round. He moved, like a blacker patch of night, crowding her in the narrow treacherous space. But what she had always seen as a threat now seemed oddly empty, defenceless.

"He told me everything."

"Everything? He would have married my mother if that foreign trollop had not come. My mother was well enough born. But no, all he could see was that inconstant bitch from Strath-Clòta. And her children, his or not."

The black shape leaned over her, like something that could take the light from her. The way it always had. Abruptly, it wrenched away, leaving only the restless beat of the east wind. She spoke into its power.

"Do you want to know what else he said to me?"

"No."

She grabbed his arm, the way he had grabbed hers, swift and vicious as a hunting cat.

"He said that the only child of his who ever truly belonged to him was you."

The arm under her hand was tighter than a bowstring before the shot flies.

"Do you say that in truth?"

"I would not say it otherwise."

"No. I do not suppose you would. Do you know how much I hated Modan the firstborn all these years?"

"Yes."

The arm was not steady.

"And you. But then the feeling was mutual, was it not?"

The arm would have pulled out of her grasp, but she held on to it.

"No. Although it would have made my life much easier if I had. But I always thought of you as a true brother."

"A brother…"

The shadow of his head bent, as though he were staring at her hand where it rested on the blackness of his sleeve.

"It was you who would not believe it."

"You little fool."

This time she could not stop the movement of his arm. It flicked up with a trained warrior's strength and then his hand caught her, held her in the same grip. It hurt.

"You will not have to bear with me much longer," she said to his black shadow. "Maol has agreed I may go to Strath-Clòta." She spoke very evenly through the deliberate pain of his grip. She was not afraid.

"Do you not have it in you to wish me Godspeed?"

He moved, one pool of blackness forming and re-shaping itself out of another.

"Yes. I have that in me."

His voice was lightless as his shape. Black as she felt. His breath hissed past her ear.

"Then do so."

She raised her head, but the hissing sound against her frozen skin was laughter, mirthless, striking at both of them.

"Nay. I will not. There are limits, Alina, even for me. I would have thought there should be for you. It was not Maol I believed you were with this day."

Her heart thudded.

"Where else could I be?" The thin laughter hissed like daggers through her skin. She gathered her breath. "You do not know. You cannot know what he has done. It was he who made my father let me go to Strath-Clòta."

"So he did. I was there when he asked. I grant that you were not, but even so... I thought you were at least beginning to discern the difference between what people say and what people want."

"But—" The beating of her heart would choke her. "I do not believe you."

"No, indeed. Lack of belief, my dear…sister. Lack of belief. Were we not both blinded by it? You may continue to be so if you wish. I give you your choice. Call it payment."

"Payment? For what?"

"A life-price."

The blackness of him was swallowed up by the clear air of Bernicia.

SHE CONTEMPLATED CRAWLING back into his bed.

There was no light in his chamber now, not even a candle glow. Not even a fire.

That should not be.

She passed through the doorway. There had been no king's man outside it, no guard with red-and-white insignia, just a small heap that was a proper thane with a silver arm ring. It chose not to move when she stepped over it.

That had to be a good sign. She shut the door.

The blackness inside was complete.

Cunan, the hellhound, the true brother, had to be wrong.

A life-price.

That was what she owed. Just like Maol. Just like Cunan.

No one had more debts than she did.

She took a step into the unknown.

It was so dark. Night's cold stabbed at her. Why did he not have a fire? She crept forward, trying to remember the layout of the bower, where the table was, the wall bench, the ridiculously extravagant chair with embroidered cushions.

She stopped at the black bulk of the bed. The curtains were drawn across it. She touched heavy cloth embroidered with silk, pulled it back.

Cold air swirled across her face. So dark, so very dark. Her senses strained in the blackness to see that familiar form, to hear his breath, the faintest rustle of movement, anything but this blackness that froze her blood.

"I can never understand how you get as far as you manage to." Her fist closed over the embroidered material, nearly dragging it down on the bed.

"What did you do, break Duda's nose again?"

He was by the window. She realized for the first time that there was actually a small shaft of moonlight breaking the clouds in the wind-driven sky, finding the partly open shutters. That was where the cold air was coming from.

"You will freeze." The words were out of her mouth before she had time to stop them. Then through the fierce beating of her heart, "Did I really break his nose before?"

"Hard to tell with Duda. It does not seem to worry him."

"He showed me all that you gave him, the silver and the clothes."

"Did he so?"

"Aye."

There was the kind of silence that went fathoms

deep and was not touched by words that glided on the surface.

"Why are you sitting there?"

"Because it is cold. Why were you trying to get into my bed?"

She looked at the dark, formidable bulk gathered in beside the window, blocking out the thin thread of moonlight, seeking the same coldness that was in his voice.

Cunan was wrong.

The difference between what people say and what people want.

"I was getting into your bed because it is what I wanted. I thought you might like it. I thought we had some—" she made the next words come out "—unfinished business." Her skin started to shiver and her heart beat like a savage's.

"I thought you might show me...the rest." She spoke it in Celtic, softly. The black shadow that was him never moved, except to draw coldness round it like a shroud. The moonlight vanished, blocked by the clouds outside in the Bernician sky.

"Nay." The English word shook her. "We have gone past that, Alina. It is far too late."

You are wrong, Cunan, wrong.

"Is that why you wanted me to go back to Strath-Clòta?"

The black bulk did not move. She could not see his face, could guess at nothing, only the coldness.

"Aye."

She took a step forward.

Wrong.

"Suppose I do not wish to go?"

"Then you will go back to Pictland and sooner or later Nechtán will make another match for you, and your father will not be able to prevent it, even if he should wish to."

She could feel the coldness gripping round her heart, the coldness of the room, of his voice, of her future without him.

"There is naught else, Alina. Nothing left."

The coldness would surely kill her. She took another step, but her foot would not move. There was no strength in it. She had no right to be here. There was nothing she could say or do that had any power over the future, or the past.

Moonlight struck through the blackness and just for a moment she could guess his face.

The space between them vanished.

"I will not go." Her voice was as strong as steel. "Not to Strath-Clòta, not to Pictland, not anywhere. Not yet."

"What do you mean?" The steel was met in kind. She struggled for her breath, to hold on to that one glimpse she had had of his face. *What people want.*

"I mean that I have somewhere else to go first."

"What are you saying?" The dark bulk rearranged itself with a suddenness that drew crawling fright down her backbone. He was naked. She could sense all the power of him, leashed, burning through his fine supple skin. She closed her mind against the memory of the way he had looked when he was baiting Cunan, poised and ready to strike.

Cunan the hellhound, who for once in his life had to be right.

She tilted her head.

"I have told you already." She undid her girdle with a speed that defied sight. "Your bed."

"You—"

She ignored the danger and stepped into the twisting serpent shadows of the moonlight. The girdle hit the floor.

Duda had said his master was not as good at being impulsive as one might wish. This was her test. She undid the ties of her gown.

"If I am going to be another marriage sacrifice, or if I am going to live out my own life at Alcluyd, I will not go without knowing all there is to know about you, about…" Her voice failed over the word. She swallowed. There were only moments. That was how life was. But sometimes moments could hold eternity.

"I want to know all about love," she said. "Not just the pleasure, but all there is, whatever it means and whatever the consequences."

She dragged the gown over her head, in one sweeping movement. Her shift was of Byzantine silk, woven so thinly it was almost transparent. All the curves and hollows of her body must be visible in the moonlight.

Coldness struck at her skin like claws. There was no protection from it.

He did not move.
She said the last piece of truth.
"I am afraid."

CHAPTER SIXTEEN

SHE BURNED HIM, inside and out. The touch of her skin on his was like fire. Because he was some frozen creature out of the depths of hell. But she burned it away.

His mouth took hers, crushed it, crushed her. Because she was the only thing that could drag him out of the freezing dark. He heard the sound of her breath and felt the hot softness of her flesh cleave to his and there was nothing in the world except that, and he was falling, with her, joined, his own body twisting beneath her like a rolling battle fall to take her weight. Shoulder and hip touched not the rush-strewn floor but the softness of the overstuffed bed. He had no recollection of carrying her there.

No recollection.

Which only showed what a *hell-thane* he was. And she had said she was afraid.

His hands froze on her body.

"Alina, do not try and do this." The words were harsh blackness against the deeper night dark of her hair. "I am not worth it." His breath rasped. "I cannot—" The word he never said choked off in his throat. There was darkness. And the small brutal sound of her sobbing breath.

He rolled away and that movement brought all the pain he should have felt before and had not. He kept his body and his mind utterly still, staring at the blackness above.

He had to speak.

"I cannot—"

"I understand what you would say and I understand why." Her voice cut across his, clear and bright as a blade. She was still speaking in Celtic.

"You cannot forgive me for all that happened."

Her words struck through him.

No, it is not that. The denial, instant, blood-searing, beat against his mouth with a force beyond thought. But it was the abandonment of the mind's power that held hell's torments.

"I understand why," said the brilliant clearness of her voice. If he said *yes* she would leave him. She would go back to Strath-Clòta and she would be safe. Always.

"It is because it is my fault." She was shaking. He knew that, even though he was not touching her. He did not have to touch Alina with his body. "I understand that—"

The untruth of it would eat through bone. It was beyond him to let her believe it.

"It is not true." His voice obliterated hers. "What happened was not your fault, none of it."

"But—"

"The blame lies with Hun's brutality and Goadel's ambition." He tried to master the black fury at the damage that had been done, the thought of the far greater harm that had so nearly happened.

"They are dead now, both of them—" He could not think of yesterday.

He turned back to face her in the dark and the bruised bones jarred with a pain that made him grit his teeth. But it was ordinary. Quite ordinary.

"They are gone and the only way they can cause more harm is if you allow them to. Let them lie."

He heard the long drawn-out thread of her breath.

"But they should not have had the power to harm you or your brother when all this began."

"We were Cenred's kin. Harm would always have come to us. That harm should not have touched you."

"But if I had not gone away with you, if I had not done something so madly reckless, made you do it—"

"The decision was mine."

"It was madness."

"No. What I did was no fleeting impulse to be disavowed later." He caught his breath on such dangerous ground, but he could see the small restless movements of her body, like a soul that can find no peace.

"You cannot mean that."

He could not watch that sort of pain.

"It is true. I tried to tell you so that day when I spoke to Cunan. It was you I wanted to speak to. Your understanding I wanted."

But the agitated movements increased. He wanted to still them with his touch, to take that small fragile body in his arms and take its pain and its hurts with all the dammed-up force of love inside him. But his love was not right for her and it was her very fragility which defeated him.

"You do not have to tell me why you rescued me from Hun," she said. "I know that. You did it because of what you are. Because you see too much and understand too much about people and why they do all the helpless, selfish, inadequate things that they do. And you are not put off by it. You have too much pity and too much...too much kindness for people. For me. Because when it came down to it, I was as helpless and inadequate as all the rest."

"That is why you thought I took you from Hun? Because I felt sorry for your...your helplessness and inadequacy?" He tried to get breath through the battered wreck of his ribs. But all the air in the room, all the cold piercing freshness of Bamburgh had vanished, leaving nothing in the pain-struck mass of his chest.

"Yes. And that is why I left you. Because you had too much honour and too much pity and I could not stand it. I could not stand the price I had made you pay for me. I took everything from you—the life that you lived, your honour, your home, all that you owned. I thought I had killed your brother. That is why I went."

"You—you left me for my sake?"

"Yes. But perhaps there was a thread of selfishness even in that." The bitterness in her voice tore through all that was left of himself.

"Perhaps in my heart I would rather that you hated me for leaving you than for staying. And yet despite all the…the helplessness and inadequacy in me, I would have walked barefoot the length of Britain if I could have taken any of that pain away from you."

"To take the pain away? Do you have any idea what it was like to think that you were dead? To believe that being with me was so insupportable to you that it forced you into a flight back to a creature who would destroy people for greed, or for enjoyment? That your flight was so wild and so desperate that it caused your death?"

He felt her move in the stifling engulfing blackness of the bed. He stopped his voice. What he said belonged to that blackness, intensified it. He fought for control over voice and breathing and all the wildly pressing feelings of his heart.

"I thought you had left me because of all I had lost, because I had nothing left to give, not even adequate protection. You asked why I was so ready to believe you were dead, that you would not come back. But I knew it would happen, somehow. It was almost as though part of me expected it, as though your leaving had to happen. Because what we had could not last. Because such things never do."

The need to touch her, to force some connection out of the blackness, was almost more than he could prevent. But it was not fit and even as he moved, her body twisted, sliding round in the dark, widening the space between them. The words he had to say to set her free came out.

"I failed you."

He got up, because he could no longer bear to be so near her and not be able to touch her. Because the separation between them was something that could not be overcome. Nay, worse: something that should not.

The welcoming cold struck his naked body. Somehow he got as far as the window and the air. He wrenched the shutter fully open and the ice wind of the coming autumn beat against his skin, cutting through it as though it was not there, until it found its place round his heart.

Behind him he could hear the rustling of the bedcovers as she moved. She made a small sound like someone in torment and he turned his head because he always would for her, even if she were not his.

Perhaps she still felt pity for him. The kind of pity that had driven her through heaven knew what dangers into Wessex, because she did not want to harm him. Her pity was like a rope made of steel, if such a thing could have been fashioned. It never let go, not even of her dangerous and tormented family.

"It is over, Alina." The words seemed stuck in the frozen column of his throat. He forced them out. "There cannot be a future for us, however much we have tried to make it so. I cannot undo the harm I have done you, but I would not cause more."

"That is not what I fear."

But it was. *I am afraid.* The way he had touched her with such wildness. The way he had slipped the bonds of control when he had killed Goadel. Such a thing would never be out of his mind. That he was like a savage. Because of what was inside him.

He had to cut the tie of her pity. He stared back into the blackness of the room.

"If you are not afraid, you should be." The coldness of the air, blessing and bane, took everything. She must have heard it in his voice, sensed the death grip of it.

"You must go, Alina, while you can. Go to Strath-Clòta. There will not be another chance." It was so hard-won, that freedom for her, so fragile just as she was.

"You will be safe at Alcluyd. You said it was the only place you were ever happy. That what you wanted was your own place in the world. I could not give you that before. I can now."

He turned back to the open window and the cold seared him as though it had the sting of fire.

"Take that of me at least." His voice splintered on the ice. He forced the last words out.

"I have nothing else."

ALINA CRAWLED OVER THE BED.

She stared at the lethal black profile outlined in the

wash of moonlight. Shadows and silver light like ice crystals.

The wildly tangled bedcovers slid off her legs. There was silence. Nothing moved except the thick, painful beating of her heart.

The moonlight showed her every plane and every ridged muscle of his shoulders. The rest fell into the unknown dark. The only other gleam she could make out was the white line of the linen strapping round his chest. She could not even see the goldness of his hair.

She swung her legs over the edge of the bed. Coldness. Freezing.

There were choices and there were things beyond that.

We will abide this together. Always.

His skin was colder than it had been when she had thought he had drowned in the clear rushing water of the river. Rigid muscle moved.

"Don't—" It was not so much a word as a sound, a sound that had the intensity of some great beast of prey that would kill itself or others before it would fall to a hunter's spear.

She kept her hand where it was and the coldness of him seeped through her fingers.

"I will not go." Her hand spread out across the frozen flesh. She hoped it was not shaking. "Not yet."

"Not *yet*." The great head turned with a speed that was savage. His eyes, in the shadows, were not gold at all but black.

"Not yet? Then when? When we have completed

our—unfinished business? When I have bedded you as though I were some stag in the rut? Because that is what I would do, Alina. Is that what you want?"

She saw the direction of the black gaze, on her hand where it lay on the moon-silvered skin of his arm.

"Believe me, it is not what you would want."

The harshness in his words, in his gaze, hurt like the cold.

"I—"

"What? What will you say? That that would be a fitting ending to all the futility that we have shared? That after it you will go?"

She could feel the coldness right inside her now, blighting all she had. It would freeze her mind and she would not be able to think. Already she felt the dizzy sickness of that cold. It would freeze her heart, rob her senses and she would drop where she stood, right here on the floor among the rushes. Just like—there was no reason to think of her father. None at all.

"Go now, while there is something left that is not marred."

No reason to think of her father. Brand was not like him.

But he had known, where she had not, that her father had not been able to express what was inside his heart.

Her father with his desperate love. With his desperate selfishness.

Brand did not deal in selfishness. He did not try to trap people.

She looked up.

"I will not leave, either to go to Strath-Clòta or to Pictland." Her words cleaved through the darkness. "Where I will go is to Lindwood near Jarrow. I will not leave until you come with me."

He did not speak and his eyes did not change. Neither did his will. It was the way a warrior defeated an opponent in battle. She did not have what it took to withstand that. She did not have what he needed, and her defeat seemed final.

But she was touching him, with her fingers splayed out on his flesh as though she were the lover she was not. The skin of palm and fingertips, more responsive than thought, lay against his. And so she felt it, through painfully stretched senses, the jolt inside that he could not disguise. She felt its rawness and uncontrollable depth, and it was doubly grievous because he would not let that break either the warrior's training or the steady citadel of his mind.

She did not know whether what she did held any rightness at all, or only more harm. She only knew that she could not stop.

"Then tell me," she said, holding her head as though there was no fear and no possibility of destructive loss. "Tell me why not."

"There is no need of words. You have seen it."

They were not the words she had expected. No bitterness. No blade-sharp assessment of why she was not good enough. Just a statement of something that was, and behind it the grief held in.

"I do not understand."

"You saw what lives in me. Yesterday. When I fought Goadel. You saw what happened, and I saw the horror of it in your eyes."

"No..."

"There is no longer room for lies between us, not even a lie out of pity. You were horror-struck. You were afraid of me. You still are."

"No." Her fingers tightened on the tense, lethal pad of muscle under her hand and she knew it would not harm her. It would die first. That was what she had seen. "I was not afraid of you."

Her eyes caught the darkness of his gaze, tried to hold it. There was gold there, somewhere. Gold was imperishable. She saw it in the gleam of moonlight as his head turned to hers as though drawn by some invisible thread. Like a Saxon's fate thread.

She did not know whether the light she could see was fire or ice. Both burned, and it was not mere gold that was imperishable, it was the essence of him, the measure of the soul's power. His eyes held hers.

"Can you not see the truth of it, Alina? Can you not know that I was afraid? Of myself and of what I did."

It was not a truth any man ever admitted. But the soul's power never wavered. The words hung in the air, like a gift made beyond price. She could not requite it. She did not think she had that much courage, or clearness of mind. Or unselfishness.

But she could not leave him like this.

Her hands tightened on the warrior's muscle adorned with the gold that betokened his rank.

She and her brawling arrogant family had taken from him something there was no way to replace.

"You must hate me so much."

"Do you think I could have done what I did from hate?"

Clarity of thought. Single-mindedness. He had said that she had that. He had seen in her things that she had been too afraid to see for herself.

Perhaps she had the courage.

Perhaps she could see, with his eyes.

"You loved me, all the time. But I never let myself believe it was so."

The moon darkness covered everything and the silence held, so that the truth, if it was there, stayed hidden.

But even if she had destroyed what had been there for her, all that he had given and she had not seen, even if it was dead, there was still so much left to be redeemed.

For him.

Her fingers left small white dents on his skin.

If she could.

Her broken fingers straightened out on his frozen, unmoving flesh. There had to be warmth there, somewhere. She would find it. In her head, she started praying to Saint Dwyn. For the right words, the ones that would set him free.

"You thought you were like a berserker, did you not?" The arm nearly ripped out of her grasp but she held on to it. Even though she had no strength, not in that hand. She looked at the crushed shapes of her fingers on his arm. He knew her weakness. He would not use one quarter of his force in case he hurt her.

She began to know what to say.

"You thought you had called up a berserk fury like a wolf skin." She knew the kind of nightmares that haunted Saxons. "You thought you were like one who is so mad with it that they feel not their wounds and kill whatever they see. You thought the way you had fought Goadel was like a *berserker-gang*."

"How else would you describe it?"

"Quite differently."

She sat down next to him on the wall bench. She slid her hand down the lethal length of his arm, so that she ended up with his hand caught in hers.

"You think it was the result of a complete lack of control." She arranged herself with careful elegance on the cushioned seat. "I would say it was the result of too much control."

She tilted back her head and stared at him.

His eyes were like twin slits of ice.

"You were afraid of me. You still are."

Northumbrian bastard. He could tell she was trembling. She wished for once in his life he would stop weighing things up.

His eyes pinned her.

"You told me you were afraid."

She glared right back.

"What I am afraid of now is the same thing I was afraid of yesterday, and that is of losing you. And," she said, before he could draw breath, "if you are going to catch me with my words, I will catch you with yours. You said you could not have done what you did from hate."

She heard the trapped breath. She would catch him indeed. She lunged like a fighting cat.

"What you did was no random act of mad fury. It was a carefully calculated decision. You made it because you had already been hurt rescuing my half brother, who has a much better claim to craziness... And because what I did forced your hand."

"No," she said to the sudden move of his head and the fierce glitter of his eyes. "Let me say what I will. You made a tactical decision, just the way you always do, even though it meant that you had to do the one thing you hated above all else, something that must have made your skin crawl with loathing, something your soul recoils from even now."

"Alina—"

He might thrash about in her trap but there would be no escape.

"You did it for me." She took a breath that made her lungs shake. "For me and for my appalling family and for everyone else who was there, so they would not be killed. Do you deny that?"

"For me to fight with Goadel was the only sane choice. It—" He broke off. He saw the trap. She felt the breath that he took and the pain of it, as though it were hers.

"It was the way I did it, not what I did."

Black muscle moved beside her. Outside the fine chamber, the restless sea beat against the rocks. The darkness poured in through the open window and with it the cold.

But there was moonlight. It silvered his skin and the coiling richness of his hair.

"I do not think you had any other choice once you had made your decision."

"The other choice—"

"Would have been to sacrifice my father and perhaps me, and to take all of Goadel's men by battle. I do not think you would have chosen that. You did not want such harm."

The black muscle condensed. She would not be able to hold it. The trap would not be tight enough.

"You did not want harm to come to me." If she watched his eyes, she would be able to see past the ice.

She tried to hold his gaze with all of her will because even now he would be able to escape her with one turn of his head, with the slightest movement of thick-ridged flesh against the useless barrier of her hand.

She fixed her face into a line as implacable as his.

"Do you know what else I think? I think you did not actually achieve what you believe you did."

He was like a great black shadow, moonlight and moving air currents wrapped round him.

"Nay. In that you are utterly wrong."

He had not denied anything else. Her heart hammered.

"It is you who are wrong."

Flexible muscle slid against her flesh.

"You were wrong. I believe that you thought, even in the middle of what was a death struggle. You had planned it all, what your men should do, how they were going to protect my father and me. You wanted to see that carried out. I think you waited until everything was in place before you really struck. That is true, is it not?"

The moonlight showed her his eyes.

"Tell me of a wounded berserker who could do that?"

"I did not even feel the wound. I did not know."

"I think you would not let yourself feel it because it would have disabled you. Such things are possible."

The trap was all around him. It would hold him. She would. Her hand tightened on his, but that was a mistake, some terrible miscalculation, because the thick flesh under hers flexed and there was nothing under her hand, emptiness. She had lost even the touch of him.

"Brand—"

Her hand reached out in desperation for him, sought his hand, his arm, *him*. He stilled. But his face was frozen.

"Do not touch me."

She followed his gaze to look at her hand on his

arm, the pathetic fingers that could not hold his strength, and she understood.

"I know what you are truly afraid of. You are afraid you might hurt me." The snare snapped tight.

His arm slid out from under her grasp and he was too strong for her to hold him, even though the noose was tight round him like something he could not escape. She had not foreseen the cruelty of that.

"It is not true. I know it. You would never harm me."

"You are afraid of me, even now. I think you have always been afraid of me."

"No..." Her voice sounded horror-struck and she cursed her weakness because he would not understand why. She cursed her fears through all the times she had known him, and the times she had let him see them.

She stared at the moonlit dark.

"I have been afraid of so many things. But never that you would harm me, not even when it seemed as though you had every reason. All that you have ever done since I have known you has been for my good and not for my harm. I have never trusted anyone as much as I have trusted you."

She thought he would turn away from her. He did not. The soul's power.

"That is what I cannot break," he said.

She could not touch him. He would not allow it. But she did not have to touch him to know the tension in every ice-sheeted muscle. Even if she had not been able to see him, the very air around him would have told her.

"You could not harm me, not you of all people."

She sensed, as much as saw, the rustle of his movement, the way all that matchless strength collected itself into one force of intensity.

"How can you say that? How can I?"

Saint Dwyn grant me the words.

"Because I know you. At last. Completely and beyond mistake."

"You do not. You have not understood." The intensity of the way he felt would withstand fire. She could not break it. All she could do was help him to break it.

"I do not believe you." It sounded merely stubborn, willful. Yet she felt the intensity sharpen. That was good. If he was angry, that was very good.

She stood up, head high. Somehow she found the power to keep her feet. Her stance settled into the same seeming willfulness as her tone.

She could feel his anger. She guessed all that it hid.

"Alina, can you not understand?"

"No."

True and not true, as ever. She left it at that and walked across the room, her thin shift billowing in the moving air. The cold seemed to burn her skin, like his gaze. She took her time over every step, the way she used to walk across the great hall at Craig Phádraig when the kind of baffled rage he was feeling pressed on her own heart.

But she had never had to face what he did.

She found what she wanted in the blackness beside the richly curtained bed. Simple. She picked it up.

"Because I do not understand, you will have to show me." The snake-patterned hilt slipped into her hand. She adjusted her grip, moving her thumb all the way round the gold-wired hilt. She unsheathed. The rune-blade made a sound that was colder to the human ear than the winter frost that could crack stones.

"What in the name of the saints are you doing?"

One saint.

The saint who took pity on lovers.

She cast the gilt-chased scabbard aside. She turned round with a length of three feet of lethal steel in her hand.

"I do what I will. Always."

"Put that down—"

She jerked the sword upright in her hand as a length of about six feet of lethal Northumbrian uncoiled itself from the window seat.

"Make me."

She tightened her grip.

"I do not know what you think you are about."

Making you angry enough to want to kill me. But you will not, because you will not be able to.

"Put it down. You will hurt yourself."

Perfect reply for an insane berserker.

"Take it off me then. It will be the only way."

She waved the blade, it tilted crazily. Light sparked off its edges. She could see the elk-sedge rune on the cross guard close to her hand, moon-white in the darkness. Her eyes dazzled. Brand moved.

The shadows and the moonlit ice that made up his body blocked everything else from her sight. The brutally shadowed gaze caught hers. There was gold behind that darkness. She knew there was. She got the blade under control. More or less.

"I will take the sword."

So you will.

Shivers ran down her spine as he began circling her, moving to the right, out of the sword's range but crowding her with his size, the precisely placed movement of his naked feet. Her own body twisted round, following that deadly quiet pacing so that she could keep him in sight.

Despite the pain in his ribs that he must feel, he moved with a sinuous ease she could not match. His gaze seemed fastened not on the flickering gleam of the sword that she could not hold steady, but on her eyes.

Modan had said that you could tell what your enemy would do by looking into his eyes.

She could not tell anything.

She tried to hold that black gaze, but she could not even do that much. Her eyes kept straying to the light and shadow of his body as it moved in that feral dance, lithe despite the wounds, utterly full of purpose. Solid, close-linked muscle tightened and stretched under gleaming skin, everything collected into a controlled, sinuously moving power, from the wide shoulders, the dense torso and compact hips to the springing, curving line of arm and leg muscle.

Controlled.

She smiled. Even though her heart beat so fast it would choke her breath.

The circling steps moved closer, pushing her back towards the wall. She fought for breath, forcing the instinctive smile to broaden, change, become taunting at the edges.

She straightened her arm, extending the sword in a futile attempt to widen that dangerous circle. Her muscles ached already from the awkwardly held weight of the blade, from trying to control its blinding power. She could not imagine how people fought with such things, except that was what she was doing. For him.

That was the key. It was a sword of protection. It was branded as such, with an Atheling's rune. She was no runemaster but she and Brand had been born Athelings, princes. The sword had spoken to her. She knew it spoke to him.

The smile on her face stretched her skin.

"What are you waiting for?"

She waved the tip of the blade. It sliced small deadly circles through the charged air. He did not step back, so she did, her breath catching. Because the battle-sharp steel was far too close to the bare sheet of his skin.

"Well?" she said, pinning the sneer back in place. She could not take much more of this. Her uncertain feet stumbled, nearly sending her sprawling backwards over a stool she had not seen behind her. That made the narrowed intensity of his eyes flash with all the fury she could wish for.

She realized she was cornered. She blundered left, but there was no room. She stumbled, fighting for balance, trying not to wave the sword in case she hit him.

"Stay away—" she yelled, her voice not taunting but deadly earnest this time, because she did not know whether she could control the lethal length of steel.

Idiot, shouted the sane half of her brain, *reckless idiot.* But then he was there.

She saw the moon-silvered shape gather itself, the solid thigh muscle flex, the abdomen tighten. The wide shoulders became straight. Her vision filled with the dark-gleaming wall of his chest, his hand found hers, found the sword hilt, yanked it out of her grasp with a strength that was full of wild fury, matchlessly reassuring.

The breath left her throat. She did not so much as attempt resistance. Because what she had done was far too dangerous, more so than she had thought.

Because she had what she had wanted: him armed and dangerous, angry beyond belief.

CHAPTER SEVENTEEN

No one moved.

He was jammed against her in the narrow space between the massive curtained bed and the wall.

Alina could feel every part of Brand's body, the flat tautness of his belly, the sinfully rich swell of his thighs pressed against her. Her gaze saw nothing but the broad immovable barrier of his flesh, the skin ice-cold, bleached of colour by the moon's light. She could see its whiteness and its blue-black shadows, so close her sight could pick out each of the small dark body hairs that dusted the centre of his chest, blossomed round each taut flat nipple.

The wildness of his breath fought against the ice-locked wall of his chest, swelled the tight curve of muscle above the confining band of linen.

"Why in the name of all the saints would you have done such a thing?"

For Saint Dwyn's sake, who can release people from bonds of frozen ice.

"You could have been hurt."

She raised her head.

"No. I could not." She did not know why Modan

had thought it was possible to hold your opponent's gaze during a duel to the death. "That is the point."

She watched the rapid leap of understanding and all that came after it.

"Do you mean to say that is what all this madness was about? Some insane kind of test to see what I would do?"

"Nay. I knew what you would do. It was only you who did not."

"I should run you through with the blade for that."

The sword rested in its natural home, like some obedient extension of his lethal arm. She stared at it, as the less deadly alternative to looking into his eyes.

"Nay, Atheling, we both know that is an empty vaunt." She felt all the hard-packed muscle crowded against her tighten into steel. If you questioned a warrior's boast, they had to prove it. Always.

She felt a large, battle-roughened hand close over her jaw, lifting her face with an exquisitely slow inexorability.

"Why?"

She did not know what the question was. She was just utterly lost in his eyes.

She answered what had suddenly become the smaller question, because she could not cope with anything else.

"Duda says you do not know yourself."

"*Duda?* What has he got to do with—"

"He says you are not nearly as good at being impulsive as you think you are. I think he is right. I...I wanted you to know. Now that you do, it is all right. I...I will go to Strath-Clòta. As you wish."

The Northumbrian word he used did not lie within her knowledge of English. But she did not need to know the finer details. She could see through the brightness of his eyes. She could see what her heart wanted to see more than anything, the knowledge that inside the anger he had been afraid for her. Her heart clenched and the world's shape changed again.

His eyes were not cold, not ice locked at all. They burned, with a heat that could sear straight through her. The same heat was in his skin, in the touch of his hand on her flesh.

She stared at him, at the naked, fiercely-honed strength, the thickness of each separate male muscle, the finely-held stance, the sword balanced easily in his hand. She stared at his eyes, the heat and the wild edge and the liquid melting depths. His eyes were quite gold. No shadow could disguise that. They held the fascinating hint of bated dangers and all the achingly needed safety of tenderness.

The haughty mask that had served her for so long slipped. She could not keep the consciousness out of her face because she knew, now, how things were. He had stirred that knowledge in her with his touch and his passion and his own knowing, and she would never be ignorant of it again.

His eyes read what she could not hide: the need inside her and the wildly-beating wanting that were the mirror image of his. That recognition of her desire, the flare it brought in the flame-gold eyes sent an erotic jolt through skin and sinew and blood, and the way he held her, flesh joined to flesh took on a different edge. His strength was the most blatantly exciting thing she had felt. Her body thrummed with an aliveness, a hunger, it was impossible to deny.

The proud head bent to hers. She watched it and her skin tingled because of his nearness. His face blurred, just the harshness of dark gold stubble, the fierce rise of his cheekbone.

"I would rather take up your first offer."

"What—" Her breath whispered with his, joining with it in the same heat.

"My bed."

She caught the gleam of his eyes. The softness of the mattress hit her back with a satisfying thud. The thick bed linen smelt of herbs. Vervain that conciliated hearts. Her breath caught and she clung to him.

He did not let her go. His touch held all the thwarted passion and all the savage pain of what had been. Yet there was nothing in it that could make her fear and as his body moved against hers, his skin and his hair caught the slanting gleam of the moon's rays through the open window. That was what she saw and what she felt, the brightness of the light.

She held him softly because of the wounds, moulding the slightness of her body against his so that he would feel the warmth. She ran her hands over every undamaged inch of him so that she could stroke his skin, know with her touch each of the battle-hard mus-

cles she had seen, learn every lean length and every
tight curve, every taut expanse of rough-smooth warm-
ness or satin heat.

But mostly so that he could know she was there.

She felt only the madness of excitement when his
hands freed her of her shift. His gaze touched her
with the same fiercely felt hunger as his hands.

The effort it took to lie quite still, bared to the cold
silver light of the moon and the molten heat of his
gaze, was not what she expected. Her mind antici-
pated the cloying rush of shame but it did not come,
or else the heat in his eyes burned through it.

There was nothing but the glittering awareness of
desire, fathoms deep and real, all the searing intensity she had believed no man could feel for her. The
knowledge that it was there sent a surge of pure wildness through her blood, so that her body arched and
writhed, just because he watched her. The heat
washed through her in waves, gathering the tightness
in her lower belly, making her ache for the shattering
release he had given her before under the wideness of
the summer sky.

She touched him. Her hand found the richly taut
curve of his bent thigh, the hot flesh, then the dark
springing hair and the smooth living hardness she
had touched once before. His skin was damp. His
heat scorched. Her hand slid round, feeling the first
beading of his seed, slippery and hot between their
joined skins.

The jolt that went through him might as well have

hit her own heart. She heard the rough sharpness of his breath and then his body pulled away, beyond her reach. The small sound of desperation on her lips was something she could not stop.

"Nay, wait." His voice was harsh, night-black. But she felt no fear. Her own voice, locked in the tightness of her throat, might have sounded as harsh if she could have formed words, and the dark was not deadly, but something shared. Lovers' night.

She felt the faint tantalizing brush of his hair as his head bent over her, the warmth of his breath on the pulsing dampness of her skin. Her hands sought his arms, the glistening width of his shoulders, holding him harder than she meant.

"Hush, I will not leave you." The words were in her language, like music, like clear running water.

"That is what I want." Her voice was no more than a whisper of breath in the darkness and they might have been back on that first night, flying through the dark from this very place. Together. But this time she could not bear restraint because of an uncertain future. She would not.

"I want all. For us. Now."

"And so you shall have all you wish. But let me show you as I will. There will be some hurt for you the first time. I cannot help that. But also what pleasure there will be, you know."

"Because you showed me that."

"Not all. Not yet."

The heat and the promise and the feel of him so

close made her head dizzy and her body ache with the need of him. Her hands tightened, her fingers digging into his flesh so that she must have hurt him, but he did not move.

His eyes watched her face as though they sought something there, and she wanted to blurt out with all her soul that she loved him. But she did not, because she did not know if her love would be peace for him after this, or another burden. She only knew that what they had now encompassed all, in a single moment.

"Then—" Her voice choked.

"Then tell me whether you want this."

"I do." Her mind sought for the words that would break the last of the ice and the lightless dark for him. "I trust what you do. I have always done so."

He was not quite swift enough to mask his eyes and what she saw brought a rush of feeling that the needs of the body were not enough to express. Yet she had nothing else, and then it was all right, because his head was bent over her heat-flushed skin and he could not see the tears that spilled out of her eyes.

Her hands slid over the thick flesh of his arms and his shoulders with all the tenderness and all the possessiveness and the terrible desire she could not speak.

But he knew her need. His hands caressed her shivering skin, mounding her breast to the wild hunger of his mouth, moving, his strong fingers finding the aching source of her desire. He touched that wet aching heat at her core until her body twisted fiercely, out of control and the cry she made sliced through the dark.

Her whole body shook as though it would break except that he held her, so close, against the wild beating of his heart and that was what she wanted, to be so close to him. Only one thing could be closer. If he could feel as she did. Even if it was only now, just the moment that was her eternity.

She moved against him, with the kind of courage that comes only when all other choices are gone. The magic was there. She could feel it in the instant response of the tight harshly-controlled mass of his body, the sharpened gasp of his breath. She pushed herself closer, still trying to hold the pressure of her body lightly, because of the damage hidden by the thick strips of linen. But not letting him go, touching him, his legs, his hips, swaying her body over hot thickened flesh until the ragged breathing became a harsh cry.

He rolled out of her reach, breaking her grip with not a quarter of his strength, but he did not leave her. His mouth sought hers in a kiss that burned her senses, then moved away, carrying the trail of that remorseless fire across her throat, her breasts, her belly, until that moist heat touched her where he had before so that she writhed.

She was caught in the snare she had wanted to use to hold him. And yet she could tell how harshly won his control was this time, even as his mouth and his tongue found what they sought, touched her so softly she made small sounds of desperation.

She felt the sliding thrust of his fingers as she had

before but she did not draw back. The only sensation in her mind was of her need, her desperate, graceless, heartfelt need for him. It gathered and shattered, the fierce limitless pleasure of it leaving her gasping. Wild.

So that when his body covered hers, her hands sought the dark moonlit shadows of him, fastened on the heavy living warmth, the sweat-damp skin, the thick muscle that had fought to save her life and her family's.

She hoped he would not see her tears in the dark as her body pressed against his, wanting him so much it would kill her heart. She let his body, all the heat and the power of him, show her as he would all that love could mean.

His mouth sought hers as he leaned above her, the heat and the broad hardness of him pressing against her moist skin, sliding inside her, slowly, until her body arched, controlless.

"Brand…"

She was moving as he thrust. She felt the sharp pain at the greater fullness of him deep inside. The last barrier broke. Her body curved round his and he held her as though the moment of bright fire could hold the endless future.

And then there was only him, so close it was impossible to be closer. All the passion and the hunger in his heart was hers. It wiped out everything, all consciousness, leaving only the fierce joy that had been theirs the first moment they met.

SHE LAY SO VERY STILL. He watched her face, pale in the dark shadows. Her eyes were closed so that he could read nothing.

His heart beat against the pulped mass of his ribs. The pain was nothing to what was in his mind. But it still made him move, sliding his shoulders round against the mattress, clamping his jaw shut so that he would not make a sound.

Her eyes flew open, fastening on his face as though she did not know where she was and then her gaze sharpened. He watched her eyes. Because he had to know. What she thought and what she felt were more to him than his life's breath.

Her gaze met his without the slightest shadow of fear or regret and that made his heart lurch again in the painful wreckage. Because he had once believed the world could hold miracles just from looking at the night-dark depths of her eyes.

But even the deepness of her eyes did not tell him the secrets that were locked inside her head. He could not truly know what she felt, whether it was no more than the driving madness between them that had waited half a year for its fulfillment. Whether it was the guilt. Like her trick with the sword.

It could not be the appalling possessiveness that gripped him, the burning primitive consciousness that she was his and only his at last; with the gift of her blood still on his skin and her hand clasped against his fingers as though she wanted him.

He did not know what she truly wanted.

He should move away, ease the vicious pain in his chest that was only half physical. But his body had its own ideas. It moulded itself round hers with all the possessiveness that lived in his heart, like a shield against harm.

The thought that the harm might come from him still coiled like a viper waiting inside him, with the power to strike through his soul.

He could not bear how fragile she looked, doubly so with the marks of his loving on the paleness of her body.

"Alina…"

She was shivering. The air in the chamber struck like ice shards. How could he not have known that? He reached across to pull the thickness of the bedcovers over her but the movement, stretching muscle over bone, was not quite as controlled as he would have wished.

Her hand caught the heavy wool, then his arm.

"I am sorry. There must be so much pain."

Her distress over that caught at him. It seemed one small thing he could make right for her.

"Aye." He found the teasing grin that never failed in its purpose. "To think I actually wanted to feel such pain. How thick-headed is that?" Her dark eyes snapped in the response that was instant between them, but then the spark faded into the deepness.

"Did you want to drown in the river water?"

His breath stopped. The question came out of nowhere. It had nothing to do with now. Yet it did, and she knew that. Because she was Alina. Because the connection was getting deeper than it should. Her eyes held his unwaveringly, but inside they were stricken.

"No," he said with all the force he could to that stricken look. "That is not so. When you found me, when I heard you out of the blackness, I was already trying to get back to the riverbank. Did you not see that?"

"Yes…I thought… I told myself so. But I knew how you felt and…such water is very, very powerful. Not everyone understands its power. I think you do. I think you must have felt its power before."

His heart seemed to stop beating. He did not say a word. But she did.

"Was it when your parents died?" asked Alina.

"I know they died in much pain," said her voice across the splintering edge of darkness. "And that you saw it and no one knew whether they were murdered or not. And that you were only twelve."

She turned over. She was very close.

"What happened to you?"

It was only the moon's light that let him see the sheen of tears. Otherwise he would never have told her. But he had taken her maiden's blood and she had suffered exile and aloneness for his sake. He owed her all.

"I was there when they died." The wide compass of the chamber at Bamburgh, the moving air that spoke of the stars' light and all the sea's wideness, narrowed into the hell of the sickroom at Lindwood. To the ways in which all that was once strong and prideful and fair could be brought down. The screams rang in his ears.

"I stayed with them all the while. But there was naught I could do. Naught a physician could do. Certainly nothing a child could say. I am not sure that they actually knew I was there."

"But you were." She said it as though it meant something it could not. Her eyes watched him. He did not wish to say any more, but he owed it.

"There was nothing left without them. Just an empty hall like a cavern and...naught. What I remember most was sitting in sudden nothingness. Just me and two small sisters who were too young to understand. There were other people there, but I do not remember them. My brother came back from the school at York. But there was nothing to say, even to him. Poor Wulf, so much was thrust on him because he was the eldest. I can only remember the nothingness."

Her fingers caught his, her hand clamping over aching skin and bruised knuckles. She should not have done that because it could make him feel that the nothingness could be conquered.

He set his mind back to the task of telling her.

"I went out in the boat. The sea was rough, with a storming wind, and I went out too far. I did not have enough care. The boat would have been swamped. It was only small and the planks were old." The tang of salt scored his throat, the coldness of the water paralyzing his limbs.

"You could have let it be swamped."

Her words, just that one sentence, exposed all that there was in him. The emptiness that was never assuaged because whatever tried to fill it never stayed.

"But you chose not to let it." It was a statement, not a question. Her voice again lending a meaning to the words that he could not see.

"I could not. There would have been no one left to help Wulf. Even though I was only twelve, I was all that there was. I had to go back because of him."

"Because you loved him. And you loved your home."

Lindwood. With its high chambers and its paved paths and the wildness of wood and hill. He had not known then that he loved it. It had seemed one more thing that would change and betray him.

He had not understood.

"I went back. I made up some story or other about fishing and getting carried out by the tide and that was it. I laughed it off. But Wulf knew."

Just like you.

Her hand tightened on his. As though it would stay there.

"Why? What did your brother say?"

"Naught. We never do say things." *We just know.*

A small streak of light seemed to wash through the darkness, lightening Alina's skin with silver. He kept his gaze on the light, as though he could draw on its strength.

"But he did nearly break my jaw. I suppose that told me."

"Saint Dwyn!"

Alina's favourite saint. The virgin. His hand tightened over hers. The tears had stopped now. Her eyes were wide, wondering. If only it were possible to make her smile, that the light might be inside her. He did not want her haunted by such dark things.

"It was a lucky blow. And I was not ready for it," he added, in the tone of an aggrieved brawler who had got the worst of it in a fight at the mead bench. "Besides, it was an unfair advantage him being four years older. Ask any brother."

Her shaking lips curved upwards. He knew what he had to say, even if it meant stripping away all there was of himself.

"After I had fought with Goadel, I went into the water because I wanted it to wash away what I had done. So that I would feel something, even if it was only the bite of such coldness. That is how it was, nothing otherwise. I wanted to come back."

She did not speak. Her hand was locked in his, like a point of warmth in the wasteland.

"I knew that there was so much I still had to do. But what I thought about, what meant more than anything to me, more than wounds or madness or right or wrong, was you."

Her hand rested in his. The quality of her stillness

and the silence was bone deep. Outside, clouds raced across the moon, sending ever-changing shadows. He spoke into the silence.

"Alina, that is still so. It always will be so for me. But what I would have you do now is what you wish. And before you say a word, I would have you know that the past is accounted for, that it does not have any power for ill anymore. There were never any debts for you to pay. What you do will be your choice. Free."

He heard the rustle of the mattress as she turned. With night-blind eyes he could not see whether she turned towards him or away. But her hand stayed in his, tentative, equally blind.

"Then I would go to Lindwood."

HE DID NOT LET GO of her hand. But that was how he was. Alina looked through the shadows at the small glimpses of tightly drawn flesh. He might have been carved of stone. But that was only what the eyes saw. Her touch and her ravished senses and her heart knew the living warmth and wildness and the power that was strong enough to be able to give.

It was the giving that could defeat her now, not the stone.

"If I asked you, would you take me there?"

"Yes."

She could feel the warmth of him next to her in the dark. He was so close that if she moved the smallest muscle she would touch him. She knew what that would be like. She knew his body in every last detail.

She knew how he breathed. She knew if she touched him exactly what he would do.

He would give all that she wanted.

She did not move except to draw the pain of breath.

"If you took me to Lindwood would it be because of what you said before? Because even though I brought ruin down on your head you thought you had not provided for me?"

The words fell through the silence like stones down a well, taking an age of time to reach the water.

"You mean a payment made in honour?"

"Yes."

"That is what it should be," said the familiar rough-smooth voice of dreams. "Because of all that I have cost you and all that you have given." There was no smoothness in the voice now. Only the harshness that must come with breath as hard fought for as hers. "It should be in payment for that."

Debt payments. So many of them. Inescapable. The cruelty of their weight crushing her. Her heart could not bear them. It would choke and kill her with the graceless desperation of its need. She forced speech.

"A debt payment—"

"I cannot say it." His voice cut her off, the rawness of it striking through her. "It is what I should give you in all honour and I cannot. You have asked me for the one thing I cannot do."

Her body moved, angling round in the tangle of the warm bedcovers. She could not stop it because she was need driven and honourless. She touched him. She saw his face and his eyes. She saw all. Gold held her gaze so that she could not look away.

"I cannot give you a debt payment."

Time seemed to stop and with it heart and breath and all that she was.

"It is not what I want."

Their bodies touched. His heat scorched her skin. Age-old longing and newly-made memory fired her blood. But he did not move.

"I do not know whether you can want what I can give. An honour payment could not contain what I feel. What I feel for you is not bound by that."

His body seemed to vibrate, with the same restlessness as hers. But behind his body's strength she could see all the pain that she had put there.

"What I feel for you is not bound by anything. It is not…it is not an honourable love. I said that when I took you from Hun there was thought and that is true. Because with you I saw what I had not believed in—a future, not just the moment."

The sharp edge of his breath must be like a double pain, the physical and that which was not.

"But the madness was in it, too, the recklessness that does not know limits. That is how I love you. With all that there is in me. But I would not…I would not force that on you, the kind of love that will take everything. I think you have seen too much of that. You cannot want that as your life." The pause and the painful breath were something that she felt in her own chest.

"Go." It was the harshest sound she had ever heard. "Take your freedom while it is there."

All that was in her mind and her body seemed to gather itself into what he had called single-mindedness and she named courage.

"I will not go. The only freedom I have ever had has been with you." She thought her voice sounded as harsh as his. Because she felt so much. Because of all that she risked.

"I told you the kind of love I wanted. It was a love that valued me for what I was, not for whatever potential power over others I represented. Only you gave me that. Not my father or my mother, or even my childhood dreams at Alcluyd. It is the kind of love that I would give in my turn, if you would let me."

She let her body rest against his and felt his warmth.

"You do not know what your love is. It is so complete because it gives. If you had been a man like my father, you would have used all the strength you have, and what you are pleased to call madness, to constrain me regardless of what I wanted."

She took a breath. "You had the right to kill my father but you did not. If you had fought only for yourself you would have used the sword's power to take. You would not have used it to protect me and everyone else. You would not have given me back my life and the freedom to go to Strath-Clòta."

She touched him and yet he held back. Because he had more control than her, always. He watched her and she tried to hold that gaze, to meet its terms.

"You wanted me to have what no one else has ever thought for me to have. You wanted me to have power over my own life."

The faint flicker in the gold eyes was all that she needed. Perhaps. With a recklessness that should have outshone his, she staked the last throw of the dice.

"I have made my choice. I will go to Lindwood with you. Not out of guilt, not out of fear, not even out of the obligation I have to you that is more than I could ever repay." She forestalled the sudden movement of his body with a quickness that exceeded mere thought.

"My choice is just as selfish as you could wish." Her voice trembled against his skin. "The way I love you does not know any restraint at all. You are what I want and what I have always wanted. My happiness does not lie in Strath-Clòta or in Craig Phádraig. It lies in you."

Her body slid across his, gently, with all the slowness of a lifetime's promise.

"If you take that happiness away from me, you take everything. I tried…I tried once to do without you and I could not. It was like living death. I need you more than I have ever needed anyone, just as I have trusted you more than I have trusted anyone. That is the measure of my love, if you will take it."

The failing edge of her breath was caught under the wild blood-tingling deepness of his mouth and there was nothing but his heat and the knowing mind-burning touch of his hands. And the pleasure. Only that.

She could not move afterwards. Her hands shook. Every muscle in her body shook. It was bliss. It was all that she wanted. She lay, sated, surfeited with happiness while the light and the shadows danced across them on the moving northern air.

"So you will take me to Lindwood, then?"

The happiness was real, there under her hand in the hot flesh and the scent of him. She felt him sigh, a sound that was drawn out and filled with suffering. The cool edge of it teased her burning skin.

"Aye. I suppose I will have to now."

Northumbrian hell-fiend.

She tried reaching a hand out to hit him, preferably across the ribs, but it was too much effort. He pulled the wreckage of the bedcovers round her but she did not need that. He was her warmth. Now. For ever. Even though she had thought she had lost him to the ice cold. She closed her eyes and her thanks went where they were due, straight to Saint Dwyn, who guarded lovers.

"Aye," she said in Northumbrian, staring at starlight beyond the window. "Now that you have seduced me—" she produced a sigh to rival his for poignancy "—you will have to marry me."

"Nay… Will I have to go that far?"

"Yes."

She twisted her fingers in the rich gold tangle of his hair and pulled. Hard.

"Argh. Well, if you are going to browbeat me into it—"

"I am. Give me two minutes and I will have the sword at your throat again. Ah—"

"You were saying?"

"Possibly that I would never touch the sword again. I do not think I want to know where you learned to kiss like that."

"Some Pictish wench I met."

His flesh filled her hands. She felt very, very safe. "What do you think my...my father will say?"

"Yes."

Her fingers tangled in his hair again while she digested this spare Northumbrian reply. "I will marry you anyway." Her fingers snagged in living gold. "There will be no escape. But...what if he does not say yes?"

His own hand, lost in the wild and longer tangle of her hair, was much more gentle. Probably because he was kinder than her. He appeared to be considering.

"Then I suppose I will just have to abduct you again."

She let out her breath.

"Would you do that?"

"Well, think of all the practice I have had. Be a shame to waste it, and I might get it right the third time."

"Aye," she said in her best Northumbrian. "You might..." She allowed a certain inflexion of irony. It was rewarded with the kind of kiss that stopped breath. It was quite enough to stop her heart.

"Do you think that—" Her voice faltered and she tried to collect it. "Do you think that people, the people at Lindwood will accept me after all that has happened?"

"No one who sees you could fail to fall under your spell."

"Nay, but…you just say that because you are susceptible." She proved it with the boldness he had taught her, but her hands clung to him with a need for reassurance that he recognized. Because he knew her. She was drawn into the utterly warm, utterly quiet circle of his arms. Safe. No one could combine such safety and such wildness. He stroked her hair.

"They know who is to blame, and it is not you. There is much to be made up to them and I would do it."

"They haunted your bower while you were ill. They love you—"

"As they will love you."

"I would do all for that."

She thought of the dead. Hun and Goadel. They had no more power. Not unless she gave it to them. She turned her face towards him.

"I would help you rebuild your home if I could."

"Our home. Then that is what we will do. And whatever happens we will abide it. Together."

"Aye."

She leaned her head against his shoulder and the promise filled the intimate darkness of the Northumbrian air.

EPILOGUE

Lindwood, Northumbria, 718 A.D.

ALINA WATCHED the cloud of dust rising in the summer heat. Two years and the circle was almost complete. At her back stood the people of Lindwood, in front stood Brand, like a shield against harm. Always.

The riders swept to a halt and the leader sprang down, lithe and powerful as the creature he had been named for.

"Wulf." Brand did not move. She could not.

The man so like and so unlike her husband scanned what had once been his home. His eyes were very different from Brand's, grey, dense as slate.

"You rebuilt the chapel."

"Aye. Do you want to see what else is here? Something you can take back to benighted Wessex with you. Books."

"You? And books?" The grey eyes struck light. They were not hard at all. They were like Brand's eyes, full of the strength that allowed people to give.

"Aye," said Brand, but it was buried under his brother's embrace.

"Benighted, indeed," drawled the soft tones of Wessex that belonged to Wulf's elegant, fair-haired wife. But whatever else she would have said was lost in a round of embraces that never seemed to end.

It was like a miracle. They went inside and the soaring roof and the painted pillars of the hall reflected laughter.

There seemed so much that required laughter. From all of them. The bright-eyed girl of the lady Rowena's first marriage giggled, her eyes resting equally on her mother and Wulf. The lady's little son by her marriage to Wulf crowed loudly, hale and lusty with health.

Alina watched them, cradling her own son, the small weight of him in her arms like heaven's blessing.

The lady Rowena wanted to hold him. But when she did, her fine blue eyes softened with tears.

Alina stared at the elegant fairness and the intimidating beauty of Wulf's wife. "I thought you would hate me for the harm I have done."

"Nay." The lady watched the child. "I know too much of what it is like to be caught in events beyond your control."

It made Alina dare the next words. "I was afraid that your husband would hate me for having Lindwood."

"So was I." There was a pause and then Rowena said, "I did not want him to regret what he gave up to be with me."

Alina's heart caught and they looked at each other with an understanding that did not need words.

Rowena's gaze slid away to where Wulf sat with Brand, their heads bent over the books Brand had had copied at Jarrow for his brother. At that moment Wulf looked up and something in the slate-grey eyes made all the cool fairness of Rowena catch fire.

She watched Wulf's smile broaden. It was shadowless. Then Brand's gaze caught her own and there was nothing but the brightness of him, the light and the fire. All the possibility of regret seemed swallowed up by the greater power of the future.

"Wulf is happy," said Alina. It was hours later. They were lying on the great canopied bed and the darkness was threaded with firelight.

"Aye."

It was all that Brand said, but she could read Northumbrians. They could pack something as large and unfathomable as redemption into one short word. She thought the past was healed and the sorrow was gone, even the blame that Brand had kept for himself.

"Will you keep any of the books?"

"Just one."

Brand shifted the weight of their son against his chest.

"Even if it gets into your head and stays there forever?"

"Why do you think I had another copy made of Boethius?"

Boethius who wrote not of transience but of the permanent joys of the spirit.

The firelight flickered in the Bernician air but it was nothing to Brand's warmth.

"Because you are happy?"

"Aye."

Alina leaned her head against his shoulder and the peace stole through her heart. The circle was complete.

HISTORICAL NOTE ON THE YEAR 716

THE NORTHERN ENGLISH KINGDOM of Northumbria lived dangerously. Its sporadic fights were internal, as well as with neighbouring kingdoms such as that of the Picts (northeastern Scotland) and the Mercians (English midlands).

King Cenred reigned two years before being replaced by Osric, brother of his predecessor and rival, King Osred. But a compromise must have been hammered out because Osric named Cenred's brother Ceolwulf as his heir.

Ceolwulf managed to hold the throne (with one interruption) for nine years and was immortalized as "most glorious" by that most famous Anglo-Saxon historian, Bede.

Bede believed that if history recorded good things of good men, the thoughtful hearer would be encouraged to imitate what was good.

Arts such as the writing, copying and reading of books flourished in Northumbria with a success that defied political turmoil.

Apart from the kings, all the characters in the book are imaginary. The background against which they struggled and triumphed is as real as the author can make it.

* * * * *

Dear Reader,

Sometimes we meet another person by chance and sometimes we seem to meet a special stranger by fate.

I wanted to create a story for a woman who finds just such a magic stranger at a desperate crisis of her life.

The lady Gemma knows the danger of helping the unconscious man lying at the forest eaves, but she will not leave him to die. As the wounded man recovers, her faith seems justified. But the stranger hides secrets. He is a man trapped between two worlds, belonging nowhere.

Ash lives under the taint of disloyalty, haunted by a past he can share with no one, least of all with a lady, a skilled goldsmith dedicated to her task of creating beauty. He is a warrior, sworn to the service of a king who stands alone against the invading Viking armies.

But Gemma and her captive brother face danger. Ash stands at the crossroads, between the demands of his mission and keeping faith with the woman whose trust he would win above all others. The prize is beyond hope—the kind of love that would bring him home.

The king to whom Ash swore faith was real. Alfred the Great, King of Wessex, finally turned back the sweeping invasion of the Viking forces. I hope you enjoy *A Fragile Trust*, the first of my tales that celebrate the spirit of the men and women who kept faith with their king in those dangerous times.

Helen Kirkman

A FRAGILE TRUST
by Helen Kirkman
Coming in April 2005 from HQN Books

The Mercian border, England
Spring, 872 A.D.

"STOP," SHRIEKED GEMMA. "The man is alive."

The horse and cart lurched to a halt so abrupt it nearly threw her.

Gemma's gaze fixed on the heap of rags beside the track. She could make out the startling breadth of the man's shoulders under the torn wool, glimpse the bare thickness of a muddied thigh.

She leaped down while the cart was still rocking.

"Don't! Lady, stop. There could be others, waiting for you to go near the trees—"

But she would not stop. The figure of the man drew her. She watched the dark shape: motionless, damaged, infinitely mysterious. The pale gleam of uncovered flesh.

The naked skin belonged to the strong sinuous length of his leg stretched out in the damp bracken beside her. She stared at the gaping cloth, the taut swell of muscle exposed beneath; at the blackened slashing line of what could only be a sword cut.

Naught about him was what she had expected. She had thought him one of the poor, starving wretches who haunted the countryside in the wake of the Viking raids. Heaven knew there were enough of them.

But swelling muscles did not belong to starving men and while his wounds could be those of a robber's helpless victim, she felt in her bones that this man had fought. And there had been a skirmish, quite recently, which the Vikings had won. She had heard their boasts.

He was filthy. He was completely alone.

He was lying facedown. The broad battered width of his hand was wrapped, nay clamped, round a tree root, as though if he could no longer walk forward, he would crawl.

A warrior's hand.

She despised warriors.

The temptation to give in to good sense was almost overwhelming. The battered man was a stranger, worse, a soldier. For all she knew he could be Danish, some Viking ambushed in revenge, set upon and left for dead.

She let go of the man's sleeve, wiping her hand clean. Dried leaves shed cold and dampness against her skin. Mud and...blood.

What if he died?

She could not tear her gaze from the stranger, from the heavy, outstretched warrior's hand.

Her own hand slid forward, reaching out until her fingers touched the stranger's flesh. She could feel each separate knuckle of that fierce grip. His skin was freezing. She could not pry his fingers free.

"I cannot leave him." She scarce knew whether she had spoken aloud.

In that moment, the stranger moved.

His eyes were the colour of the forest, dun shadows and green light, so deep they did not seem to belong to a world dweller but to a spirit, a *wood-wose*. Deep beyond imagining.

Sudden fire seemed to erupt around her, despite the cold—wild, fast forest fire. The wood-dark eyes burned into hers. The spine-crawling silence of the air beat against her ears.

"Who are you?" The English words, deep as the earth's fastness, seemed not to break the tingling silence, but to be part of it. His voice demanded an answer. Yet it hurt him to speak. She could tell that from the tautness of his mouth, the heaviness of his breath. His speech was not Danish. It was as Mercian as hers.

That did not take away one iota of the danger.

"I am Gemma."

"A jewel, then."

His gaze held hers. The strange wildfire inside her kindled, coursing through her veins, making her whole body burn, so that sight and feeling and sense dizzied with the power of it. It was like the rush of the strongest mead.

The mysterious male creature under her hand had made her feel that.

Beside her the lifeless fronds of last year's bracken

crackled and the sharp snap of winter-hard twigs broke the spell.

A kind of panic leaped inside her. She was mad to linger here beside the dark bulk of the forest filled with outlaws and thieves and the bitter dispossessed.

"Lady, come away."

The hazel gaze flickered past her to the grimness of her escort's face before turning back to her. All at once, the strained face seemed not that of an other-worldly spirit, but man-kindred, human, and therefore vulnerable despite its evident will.

He would ask for her aid. He must. She knew, with a startling completeness, that she would not refuse him. The urge to reassure him, to respond to the humanness that she saw, to tell him he was not alone, cut through mind and flesh.

"It is all right. I will not leave you. I will help you—"

"Nay." The word was forced out of him, like an act of will, and she understood what she should have known the moment she had seen his hand. He would not beg for anything.

"You must leave me—"

Not a reproach, not a plea. It was a command.

"No—"

"You must go. I will bring you danger."

Danger. Her skin, the very air around her, shivered with it.

`"No."` She tried to hold the shifting brightness of his eyes, to tell him without words what the breathless tingling air told her. Things she did not know herself. That there was more to this than a chance meeting of strangers, that a bond had been made, of what kind or how was beyond her understanding. It was just there.

But the forest-green gaze slid beyond her to fasten on her escort.

"See her away—"

"No…" she began, but the gaze was gone, far beyond both of them, into some realm she could not follow. She watched the thick brown lashes drift closed, cutting her off. She could not hold his gaze, could not hold him. She let go of his hand.

She could not afford to upset her Viking masters. She could not bring an unknown and dangerous fighting man into the camp, an Englishman.

She looked at the cut on the muddied swell of his thigh. He was not her responsibility. She had more responsibility than she knew how to endure. She should leave this man, this stranger, this warrior creature to his own fate.

Even the stranger had seen the truth of that.

She knew what her decision was. She straightened up.

She would have to be quick. Very, very quick.

**#1 *New York Times*
bestselling author**

NORA ROBERTS

**From the master of romance—
two extraordinary tales of heartfelt reunions.**

R E U N I O N

Set in a world where love the second time around
is the greatest treasure of all, these two full-length
stories are back in print after more than ten years.

December

"A storyteller of immeasurable diversity and talent."
—*Publishers Weekly*

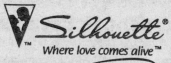

Silhouette®

Where love comes alive™

helen
kirkman

82629-5 FORBIDDEN   ___ $ 6.50 U.S. ___ $ 7.99 CAN.
(limited quantities available)

TOTAL AMOUNT $_____
POSTAGE & HANDLING $_____
($1.00 for 1 book, 50¢ for each additional)
APPLICABLE TAXES* $_____
<u>TOTAL PAYABLE</u> $_____

(Check or money order—please do not send cash)